BIRDIE
AND
ME

J. M. M. NUANEZ

PUFFIN BOOKS

FOR MY PARENTS—ALL FOUR OF THEM

PUFFIN BOOKS
An imprint of Penguin Random House LLC, New York

First published in the United States of America by Kathy Dawson Books, 2020
Published by Puffin Books, an imprint of Penguin Random House LLC, 2021

Copyright © 2020 by J. M. M. Nuanez

Illustrations copyright © 2020 by Jessica Jenkins

Puffin Books & colophon are registered trademarks of Penguin Books Limited.

Visit us online at penguinrandomhouse.com.

THE LIBRARY OF CONGRESS HAS CATALOGED THE KATHY DAWSON BOOKS EDITION AS FOLLOWS:
Nuanez, J. M. M., author. | Birdie and me / J. M. M. Nuanez.
Description: New York : Kathy Dawson Books, [2020] | Summary: "Ever since their free-spirited mama died ten months ago, twelve-year-old Jack and her gender creative nine-year-old brother, Birdie, have been living with their fun-loving uncle Carl, but now their conservative uncle Patrick insists on being their guardian, which forces all four of them to confront grief, prejudice, and loss, all while exploring what 'home' really means"—Provided by publisher.
Identifiers: LCCN 2019020270 (print) | LCCN 2019022239 (ebook)
ISBN 9780399186776 (hardcover)
Subjects: CYAC: Brothers and sisters—Fiction. | Loss (Psychology)—Fiction. | Sex role—Fiction. | Uncles—Fiction. | Home—Fiction.
Classification: LCC PZ7.1.N7 Bi 2020 (print) | LCC PZ7.1.N7 (ebook) | DDC [Fic]—dc23

Printed in the United States of America

Puffin Books ISBN 9780399186783

10 9 8 7 6 5 4 3 2 1

Design by Cerise Steel
Text set in Joanna MT Pro

CONTENTS

1 How to Move Again 1

2 Dinner with a Clam 14

3 The Tornado 24

4 The Long Way to Town 34

5 Looking Out 51

6 A Dog with Sneakers 67

7 Shopping with Patrick 82

8 The Proposal 94

9 Suspension 109

10 When to Use the MicroBlaster 119

11 Gifts 127

12 Cracks in the Ice 139

13 A Drastic Thing 153

14 Islands on the Lake 171

15 Picking Up the Pieces 180

16 An Enigma 197

17 One Island Next to Another 203

18 A Small Wooden Thing 209

19 Bright Spots in the Dark 218

20 What Hope Looks Like 231

Epilogue Journal Entry No. 1, December 13 245

CHAPTER 1

HOW TO MOVE AGAIN

Today is Saturday, the day we usually eat Honey Bunny Buns for breakfast and read the back page of the newspaper with Uncle Carl while he drinks coffee and smokes on the porch. The back page is the section of the newspaper that has weird news about things like two-headed llamas or people who get themselves stuck in air-conditioning vents or pets that are accidentally sent through the mail and survive.

But today isn't just Saturday. It's also moving day. And right now my little brother, Birdie, is on the couch waiting for me to open my eyes. I pretend to sleep, but even in the half-light, through squinted eyelids, I can see he's got Mama's old purple eye shadow on and a towel draped around his head like a glamorous headscarf.

"Jack," Birdie whispers. "Miss Jackie Jack Jacko."

"I'm sleeping. You should too," I say.

"I can't sleep any more."

He creeps across the couch, down to my futon, and lays his head next to mine. The smell of Dr Pepper lip gloss fills the air. In my ear he says, "I've got a stomachache and it's probably critical. I don't think we can move today."

I open one eye. "Critical?"

Birdie leans toward me and whispers, "Critical is the worst stage."

"You're not critical," I say, sitting up.

"Okay," he says, "but I do have a stomachache."

I peek out the dusty blinds. Patrick will be here to pick us up in two hours. "I do too, Birdie."

Birdie straightens his towel scarf and rewraps it under his chin and says, "Do I look like Audrey Hepburn? With my scarf?"

"Who?"

"Audrey Hepburn. You know. *Charade. Breakfast at Tiffany's. My Fair Lady.*"

I wait for him to say something about Mama and her obsession with these old movies, but he doesn't.

"You'd look more like Audrey Hepburn if you had sunglasses," I say. "But it's not bad."

He smiles a little, but unwraps the scarf and drapes it over his head like a lampshade. Then he takes a fashion magazine from the coffee table and opens it on his lap. "Maybe we should go to the library today," he says.

I don't say anything because even though he might pretend that today will be like any other day living with Uncle Carl, I see that he's already packed his backpack and two duffel bags. Birdie's only nine, but he knows there's nothing we can do about this move. Uncle Carl messed up too many times and now we have to move in with our other uncle, Patrick.

Two hours later, Uncle Carl comes out of his room in his shiny gold boxing robe. He salutes us, and then leaves the apartment with his empty coffee mug. His first cup of the day is always the free coffee from Juan at the Stop-and-Go down the street. He told us that him and Juan have an understanding. I don't know what exactly they understand, but as long as Uncle Carl brings his own mug, he comes back with free, steaming-hot coffee.

Birdie puts one magazine down and picks up another.

I try writing in my observation notebook, but my pen doesn't write anything except a giant question mark with a lopsided circle as its dot, which I color in until my pen starts to run out of ink.

I make a second piece of toast because Mama used to say that toast was good for stomachaches and other ailments like sadness and nervousness and writer's block. But after eating it, my stomach drops when I see Patrick's truck pull up.

Birdie must hear the engine, because he looks up from

his magazine and says, "But Uncle Carl isn't back from the Stop-and-Go yet."

"I think I see him now," I say.

Uncle Carl and Patrick meet on the sidewalk and stare at each other, and for just a moment, it's like Uncle Carl is standing in front of a mirror: the same white skin, same wavy gray hair, same bushy mustache, and same lanky frame.

But the mirror image isn't wearing a gold boxing robe, sweats, and worn-out leather huarache sandals.

Instead, Patrick's wearing what he always wears: an old Chevy baseball hat pulled low, a tucked-in plaid shirt (rolled to the elbows, arms crossed in front), jeans, belt, and work boots.

"Are they ready?" I hear Patrick ask Uncle Carl.

"Of course they're ready." Uncle Carl starts up the stairs. "You going to come up? Or should I send them down so you don't have to step foot in my apartment? Wouldn't want you to break your—what—almost yearlong streak?"

Patrick watches Uncle Carl climb the stairs to the second-story apartment, his hands now on the hips of his belt.

When Uncle Carl blunders in, I start holding my breath.

Birdie and me stand up from the couch and go behind the coffee table, which holds Marlboro, Uncle Carl's two-foot-long taxidermied bearded dragon. Birdie is still kind of freaked out by her glassy real-looking eyes and her spiky skin, which Uncle Carl insists is second to no animal's in radiance and beauty. I keep thinking that Birdie will be less afraid of the giant lizard now that she isn't alive, but that doesn't seem to be the case.

It's ten heartbeats before Patrick shows up in the doorway. Birdie and me stay behind Marlboro.

"They're ready," says Uncle Carl, after taking a long drink of coffee by the kitchen counter. "All packed just like you asked."

We haven't been in Patrick's truck since that seven-hour drive almost ten months ago from our home in Portland, Oregon, to here in Moser, California (aka a small town in the middle of Nowhere, Northern California).

Patrick gathers up our bags that are piled by the door. He looks at Birdie in his yellow shirt that has polka-dot strawberries all over it and his rainbow sneakers. At least his leggings are just plain black and the purple eye shadow has mostly rubbed off. He cradles his favorite purple jacket like a stuffed animal. Patrick won't stop staring.

Then he silently goes out to his truck with our bags. Uncle Carl turns toward us.

"Phew. Okay. I have some parting gifts even though I fully expect to see you tomorrow. I know it's a bit of a walk from Patrick's, but I promise a sundae from the Fry Shack or something better if you come visit me."

"We're going to visit you," I say. "You don't need to use bribery."

"Okay, but I have to make a grand gesture so I don't cry. Now here, just take them."

The big paper bag in his hands is full of individually wrapped Honey Bunny Buns, the mini cinnamon buns they sell down at the Stop-and-Go for fifty cents each.

Before we can thank him, he puts a hand on each of our shoulders and says, "Now, look. I should have paid better attention to your schoolwork and your teachers, but how was I to know there are truancy laws, right? And I didn't mean those things I said about your teacher, okay, Mr. Bird? You know I was just really broken up about Marlboro." He stands up straight and rubs the back of his neck and looks away. "All I'm saying is, things are going to be different for you at Patrick's. That goat has lived alone for thirty years, so who knows what he's going to think of living with two kids. But just because you live with him now doesn't mean you can't come to me if you need anything."

He takes a deep breath and I think he's going to continue his speech, but he doesn't. Then all of a sudden he's ushering us downstairs to the truck, where Patrick sits in the driver's seat with the passenger door open. The engine roars to life.

We don't hug Uncle Carl. We don't even say goodbye. After climbing in and clicking our seat belts and closing the door, I roll down the window. The truck pulls away from the curb as Uncle Carl says, "I'll see you guys later." He watches us go, sipping his coffee the entire time so that the mug covers his face.

...

A week after Mama died, Patrick showed up at Mrs. Spater's, who we'd known our whole lives because we rented the unit next to hers. She owned the duplex, but she was also our friend. And even though she's eighty-two years old, there was no question that she'd look after us until family showed up.

It was the first time I'd ever seen Patrick. Somehow he looked too old to be Mama's brother. Mama had never talked about him and I never saw any family photos with him. She had three pictures of Uncle Carl, but she didn't keep them on display like she did with ones of us or her friends.

We'd actually met Uncle Carl four years before when him and his then-girlfriend rode up to Oregon on his motorcycle. Mama was not expecting to see him. He gave us all big hugs and gummy bears and two Honey Bunny Buns each, even Mama. I don't remember his girlfriend's name, but she didn't have a full right leg. The part below the knee was prosthetic and we could see how it connected with her real leg since her leather skirt was so short. Her entire thigh was covered by a tattoo of a giant red lobster, which seemed to glow against her light skin. The next morning Uncle Carl gave me a short ride around the block on his motorcycle and I remember thinking how lucky his girlfriend was to ride it all day long. Mama wouldn't let Birdie ride, though, since he was so small.

So anyway, Birdie and me were sitting quietly like Mrs. Spater told us to when she answered the door.

"I'm Patrick. Beth's brother." Patrick's voice was a quiet mountain rumble. At first, I couldn't think who Beth was exactly—I didn't make the connection to Mama. "You and your brother are going to come with me," he told us when he came inside. He seemed sad, but I didn't see him cry.

Instead of hugs and Honey Bunny Buns, Patrick just looked at us until Mrs. Spater directed him to our bags.

It was almost like he'd come to pick up a family heirloom or a piece of expensive equipment—something serious and important, but not something real. Not his actual niece and nephew.

Right then I had an urge to write that down in my observation notebook. My notebook was in a little bag slung across my back, but I didn't move.

I asked Patrick where Uncle Carl was and he said that we'd see him soon enough. He looked at our stuff and I was afraid that he'd say that we'd have to leave some behind even though he'd said we could bring three bags each. Uncle Carl didn't have much room, he'd told Mrs. Spater over the phone.

At first, I couldn't believe we actually had to leave it all. But then she'd said her daughter was coming to help her pack everything else up. She'd take care of our things. We shouldn't worry about it now. And then she gave me some of her lemon pound cake and all I wanted was to go back to a time when Mama was there to say, "This cake is so good I hereby request a bed-sized piece so I can sleep in it."

But Patrick didn't say anything about our bags. He picked them up without a word and went outside. We followed him and got into the truck. Mrs. Spater asked him if he was sure he didn't want anything from Mama's house. But Patrick put up a hand and shook his head. "No, thank you," he said in his mountain voice.

Mrs. Spater looked at Patrick through the truck's passenger window. "You take good care of these kids, Mr. Royland. And I'll make sure to take care of the rest." She pursed her lips and I know she was trying to keep from crying. "Goodbye, you two. Be good for your uncles. I know you will be." And then she took a step back. "I'll miss you."

I don't remember what I said because I couldn't decide what to say. I hadn't thought about it at all. "I'll miss you too" didn't seem to make sense. We would more than miss her. I think Birdie said her name just as the truck began backing away.

Mrs. Spater waved from her porch, her old cocker spaniel, Colin, staring at us through the window. With her other hand, she covered her mouth, so that only her eyes could be seen.

I grabbed Birdie's hand, each of his fingers with chipped turquoise nail polish, and squeezed it again and again, like a beating heart, the whole ride to California.

...

I try not to watch Uncle Carl in the rearview mirror because I hate my last memory of Mrs. Spater and Colin and their sad faces shrinking down to nothing as we drove away.

I tell myself that it doesn't matter. I'll see him soon. We're only moving a mile or so out of town.

Patrick doesn't say a word and only once looks over at us when Birdie's feet start fidgeting, which is one of his many nervous habits.

I swear I see Patrick's mustache sag into a frown.

After a minute, we get onto the highway and pass a big gray-and-black bus going the other way.

I know bus number 331 goes from here all the way to Portland, Oregon. I know that bus fare is twenty-six dollars for minors and thirty-two dollars for adults. I've known this information since our second day with Uncle Carl when Birdie and me went to the library for the first time. But that was the same afternoon that Uncle Carl bought us our first Fry Shack ice cream sundaes and I forgot about the bus for a while after that.

"When going to and from town," Patrick suddenly says, "try not to walk along the highway. It's too dangerous. There's no safe place to walk. There's another route I can show you." He turns down a small road and points to a dirt path. "It takes a little longer, but it starts near my street and ends close to the elementary school."

He turns the truck around and goes back to the highway, only to turn off onto another road less than thirty seconds later. We drive past a few houses until we come to one that has a chain-link fence and hedge around it. The gate is open and we drive through and stop in front of a small garage attached to an old house.

Patrick shuts off the engine. "Well, okay then."

He gets out and grabs our bags and heads to the front door.

Patrick lives in a shoebox. At least that's what it looks like to me, a giant shoebox with a few squares and rectangles cut out for doors and windows. The roof looks almost completely flat, like someone ran out of building materials.

Birdie looks at me and I just shrug.

Inside, we follow Patrick up a staircase without a word. He opens two bedroom doors, puts our bags down, and then opens the door to a bathroom. He doesn't open the curtains, so everything is in shadow even though it's almost ten o'clock in the morning and the sun is shining outside. Patrick walks back to the staircase and stops. A dog barks.

"That's Duke. He's harmless." Patrick's baseball hat is pulled low, so low I can't see his eyes. He rubs the back of his neck like Uncle Carl does. "I need to go back to work for a few hours. There's some eggs and cheese in the fridge. Peanut butter and tuna and other things on the shelf. Carl says you know how to use the stove all right."

I nod.

He takes a breath and rubs the back of his neck again and looks down the wooden staircase and it dawns on me that he really is about to leave. We've lived in this town for ten months and this is the first time we've ever been in this house and now we somehow live here.

"You kids know why you couldn't stay with Carl anymore, right?" He pauses. "He's not reliable. You're better off here."

We don't say anything. Patrick clears his throat. "I put my cell number and the address here on a paper by the phone. One for each of you. Carry it with you." He stares again at Birdie and then knocks twice on the wall and takes the stairs down.

Birdie picks a bedroom and goes in.

The hallway is dark.

Somewhere there is a clock ticking.

On the way here, I tried to pretend that today was a Wolf Day, Mama's greatest invention: a spontaneous amazing adventure. But Wolf Day was all about saying *yes*. Moving to Patrick's is all about saying *no*.

No to Fry Shack ice cream sundaes.

No to fashion magazines for Birdie.

No to easy walks to town.

How can it really be true that Patrick is Mama's brother?

**Observation #773: Shoebox Inventory

- 5 bedrooms, 0 decorations on the walls unless you count some painting of a ship in a bottle & another of wooden ducks
- 1 ancient basset hound (named Duke) that might be blind & also deaf
- 1 fridge (no magnets):
  - 3 pounds of frozen ground beef, 2 pounds of frozen ground elk, 2 packages of bacon (1 frozen), 1 bag of tortillas, 1 jar of mayo, 1 jar of grape jelly, 1 block of cheddar cheese, 3 sticks of butter, 8 eggs, 4 carrots, 1 cabbage
- 2 wooden cupboards (with the doors removed):
  - 9 giant cans of beans, 5 cans of tuna, 2 boxes of cereal (no milk), 1 jar of peanut butter, 2 onions, 1 jar of nuts, and something round wrapped tightly in foil and covered in a small towel
- 1 overgrown backyard with a big lonely-looking oak & 4 other smaller trees
- 1 giant circular shed on the side of the house (Birdie said it's an old grain silo that's been shortened—he saw one on some home makeover show he watched with Uncle Carl)
- 1 large something next to the shed, covered in a giant tarp on a trailer—a boat?
- 1 big living room window that would let in a lot of light if only you'd pull the curtains back
- 1 wood-burning stove with a giant pile of logs & kindling (the only thing in the whole house that is anything like home)
- 0 pieces of evidence that Patrick is related to Mama or Uncle Carl or any of us

CHAPTER 2

DINNER WITH A CLAM

After unpacking a little, I find Birdie sitting on the back of the living room couch, staring out the large front window, his face close to the glass. The curtains are open, so light floods in.

"Are you cold?" I ask. "You look cold."

He's got his purple jacket on with the hood up. It's October and starting to get chilly because of the nearby mountains, but I'm not sure I'd wear a hood indoors just yet.

"It's so windy here but with no rain like at home. It's cold sitting by the window."

"Then why are you sitting there?"

"Because if you sit right here and look out, it almost reminds me of our front yard."

I stand behind him but don't see it. Our house didn't have a chain-link fence. We had tall rosebushes and a little fig tree.

I'm not cold, but I go to the wood-burning stove and make a small bridge of wood, just like Mama taught me, and shove crumpled newspaper and wood chips underneath and then light a match. The newspapers catch quickly and I watch the flames for a moment and then close the little door.

In the kitchen, there's no bread, so I use tortillas for peanut butter and jelly, which was something an old boyfriend of Mama's used to do before she broke up with him—I'm pretty sure the tortillas were to blame.

When I return to the living room with the food, Birdie's eating a Honey Bunny Bun.

"Birdie, stop. I have real food."

Birdie looks over at the rolled tortillas and the little pile of nuts and a couple of carrots.

"I don't think I've eaten a carrot since home," Birdie says, finishing his Honey Bunny Bun. "I don't even remember what they taste like. Probably not as good as a Honey Bunny Bun—is that peanut butter and jelly in those tortillas?"

I don't think we've had *any* kind of raw vegetable since Mama's house. "You can't live on Honey Bunny Buns forever," I say.

"Says who?"

"Says me, your wise, all-knowing, Honey-Bunny-Bun-expert older sister."

"Um, if anyone is the Honey Bunny Bun expert, it's me."

"Actually, it's probably Uncle Carl."

"True."

We don't say anything else for a long time. We sit on the back of the couch and look out the window and eat our picnic lunch, and there is the faintest crackle coming from the wood-burning stove and it's finally warm enough for Birdie to put his hood down.

I'm about to ask Birdie what makes the view from Patrick's window so much like Mama's when I see it. Maybe not what he sees, exactly. But with the fire and the stupid crunchy carrots like the ones Mama would make us eat all the time, and sitting in a real living room, on a real couch (a couch we don't have to sleep on at night), I feel like home with Mama wasn't just some dream like I've been telling myself the last ten months. We *did* live in a house. We did have our own rooms, with our own things, our own real lives. It had all really happened.

When I hear Patrick return right after the sun sets, I'm lying on the rug in Birdie's room as he sorts through his binder of fashion collages. He made it from magazines and gel pens and stickers. Uncle Carl even bought him a whole stack of new magazines once. Birdie calls it *The Book of Fabulous*.

When the truck goes quiet, Birdie sits up straight and taps his pinkie on his leg.

The front door opens and Duke's collar jingles.

I sit up. Birdie and me watch the door.

Each footstep seems to echo and I catch myself holding my breath again, just like earlier at Uncle Carl's.

Patrick appears, glances into the room, wipes his hands with a gray bandanna, and says, "Dinner will be ready in about half an hour." Then he nods and disappears and Birdie and me look at each other.

"Are we really going to eat dinner with him?" asks Birdie.

"I think we have to."

"I'm not hungry."

"That's because you're eating too many Honey Bunny Buns."

He gathers up his supplies. "When we first moved here, Uncle Carl asked us so many questions. He even wanted to know about that lizard we caught that Mama made us release in the backyard. He remembered. What does Patrick remember?"

"Patrick's not a big talker. Like Uncle Carl says, he's a giant clam in pants."

"I don't want to have dinner with a clam. Especially one who doesn't like us."

Birdie pulls out his mad cap, which is this old sparkly purple knit hat that comes to a point, like an elf hat. Mama made it when she was in one of her knitting crazes, which used to happen once a year or so.

I call it his mad cap because Birdie only wears it when he's mad.

When it's time for dinner, Birdie and me go downstairs. Even before we walk into the kitchen, something perfect and wonderful hits my nose, but I can't place what it is.

At the kitchen island, Patrick slices a big round loaf of homemade bread. I realize this is what was covered in foil under the towel in the cupboard. The bread knife is small in Patrick's hand. Two iron skillets filled with steak, onions, and broccoli rest on the counter.

Duke lies on the floor a few feet from where Patrick stands.

Patrick looks at Birdie and his mad cap as he plates our food and says, "Take a seat."

Patrick sets our plates down, along with the bread, some forks, knives, and a roll of paper towels. I automatically close my eyes and inhale and the aroma goes straight down into my chest.

For a moment, I think that I shouldn't eat it because Mama wasn't a fan of red meat.

But before I realize what I'm doing, I have a bite in my mouth.

It tastes perfect.

Almost too perfect.

And I suddenly realize that we've been eating Fry Shack, instant noodles, and snacks from the Stop-and-Go for the last ten months.

Patrick sits down, drops some food on the floor for Duke, and then starts to eat.

Birdie stares at his plate, his arms in his lap.

"Need me to cut it?" Patrick asks, looking at Birdie's steak. When Birdie doesn't say anything, Patrick looks at me, like maybe Birdie doesn't understand English and needs me to translate.

"We didn't eat a lot of steaks," I say.

"He doesn't eat steak?" Patrick asks. His eyebrows might be raised in surprise, but it's hard to know for sure under his hat.

"No. That's not what I mean," I say.

"Carl said you didn't need much help in the way of food." Patrick looks back at Birdie's hat. "Are you cold?"

"He just likes to wear it," I say. "Helps him adjust to new stuff."

I give Birdie a piece of buttered bread, which he nibbles on.

Patrick finishes quickly, then he gets up, washes the pans, and goes out the front door. Duke follows.

For years, all Birdie has asked for is a dog. Too bad this dog doesn't care about anyone except Patrick.

I go out to the front window and peek through the blinds. There's a light on in the round silo shed and the glow makes it look like a UFO.

I call to Birdie to come look at the UFO lighting, but he doesn't answer. I find him at the trash can, scraping his dinner off his plate.

"Birdie—"

"I have a stomachache. Good night."

And that's how I'm left alone in the kitchen with an old green ticking clock and a hole in my chest going down to the center of the earth.

Patrick is outside for over an hour. When he does come in, he stays downstairs.

I don't want to leave the bedroom, but I can't sleep without a glass of water near me.

When I go downstairs to find one, Patrick is standing at the kitchen island again and this time he's kneading dough.

I go to the sink and try not to stare at Patrick's dusty hands as they move the dough around.

I'm about to leave when he says, "The clothes Birdie's been wearing, are those yours?"

"All the clothes he wears are his," I say.

I watch Patrick put one mound of dough to the side. He grabs another, throws a bunch of flour on the counter, and lays the dough down and begins kneading.

The clam makes bread.

He continues, "Tomorrow I will show you around the house a bit more. How to take care of the kitchen. And some things about the yard, like where to put ash if you're going to make another fire. Also, the washing machine and where to hang-dry clothes."

"Okay."

I wonder if I can go now.

He washes his hands at the sink. "Birdie needs some proper clothes," he says. "This seems to be part of the problem he has at school."

"He doesn't have a problem."

"Missing twenty-seven days is a problem."

"But it doesn't have anything to do with his clothes."

Patrick stops drying his hands. "That's not what his teacher said."

"Ms. Cross-Hams?" I don't mean for this to slip out, but I'm shocked Birdie's school troubles are being blamed on his clothes. Then again, Birdie's teacher—whose arms *are* like giant ham hocks—hasn't been a fan of Birdie since we showed up last year, a couple weeks into December.

According to Birdie, the first thing Ms. Cross-Hams said to him was that he couldn't have his purse in class.

Birdie's always been the teacher's favorite, so he didn't know what to say. And he hasn't figured it out since.

Patrick sighs again and hangs the towel by the sink. "Now that you live here, there's going to be some changes." He calls Duke, who stands at the sound of his name, and they head out of the kitchen. Right before he goes out, he stops and says, "On Monday, I'll drive you guys to school. I'm going to speak to Birdie's teacher. We'll get it sorted out. She has some ideas." Before I can think of anything else to say, he and Duke go, leaving me standing next to the mounds of dough.

Mama always let Birdie wear what he wanted. He never wears skirts or dresses to school because he says they aren't comfortable for dodgeball, which is another thing Birdie likes. Even still, most people do notice that Birdie doesn't dress like most boys. But his pink and purple shirts, rainbow shoes, and leggings covered in pink donuts, and everything else, have never really been a problem.

Of course, getting Birdie to go to school has also never been a problem.

I press my finger into a doughy heap. It is soft and still warm from being kneaded.

I want to smash it into nothing.

**Observation #774 Old Bedroom Inventory

- 81 books: novels, comics, biographies, reference books, and 6 poetry books, which I rarely opened (all from Mama)
- 11 observation notebooks
- 4 plants, left over from a science fair project
- 4 strands of twinkling lights on a fake palm tree from Birdie's 7th birthday party
- 1 Swiss Army knife
- 1 Treasure box of rocks and shells
- 9 board games, plus one I made when I was 8
- 1st place ribbons: 6th-grade science fair, spelling bees & math league
- 1 bean bag chair (for reading)
- 1 banker's lamp (found at a garage sale) on a small white writing desk (which Mama found on the side of the road, sanded down, and painted)
- 1 life lived freely (even if my room was half the size of the one at Patrick's)

CHAPTER 3

THE TORNADO

To say that Janet Rosweiler is my best friend is a little bit of a lie. I guess it's better to say that she is my only friend. She was the first person I met after Patrick drove Birdie and me to California from Mama's.

Janet lives with her mom in a house that's really a double-wide trailer on a two-acre plot of land. It sounds bad, but it's actually pretty nice. There's a big oak tree and six big cedars and the first time I saw it, my chest ached thinking of home. Janet has her own room and her mom has two jobs and like four boyfriends, so she's barely there. Which means Janet basically has the place to herself.

I've walked to Janet's from town probably twenty times and never knew Patrick lived right down the street. Birdie and me would even explore the nearby nature reserve, which stretches almost to Patrick's backyard, and still we never knew.

This morning, Sunday, Patrick and Duke left before the sun was up. Birdie was still in his room when I slipped a note under his door reminding him I was going to Janet's. My tennis shoes make little crunching noises as I cross the gravel driveway to her trailer door. I'm starting to doubt if she's awake even though she made me promise to come by at nine a.m.

"Hey loser, don't you have anything better to do on a Sunday morning?" Janet yells from a window.

"Ha! You're the one who told me to come early," I yell back.

"God, your hair is a DISASTER. I should take a 'before' photo. Get in here."

Lucky, a dog Janet found behind the Stop-and-Go, barely lifts her head from a nap. I hope they aren't waiting for her to become a watchdog.

I walk in, looking around.

"She's not here," says Janet. "It's Sunday morning, meaning last night was Saturday night, which is Ross's night, so she's probably at his place *as if* I care. You want some Froot Loops and a smoke? My mom forgot her cigarettes. Again."

I sit down to her bowl of cereal, ignoring the cigarettes as she begins brushing my hair. Janet is fourteen, a year and a half older than me, but she started smoking when she was ten. Now she says I'm already behind on my smoking career by more than two years. I don't know if I totally believe her, though, because I've never once seen her actually finish a cigarette.

Janet sighs. "I can't believe you go outside looking like this. Seriously, why am I even friends with you?"

"Because I helped get your cell phone out of your mom's locked car. And because I sometimes do your English homework."

"Okay, okay, okay. Whatever. Now tell me. What is Patrick's house like? I can't believe you live there now. I've always wondered about the inside. And what's with the giant round thing in the front yard?"

"I don't know. I think it's a shed." I swirl the cereal bowl. "Birdie says it's an old grain silo."

"Oh my God—Birdie. Is Patrick actually babysitting him?"

"No." I tell her about the note I found this morning that said Patrick had a quick job in town and would be back later.

"So Birdie's all alone doing what? He could have come with you, you know. The kid knows more about hair than you do."

"He's sleeping." That's not really true. I heard him moving around in his room, but Birdie's not a big fan of Janet. He calls her "an acquired taste, like sushi." I have no idea where he gets these phrases.

Janet goes to her room to find a spray bottle and her

stand-up mirror. When she returns, she stops in the door-way and does that thing where she pops her hip out and then scowls. "Okay. Spill it."

"What?"

She walks over and sets the mirror in front of me and then starts in on my hair again. "Is it that bad? Patrick's house?"

I shrug. "I mean, it's just such a big house compared to Uncle Carl's apartment."

"Yeah, but don't you have your own room? Like, it's got to be better than sleeping on a futon next to some grungy couch."

I shrug again.

"Oh, don't you go all broody on me. It's too early for broodiness. This is one fine day, Jack Royland. Do you know what today is?"

Of course I know what today is. Today Janet starts at Snip 'n' Shine, the one and only hair salon in town. Janet says she's been hounding Cherylene, Snip 'n' Shine's owner, for three years to let her work there. Janet even offered to work for nothing. I guess Cherylene finally couldn't pass up the free labor.

Janet tugs on a piece of her straight black hair and frowns in the mirror. "Why would God waste such beautiful curls on someone who doesn't even want to look nice? Instead, I get stuck with this hair." She ties her hair into a bun, then goes back to mine. "Anyway, today is the day. You are looking at a gen-you-ine Snip 'n' Shine apprentice!"

She turns my stool so that I'm facing her. She's totally absorbed. Three bobby pins sit in her mouth an inch from my nose.

"Maybe I could get you a job there," she says as she shoves the hundredth bobby pin into my hair. "You know, get you out of that house since you obviously hate it so much even though you've only been there for like twelve hours." She side-eyes me.

I tell her it's been more like twenty-two hours and she rolls her eyes and says, "Jack Royland, inmate number one-oh-one at Patrick's Prison: Close your eyes."

She lays the hair spray on thick.

I wish I could explain the difference between Mama's house and Patrick's. But Janet would never understand a place like Mama's.

I don't realize I'm gripping the hard plastic side of the countertop until Janet says, "Hey Hulk-Smash. Don't break the counter, okay?"

She's looking at me with that serious Janet intensity. I let go.

"I can't wait to show the girls at the salon the magic I have done with your hair. That's why I asked you to come over."

She wheels my chair around so I can see the final product in the mirror. I barely recognize myself, which is what usually happens when Janet gets ahold of my hair. My normally unruly lion's mane is transformed like magic, my bangs swept up, meshing with the twisted curls at the top of my head. I look five years older.

It's just what I'm hoping for, but I don't tell her that.

"I can't go out like this," I say, though I can't help but smile. Even my giant practically unibrow eyebrows aren't bothering me, my hair looks so good.

"Oh yes you can. I have to show Cherylene as many hairstyles as possible. That way, I can prove my worth at the salon. Because they might have people who can cut hair there, but I swear to God, no one there can style. I've seen the girls that come out of that place on prom day and it is so sad."

She tinkers with my hair a little more.

"So you're meeting me there, Jack Royland, in a couple of hours when I start my shift. Bring Birdie, if you have to. I need your head as proof." She flicks her long finger at my curls and then disappears into her room to change.

On the day we arrived in California I saw Janet through the windshield of Patrick's truck. The afternoon sun glinted off the glass and made her look like a mirage. It was the first time I got to see the Janet scowl and that stance she does when she means business.

She was standing in the doorway of the Lock & Key, the store underneath Uncle Carl's apartment that he manages. With her hip popped to one side, a skateboard under her arm, she was saying something about having left her cell phone in her mom's car and could Carl please jimmy the lock for her?

Me, Birdie, and Patrick walked up to the Lock & Key from the truck and that's when Uncle Carl came out of the store, frowning at Janet.

"Get out of here. I'm not going to jimmy a lock for you."

"But my phone. What would *you* do without your cell phone?" Janet said.

"I don't have one."

"Yes you do. I've seen it."

"Yeah, well, most of the time it sits at home in between my couch cushions, out of battery."

"But the car is right across the street, *see*, and my mom took off for the night with Ross, maybe the whole weekend. Can never tell with her. And she took her dumb car keys with her."

Uncle Carl was about to respond, but that's when he saw the three of us, me, Patrick, and Birdie, probably looking really tired after driving for more than seven hours. "Well, melt my cheese, there you all are! Look at you!"

I looked at him, but I couldn't help staring at the girl behind him. She wore a hot-pink sweatshirt that had a giant mouth with its pierced tongue sticking out on it. Her hair was elaborately done up in two buns, one on each side of her head, and even though it was December, her face was still tan and freckled from summer.

Uncle Carl came over to us and said, "I wasn't expecting you for another hour. Come on, let's go up. You must be tired or hungry. You guys want some food? We can go to the Fry Shack. Birdie, my man, look at you. You have a growth spurt or something?"

Then Janet was like, "Yeah, let's go to the Fry Shack, *across the street*, and before you go in you can stop at my mom's car, which is right in front, and open it so I can get my cell phone."

He didn't look behind him, he just said, "People, this is Janet, the town menace. Town menace, meet my niece and nephew, Jack and Birdie."

"Nice to meet you," she said quickly, her eyes zeroing on me. "Now, I wonder what *you* would say to a helpless person just trying to get her cell phone and asking for assistance. Would you leave her high and dry like her mom did and now just like Carl here too? Hmmm? How about you?" She pointed at me.

I stupidly looked around and then pointed to myself and said, "Me?"

Janet rolled her eyes and then blew a bunch of air out of her mouth and started turning away.

I can't explain why, but all of a sudden my heart constricted like a fist had grabbed it and I felt like everything about this new town was starting out poorly all because Uncle Carl wouldn't help her get her phone out of the car.

So then I awkwardly shouted, "I would help that helpless

person! I would help that person get their phone!" She stopped and looked back over her shoulder. Then I looked at Uncle Carl, who I hadn't seen or talked to for almost four years. "Uncle Carl, can't you help her get her cell phone?"

After some sighing and huffing and "talk about war on all fronts" comments he went into the Lock & Key, got some kind of long, metal tool, and crossed the street with Janet, pointing it at her like a sword, saying, "You're lucky I have a soft spot for those kids."

He jimmied the lock and she got her cell phone out and then he locked and closed the door again. From across the street she raised her hand, which had the phone, and was like, "Hey you! Girl with the hair! Best friends forever!" Then she skated down the street.

I wasn't sure then, because the whole thing had seemed impossible and spontaneous, like something that would happen to Mama. But it turned out, she'd been talking to me.

**Observation #775: Janet

She never asks if she can style my hair.
I sit down and she just does it.
Being around her is like being around a tornado
—unpredictable and chaotic
and I can't help but get sucked into her storm.
Which is fine by me.

CHAPTER 4

THE LONG WAY TO TOWN

When I get back from Janet's trailer, Patrick comes in from the backyard where he's been trimming the four scraggly trees. They look naked now, and I wonder if he knows what he's doing. Duke's outside, looking up from his nap, waiting for him.

"Where've you been?" he asks, wiping his face with his bandanna. He looks at my hair but doesn't say anything else.

"Janet's. She lives down the street."

"I know where she lives. When you go somewhere, you should probably leave me a note." He goes over to a drawer by the phone and takes out a pad of paper and a pen. "Just write it on here."

"Okay."

He looks at me and then nods and goes back outside. Patrick pats Duke on the head before returning to the trees.

I don't mention the plan to go into town. It's too hard to talk to a clam.

Later, it takes Birdie and me almost half an hour to walk to the salon. In town, besides the shops, there are some houses and apartments, along with our schools and the library. But most of the older houses with land are farther out, off the highway. People come through here on their way to the mountain but not a lot of people actually live here. Janet said there used to be a barber shop, but this town is too small to have two places to cut your hair. So I guess the guys have to go to Cherylene too.

We each eat a Honey Bunny Bun as we go. Birdie licks his sticky fingers and straightens his pink and purple lightning-bolt rings.

"It's going to take forever to get to school now," says Birdie.

"We used to walk almost as far when we'd go to the reserve."

"Yeah, but that wasn't every day. And I actually like going to the reserve."

"Well, Patrick said he's going to bring us to school tomorrow. He's going to talk to your teacher."

"Don't remind me." He changes the subject. "I wonder if Uncle Carl has any new magazines."

We're crossing the street toward the salon, and I'm about

to say that I doubt Uncle Carl bought new magazines since yesterday, when I hear Janet's voice ring across the pavement.

"Oh my God, I can't believe you haven't totally destroyed your hair. Honestly, I am truly in shock. Here, take my pulse. And gimme some Honey Bunny." She takes a piece of my bun and pokes at my hair one last time.

"Are we going inside?" I ask.

"Yes. Okay, so for the big reveal, they will be looking at the hair, of course, the masterpiece, but your posture and facial expression will affect how they see the hair. I can't have you walking in like some slumped, three-day-old chalupa that's been rotting in the sun. We can't do anything about your sad fashion sense, and the track pants that you love so much, but whatever! Be confident! Walk in like you're wearing a Bob Mackie gown!" She gives me a quick demonstration.

Birdie smiles and twirls along with her. Janet looks at him and rolls her eyes. "See, even he can do it," she says. Then she takes a deep breath. "All right—this is it!"

Bells tied to the door jingle as Janet ushers us in.

Every chair is filled with a customer getting snipped and shined. Before Janet even has a chance to announce us, Cherylene appears from the back of the building.

"Janet, come get this broom. Start sweeping. Any longer and we're going to have a problem tantamount to Captain Kirk's trouble with tribbles."

You might think that a clash between a stick-thin

fourteen-year-old girl and a fifty-year-old woman who looks more like a truck driver, except for her hair and nails, would be no contest. But this is Janet.

"Cherylene—" she starts.

"That's Miss Cherylene. Or you can call me Captain."

"Right. Miss Captain Cherylene, allow me to introduce my best and most curly-haired friend, Jack Royland." She nudges me forward and I try to push my shoulders back like she said.

Cherylene moves around me, batting me away like a fly in her ear, and puts the broom into Janet's hand. "And allow me to introduce you to your new bestest, most straight-haired friend, the broom."

She turns and begins walking to her office in the back.

"Miss Cherylene, didn't you notice Jack's hair? I styled it this morning. And I did it without any product other than a bit of hair spray. Two whole hours ago."

Cherylene sighs heavily and then picks up some towels and puts one at each station. "I noticed nothing but our trouble with tribbles." Her long, neon-orange manicured fingernail points down at the fat clumps of hair.

"But Cherylene, you have to look—"

"No, Janet. I don't have to do anything. You've pestered me for years about working here and then I said you could come and sweep and clean and silently soak up the life of salon work. I am captain of this ship, so you either want to sweep the deck, or you don't want to be here at all." She glares hard at Janet and then disappears into her office.

Janet is statue-still, but I can see her fists tightening. The rest of the hair stylists, who had gone silent moments ago, begin to move again and chat with their clients.

"Come on," I whisper to Janet. "Let's go."

"No," Janet says through her teeth. "It's time for me to sweep." With the Janet scowl, and her own shoulders pushed back, she walks onto the salon floor between the chairs and raises her voice a little louder. "Because apparently the captain can't keep her ship's deck clean."

Birdie and me head outside.

He looks back through the shop window.

"Come on," I say to him, tugging his shirt toward Uncle Carl's apartment down the block. "She'll be okay."

"I'm not worried about Janet," says Birdie. "But Cherylene doesn't know what she's gotten herself into."

When we get to Uncle Carl's apartment, we pause. Before this weekend, we would've just walked right in. I knock three times, but he doesn't answer. I peek inside, because Uncle Carl never locks the door. The apartment looks the same as it ever did. I call out hello, but no one answers.

The whole situation with Uncle Carl really started to go wrong when Marlboro died. It happened about nine months after we'd moved in, on the same day as Birdie's makeup-makeup back-to-school meeting with his teacher. It was a double makeup because Uncle Carl never went to the first two.

Maybe if Marlboro hadn't died on that exact same day, we'd still be living above the Lock & Key shop on Main Street.

Marlboro, "the most noble bearded dragon to crawl the earth," had been fine that morning. Then, at some point, Uncle Carl fed her some crickets and went downstairs to the Lock & Key. He didn't come back up for hours and by then it was too late. A fat cricket had lodged itself in her throat and that was that. Sometimes, when I think about my day at school, I try to imagine what class I was in when it happened. I know it's kind of creepy to do that, but I can't help it.

So because he discovered Marlboro like thirty minutes before the back-to-school meeting, Uncle Carl didn't show up. He spent the time at his apartment crying and I guess probably drinking too.

Birdie and me were still hanging around his school library when his teacher came and scowled like we had done something wrong. She had her big ham hock arms folded across her chest and said, "Where is your uncle?"

Birdie and me looked at each other for a second and all I could say was something stupid like, "Isn't he with you?"

"Would I be here if he was?" Her eyes were so narrowed that I couldn't see her pupils.

Her pale pink forearms flushed as she said, "This is the third meeting we've scheduled. The missed meetings combined with your brother's already poor attendance means I will have to go to the administration about this. It's unacceptable." She turned and went out the door and Birdie and me were left sitting in the quiet library with the nice school librarian looking sad for us.

Okay, so we did have some attendance issues. Birdie, who had always liked school, started claiming to be sick a lot, but he never felt hot to me except for maybe once. Uncle Carl told me to leave him alone, that it would take time. Well, nine months into it, four weeks into a new school year even, Birdie was still sick at least once a week. Uncle Carl never once took his temperature.

I'm not saying Uncle Carl didn't try to cheer us up and fix the problem. Sometimes he'd take us to the mall and we'd all share a giant Cinnabon and then walk around Scare Monkey, the gag gift store. Other times we went miniature golfing, but only on Two-Buck Tuesdays.

To be honest, I liked not having to go to school on those days too. I never felt like I was missing anything. It's not like I had any friends at school who would call me up later on and ask, "Hey, where were you today?"

Still, we didn't hear anything from Birdie's teacher until about four weeks after Marlboro died. There was this spelling bee at Birdie's school. Birdie was not keen on participating, but he was the best speller in his class by far and I think he wanted to try and win his teacher over.

Uncle Carl was in the middle of trying to get Marlboro back from a taxidermist who he paid five hundred and sixty dollars to get her stuffed and mounted to a piece of shiny wood with a cigarette hanging out of her mouth. I guess as a baby she got a twig lodged in her mouth that looked just like a cigarette. So, after carefully getting the stick out, he named her after his favorite cigarette brand and they were best friends for fourteen years before she choked on the cricket.

Anyway, Uncle Carl hadn't heard from the taxidermist in two weeks, but he went to the spelling bee anyway. It was there that Birdie's teacher approached him about the missed double-makeup meeting and Birdie's absences. I don't know exactly what happened because Uncle Carl was standing at the back of the auditorium and I was up near the front with Birdie.

All I remember is Uncle Carl yelling, "Excuse me! Who are you? Nurse Ratched or something?" Then there was all this commotion and Birdie's teacher called Uncle Carl unreliable and a poor guardian and that she would report him and then there was more shouting, this time from other parents, and Uncle Carl kicked a chair over and then stormed out. Birdie didn't want to go on stage after that and we went out the side door and walked to Uncle Carl's apartment alone.

The next day, Patrick came over so they could discuss some things. They were gone for most of their discussion, but when they came back I heard them arguing as they got out of Patrick's truck. Uncle Carl pointed at Patrick, saying that all we needed was a little help and a little time, both of which Patrick never wanted to give in the first place.

But Patrick just shook his head, his hands on his belt. "I already told you, Carl. It's too late. The teacher reported the truancy. She made sure of it after you threw a chair at her."

"Well excuse me for caring about the kids' feelings." Uncle Carl threw up his hands and then headed toward the stairs. Patrick drove off in his truck.

Marlboro came back from the taxidermist a week later and we moved in with Patrick three days after that.

I knock on Uncle Carl's door again, and Rosie's bellowing voice in her British accent calls out from the street. "He's not there. Said he was headed to Social Security. Went to buy lotto tickets more like it."

Rosie is the love of Uncle Carl's life, his sort-of girlfriend. You know the kind of person you can't help but like even when they are completely opposite of you? That's Rosie.

"Social Security's not open on Sunday," I say.

"That's what I said, but he just got on that stupid bicycle and disappeared." She rolls her eyes. "And he wonders why

I keep saying no. Ha!" About once a month, Uncle Carl asks Rosie to marry him. She turns him down every time.

"Come, then," she says, waving us down to the curb to her truck. "I'll make you some lunch. I've got some new ones to show you."

Rosie owns the Quesadilla Ship—the best (and only) food truck in town. The truck's old—it was the only thing she could afford when she left England ten years ago to take care of her mom, who has some kind of cancer and also some condition where she forgets things a lot.

She climbs inside the lime-green truck and we wait at the ordering window. With a flick of her wrist, she slaps a couple flour tortillas on the griddle and her eight bracelets ring together like bells.

Rosie wields the spatula like a wand. "Wow, look at that fantastic hair. Janet got ahold of you, looks like. Now pick your poison. You can try my new garlic fresco quesadilla. It's hot off the presses, that new recipe." Her smile is so big it's about to break her face.

"Sure, I'll try it," I say, because I always try Rosie's new recipes.

"Just a regular for me," says Birdie.

A Birdie Regular is a quesadilla with Colby Jack cheese and salsa, with avocado and sour cream on top. I guess Birdie's ordered it enough times that now it's "regular."

Rosie winks, her green eye shadow flashing at me. I've

never seen Rosie without eye shadow and she always lays it on thick, making it stand out against her brown skin.

"Birdie boy, when are we going to have another sewing session?"

I wonder if she's going to mention how we live a million miles away now.

Birdie looks down and shrugs his shoulders. "Soon, hopefully."

An employee from the Stop-and-Go walks up to the ordering window and asks for a Tomato Onion Sizzle.

Birdie and me sit down on the curb. He holds out his hand and watches an ant crawling around his finger until it reaches his pinkie, which has light purple polish shining in the sun.

"Do you think this color is nice? I kind of wish it was darker," says Birdie.

"It's because you didn't put on two coats." I know this from the one and only time Rosie did my nails. I rub his nail with my finger and he snatches it away after a couple seconds. He knows how to make polish darker. Mama taught him.

Mama had a whole set of nail polish, which she kept lined up on her dresser like a little nail polish army. Birdie used to always rearrange them into rainbow order.

For the first time I wonder what happened to all her polish. Is it still lined up along the back of her dresser? Packed up in a box? And would a place like Patrick's be easier for Birdie if he had a nail polish army?

He squints at the ant. "Maybe I should take up ant farming."

I wonder if he notices that he's doing it again, that thing where he says the things Mama used to say. She was always telling us how she should "take up" some new activity.

Suddenly, there is a screech of bicycle brakes.

The wind gusts and Uncle Carl half jumps, half falls off his bike and lays it down on the asphalt in front of us. He's got a bag from Yum Yum Donuts in his hand and a little box that says *Shasta Cupcake Company* tucked under his arm. He's wearing jeans and a collared shirt, which I didn't even know he had. There's an orange balloon tied to the handlebars of his bike.

Rosie comes out with our quesadillas and one of her eyebrows goes way up.

Uncle Carl kneels dramatically at Rosie's feet. "Mi querida, mi amor." He holds up the cupcake box like he's offering a sword. "Marry me, Rosemary Wilson."

"No thanks, but I will take the cupcake." She takes the box from his hand, sits on the curb, and he plops down next to her.

"But I biked all the way to the mall for that," he says. "Throw a dog a bone. How many nos can one man handle?"

"You biked all the way to the mall just for this cupcake?" Rosie says.

"And the gourmet donuts for my favorite niece and nephew." He tosses the bag toward us. "They were handing out free balloons, Mr. Bird. Thought you'd want one." He looks at Birdie and his bushy eyebrows go up and down in exaggerated excitement. Sometimes I wonder if he thinks that Birdie is still the four-year-old kid he met five years ago.

"I thought you were going to the Social Security office, which we all know is closed on the weekends," says Rosie. "And you got all spiffed up to go too."

"Well, I was on a top secret mission and I had to throw you off my trail."

"Top secret mission?" I say as I dig through the donut bag.

"Yes, and even you two beautiful ladies and this strapping young lad won't get the secret out of me. These lips are sealed tight."

"Right," says Rosie, "just like your super-secret way of getting free cable? Is it as secret as that?"

Uncle Carl closes his eyes and shakes his head. "I can't say I know what you're talking about."

Rosie rolls her eyes and Uncle Carl winks at me as he lights a cigarette. "Well now. Looks like Janet got ahold of you," he says, pointing his cigarette at my head.

"She was helping Janet showcase her hair-styling skills," says Birdie.

"So you let the menace touch your hair again?" asks Uncle Carl.

"Don't call her that," says Rosie. The funny thing is that sometimes I think Janet likes to be called the town menace. Like that maybe it gives her some kind of power or something.

Rosie asks, "Who's going to defend that girl when I'm not here?"

In less than three weeks, Rosie's taking a trip back to England. I guess her dad is sick now and her stepmom needs some help with getting his affairs in order.

I take a bite of quesadilla, which is fried to golden perfection. The saltiness is a good companion to the sugary donut. I go back and forth, taking a bite of one, savoring it, and then taking a bite of the other. Sometimes when I'm eating Rosie's quesadillas, I feel like my life is maybe totally fine.

Uncle Carl taps his cigarette over an ashtray that Rosie keeps on the sidewalk near the Quesadilla Ship just for him.

I'm waiting for him to ask about Patrick's house, but maybe he's hoping one of us will say something first.

Or maybe all of us are pretending that nothing's changed in the last twenty-four hours.

A group of people walk up, looking like they're headed to the hot-air balloon rides, which launch from a spot across town and over the hill. They've got expensive-looking coats on. "Back to the grindstone." Rosie heads back to her truck.

"So," Uncle Carl says after Rosie is gone. "Looks like you've survived one day with the old man."

Birdie says, "And Duke the dog, who doesn't care about anyone except Patrick."

"Patrick even gave him some of the steak he made us," I say.

"Wow, steak, huh?" says Uncle Carl. "The goat's pulling out all the stops to impress you. Got money to throw around, I guess."

Clam. Goat. Old man.

Birdie shrugs. "I wish we could live with you, Uncle Carl."

Uncle Carl stubs out his cigarette and blows the last of the smoke toward the sky. "Me too, kid. But the old man's got more room, and a better job, and he's just . . . better. For you."

Birdie says, "I really don't care about sleeping on a couch. I don't mind. It's a great couch, actually."

Uncle Carl kind of laughs and then shakes his head and sighs. "Did you guys already eat all the Honey Bunny Buns? Do you need more?"

I stand up and say, "I have to go to the bathroom." And then I walk up to Uncle Carl's apartment.

In the kitchen, I dig through the junk drawer until I find the picture of a younger Uncle Carl and a teenage Mama, and the best thing about this picture is that she looks exactly like me. The same thick eyebrows and frizzy hair—not at all shiny, smooth, and styled like she normally had it. In the photo, Uncle Carl is looking off to the side, but Mama is looking right at the camera.

Under her wild bangs, her eye makeup is smudgy and dark, but she has that same look she'd get when a Wolf Day was coming. Fired up but also resolved and defiant. Her cropped T-shirt and tight jeans look strangely like something Janet would wear.

I close Uncle Carl's drawer and look over at the couch. I almost trick myself into thinking that we still live here. That later today I'll unfold the futon and lie down and try to sleep.

Birdie and me are here, but our home and Mama's things are seven and a half hours away in another state. Thinking of Mama and Janet makes me realize that I need to be more determined too.

**Observation #776: Things I Already Know About the Bus

The bus station is in the next town, 16 minutes away.

We have to take a local bus from the sidewalk in front of Uncle Carl's apartment to get there.

Then bus #331 takes 8 hours and 51 minutes to get to Portland, Oregon.

For a long-distance bus, the cost of an adult ticket is $32. Kids are $26.

Local buses cost $1.75.

I have $68.71 saved up from birthdays and Christmas.

I don't think two kids can ride alone.

But I look a lot older when my hair is done up.

And Birdie is great at acting.

And persuading too. Birdie could convince Mrs. Spater to bake a whole lemon pound cake for him, even when she was tired.

Maybe he could convince her that we are better off living with her.

That our lives stopped when we left and all we want is to come home.

CHAPTER 5

Looking Out

The next morning is Monday and Birdie neatly arranges his books and binders inside his backpack before we leave for school. He's got black leggings on along with his favorite purple jacket. I don't see any jewelry, not even his milk-and-cookies charm necklace, which he wears almost every day.

Birdie says, "Patrick didn't get home until nine o'clock last night. And now he's already out in the shed. Is he like a secret agent or something?"

"I guess he's some kind of mechanic. Rosie says he drives all over Northern California fixing engines that other people can't fix."

Birdie says, "The engine whisperer," zipping his backpack closed.

I'm about to ask him if wearing the purple jacket at

school stresses him out, when Patrick suddenly calls from downstairs, telling us it's time to go.

Birdie puts his *Book of Fabulous*, which he usually brings with him, in one of his drawers. I offer him some of my toast but he shakes his Honey Bunny Bun at me.

"I hope you're not eating more than your share," I say. "It's fifteen each."

He rolls his eyes. "What do you think I am? A bun stealer?"

Patrick waits for us on the front step while the truck idles. He locks the door behind us and I'm surprised to find the truck warm on the inside.

When he pulls into my school's parking lot, he says, "I have a job in the next county and might be home a little late again. There's roast beef, cheese, and tomato in the fridge."

I look at Birdie, wanting to tell him that it's going to be okay. No matter what happens in that meeting with Patrick and Ms. Cross-Hams, I will make sure he's okay. But Birdie never makes eye contact with me.

"Maybe you should call my cell phone when you guys get home," Patrick says.

I nod.

I can tell he wants me to close the truck door and get a move on. So that's what I do. Except I don't exactly get a move on. I stand there in front of the school steps, with students streaming around me like water around a rock, and watch Birdie disappear in Patrick's truck.

...

My English teacher, Mr. Belling, peers over his glasses at us as he hands out a sheet explaining the details of our next project. Working with a partner, we're supposed to select a poet, research their life and poetry, and then make a poster to share with the class.

More than once Mr. Belling stops, takes off his glasses, and pinches the bridge of his nose, which is something he does when someone asks a stupid question. It's the perfect class to write in my notebook because Mr. Belling has to stop so many times and breathe himself calm in the face of many clueless students.

Sometimes, when I can't think of anything to write in my observation notebook, I doodle in the margins. I draw Birdie's milk-and-cookies charm necklace, which is probably at Patrick's house, tucked away in a drawer. I guess he didn't want to wear it when he knew he'd have to sit through a meeting about his clothes.

I'm not sure how long Mr. Belling has been calling my name when I finally hear, "Miss Royland? Hello? Earth to Jack Royland."

I look up from my notebook and see Mr. Belling frowning at me. The tall kid in front of me twists his body around, and under his long, blond bangs I see him eye my notebook. I quickly close it.

"I'm trying to inform you of your partner for the poetry

project. I hate to think that she'll have to do all the work because you chose to not pay attention in class."

Everyone looks at me and I think I even hear snickering.

"I've said this before, Miss Royland: Participation is much easier if you'd just pay attention to the front of the class instead of whatever you are doing in that notebook."

His bald head has gone from white to an aggravated red and the body odor coming off the tall kid begins to suffocate every other thought from my mind. I wish he'd turn around so that his arms are clamped down again, holding in that horrible smell. I don't know what it is with the boys this year, but they do not smell good.

Mr. Belling finally calls on another student. The boy in front of me turns back around.

When the bell rings, I don't wait to find out who my partner is. I grab my things and head out the door.

I'm at my locker when a voice behind me says, "It's not your fault. He always zeroes in on the smart ones in the class." I turn around and face a girl with huge blue-framed glasses. "I think he's jealous of the smart students. My mom knows him from way back. She said he's a frustrated failed novelist who is forced to teach middle school English for a living."

It's a girl named Krysten. I don't remember her last name. But her dark complexion and tons of neatly done braids and blue glasses make her stand out. She's one of two black students in the whole school.

"I'm Krysten, you're Jack," she says.

"Ummm" is all I can get out before she starts talking again.

"Is Jack short for something?"

"Um, Jackie?" For some reason her pointed questions make me second-guess everything I'm saying.

"Oh, okay," she says. "I was just wondering because my mom's name is Jacqueline and her friends sometimes call her Jack. Anyway, I just wanted to let you know that I've noticed Mr. Belling kind of picking on you since the school year started and I heard he only does that to students he thinks are smart. You and your brother just moved here last year, right? That kid with the girl clothes who I always see you with, he's your brother?"

"Yeah."

I don't know what she means about always seeing me with Birdie. It's not like he comes to school with me.

Then I realize: She means around town. She's probably gone by us in the car or something. I sometimes forget that's the sort of thing that happens in a small town.

"Anyway, I know you're still kind of new. So I just wanted you to know about Mr. Belling. That, and we're partners for the poetry project, so maybe we should come up with a time to meet and get started."

She stares at me like I'm a knot she's trying to untangle.

"They're not *girl* clothes," I say. "They're just *clothes*."

Her cheeks get a little darker and I feel bad for saying it so forcefully when it was just an honest mistake on her part. "Right. Sorry. I like his sneakers. Anyway, I also like your notebook. The one you had in class? I've noticed you write in it a lot. It's nice to see another person who writes. I have a journal at home. Are you a writer?"

I shove my notebook in my backpack and zip it up. I say "um" again, but even that gets stuck in my throat and nothing else comes out. I've literally never spoken to her before this moment and now she's suddenly here, noticing Birdie and his sneakers and my notebook.

"You should join a club," she says, smiling. "That's what I did when I moved here five years ago. I mean, I swear everyone still calls me the new girl, but maybe that's for other reasons. Joining a club helped with making friends, at least."

"Can we talk about the poetry project tomorrow?" For some reason this is the only sentence I can get out.

She starts nodding right away. "Yeah, sure. Okay." She doesn't stop nodding. "I think my mom is here anyway. All right, talk to you tomorrow, then, Jack. Bye!"

What I want to say is, "Yeah, see you later! And thank you for letting me know about Mr. Belling. And sorry for snapping at you. The poetry project sounds interesting. And no, I'm not a writer. I just write what I see."

Because that's the normal thing to say.

I mean, it's normal to at least say *something*.

But of course it all just comes out as a nod.

...

I was eight when Mama gave me my very first observation notebook. It was striped blue and green with a binding like a real book. Along the spine, in shiny silver lettering, it said: *Jack's Journal.*

"And you know what?" she said. "My mama gave me my first journal too." She looked away from me and down at her lap. It was the first time she'd talked about her mama.

"Whenever my head gets too full and buzzy, I write my thoughts down, and maybe make a piece of toast, and then all of a sudden, I feel lighter. Like maybe I can breathe a little longer. Understand?"

"I don't have any thoughts like that," I said.

"Sure you do. I see you looking at everything. Watching people. Both you and Birdie are so quiet. How did I get such quiet kids?" She lightly twisted my nose like she often did with Birdie. "But you know what? Birdie looks in, you look out."

I remember it was the middle of a Saturday. All of a sudden, our cranky neighbor Mr. Byrne started mowing his lawn and Mama put her hands around her eyes like binoculars. "You look out," she said again, laughing. It was my favorite laugh, the one when she was in a good mood and she didn't mind sitting on my bed, legs crisscrossed up against mine like she was my best friend. We both leaned into the window and spied on Mr. Byrne.

"He's got two different socks on," I said.

"Maybe we should go buy him some socks."

"No way." I was never sure how far she'd take her ideas.

"Come on. We'll leave them on his porch with a bow on top. We'll buy all the socks in the store and make sure he's never in need of socks again. He'll thank us. He'll never be cranky. He'll never file a parking complaint against my friends when they visit."

"He doesn't always have mismatching socks."

"How do you know?"

"Because . . . I watch."

She scooted off my bed and grinned. "See, I told you," she said. "You look out."

She tapped my journal three times with her bright red fingernail. "I might still buy him some socks. Grilled cheese and broccoli for dinner, my little spy!" And then she floated out of my room, toward the kitchen.

I still have that blue-and-green-striped journal. I keep it in an old backpack, along with the ten other notebooks I've used since. Of course none of them are as nice as that first one. In fact, most are like the one I have now—small, cheap, and spiral-bound. But they are filled with what I see because I look out.

When I get to town, Birdie is waiting for me by the Quesadilla Ship, just like we agreed. There's a couple students ordering quesadillas and Birdie sits off to the side looking through a book. When I stand over him, he doesn't even say hi.

"Guess what?" he mumbles. "I have to get new clothes now because of Mrs. Cross-Hams."

"What happened?"

"She convinced Patrick that new clothes would solve all my school problems. And afterward, the only thing he said to me was, 'We'll sort it out over the weekend. We'll go to the mall.' He didn't even say bye."

I don't waste another second. "Stand up. We're going to the library."

Birdie looks up at me. "Now?"

I don't want to explain yet. I just want to go get the details.

"Come on. I have to find something for a school project." Which is true, but I have no intention of still living here when it's due.

We walk three blocks to the county library and spot the head librarian, Ms. Perkins, right away.

Birdie loves her, probably. I think it's because she's got a totally unique style and doesn't seem to care about what other people think of her. Like today it's a long denim skirt with laced-up leather hiking boots and a beaded necklace. Her gray-and-black braids hang down like twin snakes and her necklace clinks together as she leans to grab more books out of the book drop.

"Well, look what the cat dragged in. A two-for-one special," she says when she spots us.

She starts toward the door and we jog to catch up.

"So you're back," says Birdie.

"Indeed," says Ms. Perkins.

"And your sister in San Francisco. How is she? What's San Fran like? Are you glad to be home?"

The small black mole on her tawny forehead goes up as her eyebrow raises. "What did you eat for lunch? Not another convenience-store donut, I hope."

"Honey Bunny Buns are buns, not donuts," he says.

I open the door and Ms. Perkins nods her thanks and Birdie follows her to the back.

I head for the computers with Internet.

On the bus website, I find the FAQ page, where I read that there's something called an Unaccompanied Child Form.

Children between the ages of 12–16 who travel unaccompanied must have a completed Unaccompanied Child Form and pay full fare.

There's a bus leaving for Portland tomorrow morning at 7:45 a.m.

We have to be at the local bus stop in front of Uncle Carl's apartment by 6:52 a.m.

I take out my notebook.

Observation #777: Inventory of Things at Mama's House

Her sequin bag.

The nail polish army.

The smooth wooden egg.

Birdie's little vanity, which lit up.

Mama's shiny gold-and-pink kimono.

The painting of a fat cat in a tuxedo.

The drawer with our favorite takeout menus.

Our huge ticking banana clock (in hall bathroom).

My dollhouse that was actually a lumberjack cabin.

Pillows Mama made that looked like cheeseburgers.

The Tokyo Tower hat rack Mama found at a garage sale.

Mama's record player that she bought with her own money at 16.

Mama's Swan Lake musical jewelry box, with a twirling crowned swan.

Perfume, jewelry & all the pretty things Mama decorated herself with.

Miss Luck Duck, our best lamp, which sat by the front door like a sentry.

...

When I look up, Ms. Perkins is walking toward me.

I take the poet project information sheet out of my backpack and pretend to study it.

"Jack. This is for you." She hands me a little plastic envelope that says *What They Said Bookmarks*.

There are three bookmarks inside, each with a writer's face and a quote. The package says it includes Oscar Wilde, Maya Angelou, and C. S. Lewis.

"Thank you."

"So, Belling's got you doing poetry?" she asks, glancing at the information sheet.

"Yup."

"Usually I know the poet project has started when all the kids come in looking for poetry books. No other reason that many seventh graders would come to a library looking for poetry. The rush hasn't happened yet, though."

"It's not due for a while. We just started."

"Eager beaver?" She looks at me with an eyebrow raised and then she studies the list of poets. She hands the paper back to me.

"Have anyone in mind? I'm sure you do. Big reader and all."

"Not yet. I don't read a lot of poetry."

"Would you like some help? Or suggestions?"

I look over at the computer screen, which I never closed, and hope she doesn't notice.

"Maybe another day," I say. "I have a lot of other homework today."

She nods and studies me for just a moment and then says to go find Birdie. "He was a little too hyped up from the souvenir I bought him."

I tell her thanks again for the bookmarks, but she's already marching away, headed toward someone who needs help at the automatic circulation desk.

I find Birdie sitting on the floor, engrossed in a book with a picture of a crazy-looking dress that's covered in what looks like fresh flowers and moss. "Did Ms. Perkins get you a souvenir too?" he asks.

"She did. See?"

He looks over at the bookmarks and I see a yellow pen in his hand that says I ♥ SF. There's clear fluid with a little cable car that moves when he tilts his hand.

"What's that book about? The clothes look different," I say.

"It's *fashion*. By Alexander McQueen. He was a designer." He glances over at me. "He was a man, but he made dresses."

He turns the page and there's a picture of a white shoe that looks like it's carved. Birdie makes his body into a giant comma as he leans close to the book. "Do you think that's bone? It looks like bone."

"A shoe made of bone?"

He shrugs his shoulders. "It's outrageous and singular."

"Outrageous and what?"

"Singular. Ms. Perkins said it means 'unique.' This book was on her monthly display: The Outrageous and Singular."

He flips through a few more pages in silence and then says, "Ms. Perkins said her sister is sick." His voice is barely a whisper. "She didn't tell me at first but I kept asking questions about her trip. Now I feel bad because maybe she didn't want to talk about it."

I bump his shoulder with mine. "Hey, it's all right. She knows how you get when you eat too many Honey Bunny Buns."

"Yeah, my stomach hurts again."

I pat him on the knee. "I know. Sometimes it's hard for you to stop eating them."

"How come it's impossible to make friends in this town?" he asks.

I think about what Krysten said, about seeing Birdie and me around. I always figured we stood out because we were new, but I had no idea how much.

We really don't fit in here.

"What do you think of buses?" I ask him.

"They're okay," he says. "Sometimes buses smell."

"What do you think of a long bus ride? Like maybe nine hours long with a couple breaks."

I explain about the bus schedule and my idea to find Mama's things and talk to Mrs. Spater and convince her to take us back. "We can practically take care of ourselves. She'll understand once we tell her in person. I know she will."

I describe how I'll dress up like Mama or some kind of adult. I tell him that maybe if I can make my hair like Janet makes it, I might be able to pull it off. And that it will cost almost all the money I have saved, but it will be worth it to find Mama's things and convince Mrs. Spater to take us back.

"Maybe I'll have to dress up in a disguise," he says, a smile on his face. "Like a costume."

"Totally. But we'll have to get ready early, though. The bus comes at six fifty-two. I'll leave a note for Patrick saying we walked to school."

"Are you sure we can ride a bus like that alone?"

I hope that I am making the right decision. "Yes. Tomorrow is going to be a Wolf Day."

**Observation #778: Outrageous & Singular

Mama would have called Birdie's Alexander McQueen book—
WONDERFUL. SPECTACULAR. Maybe MAGICAL.

Uncle Carl would love it too. He'd turn it over in his hands &
then open it up & look at the pictures & say, "But do they make
it in a size 36?" or "Do they sell it at the Walmart?" or "I bet
that's itchy business for the lower half."

I bet Patrick would look right through the book like it wasn't even
there. Or he'd put it in the trash & then head off to work or into
the silo shed.

CHAPTER 6

A DOG WITH SNEAKERS

The thing about Wolf Day is that there isn't actually a wolf involved. It started five years ago when Birdie thought he saw a wolf in Mrs. Spater's backyard. I was pretty sure it was just a coyote, but Mama said, "Well, sometimes it's good to have a Wolf Day—a day when wild and unexpected and spectacular things can happen. You believe in them. And not just that, but you chase after those wild and spectacular things no matter what your brain might say about what's 'probably true.'"

So after that, we had Wolf Days. On a Wolf Day we'd do something unexpected and then follow wherever the day took us, saying yes to every spectacular thing, believing it would lead to something else magical. One time we learned how donuts are made. Another time, we ended up at a bat mitzvah celebration.

And we always found little souvenirs to remind us of

where we'd been, like a real-looking wooden egg we got from a family we helped move who had a bunch of chickens in their backyard.

At night, we'd always wait for the wolf. We'd sit silently in Mrs. Spater's backyard with mugs of hot chocolate and we'd stare into the trees and bushes and hope for some magic. Sometimes it was hard to be so quiet, but Mama said it was important to experience the silence as the night sky swallowed us up.

All I saw that first Wolf Day was the flash of a wild eye and the swish of a gray-brown tail. I know it was a coyote.

I guess the wolf is one of those things that you know isn't true, like the tooth fairy or something. And yet, there's still a very small, secret part of your brain that holds on to the possibility that it might be true because it's magic.

Really it was Mama's magic that made it work.

In a lot of ways, every day was Wolf Day with her.

In the morning, I wake Birdie up at five thirty. It is totally dark and Birdie jerks awake and immediately says "Jack?" in a sleepy voice.

"I'm here," I say, switching on the flashlight. "Are you already packed?"

"Yeah." He rubs his eyes.

"How long will it take you to get dressed and ready to go?"

"Half an hour?"

"Okay. We'll eat Honey Bunny Buns when we get to the bus station, okay?"

He nods again and says, "How come you're using that flashlight?"

"I'm worried Patrick will somehow see our room lights. Now remember, bring only what you can carry yourself. I'll have my own stuff to deal with. I'm not sure if we'll ever be back here."

My heart skips a beat saying that out loud.

"I know. You told me last night." Birdie switches on his own flashlight and gets out of bed. I go back to my room and finish my hair. When I'm done, I check my small duffel bag and backpack. I have to leave some clothes and books behind, but there's nothing to do about that. We still have to walk to town, take two buses, and then once we're in Portland, take the city bus to Mrs. Spater's.

I help Birdie get his bags down the stairs and lock the back door behind us with the hide-a-key.

As we walk along the side of the house, I already know Birdie is going to be too cold, but he insisted on wearing his zebra-print leggings and skirt, along with his purple jacket. He has his hair separated into two short pigtails and wears a silver-and-turquoise beanie, which I've never seen before.

"Rosie found it at the thrift shop," he says. "Don't worry, it's washed."

I put my finger to my lips as we pass in front of the house.

I hold Birdie's hand the entire way to town. Every few steps I look behind us thinking I'm going to see Patrick's truck. But we don't see anyone. It's like everyone except Birdie and me has suddenly disappeared or maybe been put under a sleeping spell.

Mama used to say that she could feel a Wolf Day coming on, like watching someone slowly swim to the surface of the lake or a pool after diving deep. They'd get clearer and clearer until finally, at some unpredictable moment, they'd break the surface of the water and there they were. Sometimes, I could tell by Mama's face when a Wolf Day was coming. She'd spend a lot of time observing Birdie and me, her eyes looking like little fires, and it was like only the three of us existed in the whole universe.

When Birdie and me get to town, the sky is purple and I can't wait to feel the sun on my face. We walk through town toward the bus stop and I nearly fall over when I hear a shout.

"What on God's green golf course are you two doing?"

It's Janet and she's sticking her head out of the salon door.

I sigh and walk over to her.

"Oh my God, are you guys leaving?" she says, glancing at our bags.

Birdie stands behind me.

"Kind of," I say.

"Kind of?"

"Okay, yeah, we are."

"Does Patrick know?"

"No."

"Carl?"

"No."

"*Rosie?*"

"No."

"Okay, so it's not just me you're abandoning."

"It's not like that."

She kicks at nothing and looks down the street toward the sunrise. "You guys know what you're doing, then? You're not gonna try to hitchhike and then get chopped up into little bits or something else horrible?"

"We're taking the bus. Please don't tell anyone."

She rolls her eyes. "I'm not going to tell anyone. Come on—who do you think I am?"

I tell her thanks.

She shrugs and acts cool but as much as I don't want to see it, there's hurt just below the surface. She's mad, she just doesn't know it yet. "Hey, you gotta do what you gotta do."

"What are you doing at the salon so early anyway?"

Janet rolls her eyes again. "Ugh. Cherylene said I couldn't graduate from sweeping the floors until I learned how to properly fold towels. And apparently they only fold towels in the morning. So here I am. Before school. Way before anyone should ever be awake."

"We have to go," I say, feeling sorry for the first time that we are leaving. I'd been trying not to think about Janet, and

Uncle Carl and Rosie. I knew if I did, then the magic of Wolf Day would be gone. My resolve would crumble. *I'll call them later, I think. I'll send them funny Portland postcards to let them know we're doing well. They'll come visit.* "The bus comes in fifteen minutes and I want to be early, just in case."

"Just don't talk to strangers, okay? And don't get into any creepy-looking vans with no windows."

I smile and say we won't. I wonder if I should hug her, but decide against it. I take a step away, suddenly feeling like she might not actually let us go.

But then she abruptly says, "Good luck," and turns around and disappears inside the salon.

The local bus number 23 arrives right on time at 6:52 and we get on with no problem. I squeeze Birdie's hand all the way to the bus station in the next town.

When we arrive, I go straight to the bathroom and check out my hair and makeup. I add a couple bobby pins, put more lip gloss on, and pinch my cheeks like Birdie told me to. I look down at my outfit—a sweater of Mama's and a pair of stylish jeans from Janet—hoping that along with my hair and makeup I will look enough like an adult.

"Two tickets for Portland, please." I practice in the mirror. "One adult, one child."

I clear my throat and try again.

"One adult and one child, for Portland."

I want to splash water on my face but don't want to ruin the eye shadow.

"I need one adult and one child. For bus number three thirty-one."

An old woman with a cane comes in. I tense up, thinking she might say something, but she barely glances my way before disappearing into a stall.

When I leave the bathroom, Birdie hops up from the bench and is like, "Can we get a hot chocolate from the machine?"

He's a little too peppy and that's when I realize he's probably eaten a couple more Honey Bunny Buns.

"Hot chocolate will make you have to go to the bathroom," I say.

"No it won't. I just went."

My hands start to sweat, and they never sweat, and I get more and more nervous as we stand in line.

I'm about to tell Birdie to calm down, when suddenly another ticket window opens up and it's our turn. I clear my throat and pinch my cheeks and walk up to the window. I start saying I need some tickets but I can't remember where we're supposed to be going. Then Birdie tugs on my sleeve and says in a loud little-kid voice, "Mommy, can I have a hot chocolate, please? *Please*? I'm cold. Please, Mommy."

I look at him for a second and then back at the ticket guy, who's kind of smiling at Birdie.

I remember my line and say, "One adult and one child for Portland, please. And is there a place to buy hot chocolate nearby?"

I give him the money, and the tickets land in front of me just like that, and the guy points to the hot beverage vending machine. I thank him and we take the tickets and go.

I buy two hot chocolates and we drink them as we wait for the bus to start boarding.

"I wish you would have told me that you were going to do that," I say, taking a sip of the hot chocolate, which tastes more like hot water with the idea of sugar sprinkled in.

"But it wouldn't have worked then. Plus I didn't know I was going to do it until I did it." Birdie swings his legs. "I'm keeping this cup forever," he says, holding his hot chocolate out. "It helped us get back home."

As the clock nears seven forty-five, I start to get nervous again but the driver barely looks at us. He seems to use all of his energy on scrutinizing our tickets. Once we're in our seats, I watch him get out and walk around the bus, checking the cargo area. He drinks three more cups of coffee and smokes two cigarettes and checks people's tickets. Then he stretches his back, gets into the driver's seat, pulls the bus out of the station, and hits Interstate Five.

**Observation #779: Bus People

<u>In front of us:</u> a lady with gray hair & a long skirt. She has
a backpack & two grocery bags. Kind of reminds me of Mrs.
Spater.

<u>Next to us:</u> a young guy with pasty white skin, black hair, black
beanie, black pants, black jacket & a ring through his nose.
He has headphones on & a skateboard. There's also a Shasta
Cupcake Company box on the seat next to him.

<u>Behind us:</u> a woman with 2 small kids, smaller than Birdie. She
spoke softly to them in Spanish, hugging them tight, and then
fell asleep before the bus even left. One kid fell asleep too. The
other stared at Birdie.

<u>Right here:</u> a brother & sister (who might look like a mom and
daughter or maybe two sisters), bags full of Honey Bunny Buns,
water, clothes, books, colored pencils. They're just trying to get
home.

...

"Medford, Oregon. This is Medford, Oregon," says a crackling radio voice.

I sit up and look around. The sun glares through the windows. We've been driving for more than two hours. I don't know how long I've been sleeping.

Birdie leans over to me, closing his *Book of Fabulous*. "I reeeeally have to go."

"I told you this would happen," I say. "The bus driver said there's a stop coming up. You can go then."

I'm not keen on getting off the bus. But Birdie is too nervous about the bad smell coming from the bus toilet and starts squirming and I realize that maybe a bathroom break is exactly what we need if I don't want a scene.

"Put everything back in your backpack," I say.

As everyone gets ready to stretch their legs, I spot the Alexander McQueen book in one of Birdie's bags. "Birdie, that's a library book. You shouldn't have brought it along."

"Mrs. Spater will help me mail it back."

He looks embarrassed and quickly zips up his bag and I feel bad for snapping at him. Who cares about one library book? And then I think of Ms. Perkins and feel kind of horrible that I won't ever see her again. But I shove that feeling down and stand up.

We file off the bus with some of the other passengers.

When I come out of the bathroom, Birdie's standing there with a wrinkled forehead. "What's wrong?" I ask.

"I didn't go."

"Why not? We have to get back on the bus." I look over at the bus, which is right where we left it.

"There are two guys in there and they are arguing."

"What do you mean?"

"They are fighting about the little dog that one of them has. About whether it's a purebred."

"In the bathroom?" I ask. I glance again at the bus.

"Well, maybe you shouldn't be going in the boys' bathroom anyway," I say, thinking of Birdie's outfit. Bathrooms are sometimes tricky things for him, but most of the time the boys' bathroom isn't much of a problem. I guess that's also because Birdie usually holds it and goes at home.

Just then I hear shouting and then barking. I say, "It's now or never."

He hands me his bag and marches into the girls' restroom. As soon as he does, the door to the boys' bursts open and the little dog is barking its head off and the guy holding it yells, "Well who asked you anyway? Dogs have a keen sense of smell and Stella here smells ignorance all over you!"

Then he turns and walks away, but the other guy follows him and yells, "It's not my fault your dog is an idiot!"

And that's when the dog, which is wearing little pink shoes and a pink rhinestone collar, jumps out of the owner's arms and runs toward the other guy and starts nipping at his ankles. Both of the guys shriek and the owner yells "Stella!

Stella! Stell-ahhh!" over and over again while the other man jumps onto a bench with his bags.

"She's crazy!" the man on the bench yells. He holds up his bags like he's trying to keep them out of water.

The owner picks Stella up and holds her close. "Purebred Chihuahuas are known to be sensitive."

"She's not purebred! How many times can I say that?" Suddenly, he looks over at me and I guess he realizes how silly he looks standing on a bench, holding his arms out, yelling at a tiny dog with shoes. "What are you looking at, kid?"

I'm in the middle of thinking that Mama would have fallen over laughing at the tiny pink shoes and would have wanted to get a dog just so she could have it wear tiny sneakers. But when the guy calls me kid, all at once I remember we are very far from home and no matter what my ticket stub says, I'm not an actual adult.

Birdie comes out of the bathroom and I grab his arm and start walking toward the buses.

"What's wrong?" asks Birdie.

"Nothing, come on."

We try to board the bus, but we're stopped by the driver. A woman bus driver.

"Excuse me," she says. "Are you kids on this bus?"

I look up at her, and then up at the bus. Number 457. Wrong bus.

"Sorry," I say, and pull Birdie away.

We look and look, but there are only three buses and none of them are number 331.

"I don't see it, Jackie," says Birdie as he holds on to the sleeve of my jacket. "I don't see number three thirty-one."

I pinch my cheeks, and then rub my eyes and I hope purple eye shadow isn't smeared across my face.

"Did the bus leave?" asks Birdie, his voice a little higher.

"I don't know," I say, even though I know it must have. The station is only one tiny building.

The sun goes behind a cloud and the temperature drops.

I only have five dollars and twenty-one cents in my bag.

"Jackie?"

"Let me think, Birdie." I take his hand, and we walk back to the benches.

The dog guy is on a bench near the ticket window frowning into his phone. I face away from him. The next bus to Portland isn't supposed to come through until tonight. Would the bus driver even let us on?

When I glance back at the guy, I see him looking at us and my hands start to sweat again.

Maybe this was the dumbest idea ever. The last Wolf Day didn't turn out well, so I don't know why I thought today would be any different.

"Should we call Uncle Carl?" Birdie asks.

"What can he do? Come get us on his bicycle?" My head is beginning to pound along with my heart.

"What about Rosie?"

"Maybe. But she might just call Patrick."

"No, Jack."

"Birdie, let me think."

"I don't want Patrick to find out."

I look around at the two vending machines, trying to decide if we can stay here until the next bus.

Birdie keeps tugging on my sleeve and whispering my name. And then I hear him say, "It's Patrick. I think that's Patrick." And I look up and across the street is Patrick's truck and there he is, standing with his hands on his belt.

He doesn't run, but when he approaches us, he sounds out of breath. "What. In the heck."

He goes to say something else, but a loud bus goes by, leaving us in a hot cloud of exhaust.

"Let's go," he says, his voice low and slow.

For one crazy moment I wonder what would happen if we refused or screamed if he tried to force us.

I say, "Please, just let us go. We have tickets."

"Under no circumstance am I leaving here without you," Patrick says. "So get in the truck."

Still, neither of us moves.

"Look. Maybe I should have told you before. Mrs. Spater fell and broke her hip. She doesn't live there anymore. She had to move in with her daughter. Your mama's things aren't there. That whole duplex has been sold."

Out of the corner of my eye, Birdie is completely frozen, looking down at his rainbow sneakers.

Patrick takes another step toward us. "I mean it, guys. Let's go."

He's so tall he's blocking the sun.

The dog guy is starting to focus on us and Stella fixes us with narrowed eyes. So my feet walk toward the truck even though I don't want them to. Patrick follows with Birdie.

When we're back on the freeway, Patrick says, "We still need to deal with the clothing issue. I was going to wait until we had more time over the weekend, but it's probably best we go straight to the mall and take care of it today."

He pauses.

"Anyway, I'm sorry I didn't tell you about your mama's house, but there's nothing you need up there. If you think you need something, let me know."

CHAPTER 7

SHOPPING WITH PATRICK

Patrick doesn't say anything else the entire two-hour drive and Birdie pretends to sleep. When we pull into the mall parking lot, Birdie opens his eyes, but then closes them again as we park.

Patrick blows a bunch of air out of his mouth. "Let's eat first."

He gets out and I open the door. Birdie still has his eyes closed.

"Come on, Birdie," I say. "You have to at least eat. I know you're hungry."

"I'm not."

"Well, you'll have to come anyway."

He reaches into his bag, digs around, and pulls out his mad cap and puts it on. Patrick glances at it but doesn't say anything.

We follow Patrick to the food court and order fried noodles, meat, and vegetables from a fast-food place called Panda Wok. We're almost finished when Patrick finally says something.

"There are a couple stores we can go to. I want to get clothes that fit. Nothing too baggy. Something good for school. Pants and shirts." He looks at Birdie. "And a new jacket."

Birdie puts his chopsticks down.

Patrick stands up. "Are you guys done?"

I'm not sure Birdie actually ate more than two bites. He dumps the contents of his tray in the trash. I do the same and then we follow Patrick down to a store call Kid's Closet.

"Pants, shirts, jacket, maybe a pair of shorts. This shouldn't take long." Patrick blows more air out of his mouth, then strides into the store. I don't think he was talking to us.

Birdie pulls his mad cap down as far as it will go and crosses his arms. "I'm not going in, not not not."

"I don't think we have a choice. Don't you want to have some say in what he's going to buy?"

"I don't want anything from that store."

"I know, I know." Patrick looks over at us from one of the racks just inside. I kneel down. "Listen. I know you don't want to do this. It's horrible. But I'm going to figure something out, okay? If you do this, I will give you the rest of my Honey Bunny Buns. You can have them all and we'll come up with a new plan."

He looks into the store and says, "I don't want to talk about it anymore. We aren't buying clothes for me. We're buying clothes for a boy named . . . Norman. And Norman only wears the most boring, unoriginal clothes." I nod at him. "And Norman can't make it today because he has a disease where he can't go outside. And he's my same height, so I'm doing him a favor." And then he goes inside and disappears in between the racks.

Birdie tries on all the clothes that I bring to the changing room. Patrick wanders around the store, sometimes picking up a pair of jeans or a T-shirt.

We repeat this two more times, once at a resale shop and once at a place called Caterpillar Kids where most of the clothes seem to be for toddlers. When we are done, Birdie has five pairs of pants, one pair of gym shorts, eight shirts, a sweater, a sweatshirt, a black jacket, and a pair of white-and-navy-blue tennis shoes. Before leaving the last store, Patrick adds a belt and a blue beanie to the pile in front of the cashier.

Most of the clothes are plain solid colors because Birdie can't stand clothes with tractors or sports equipment or superheroes on them. He says they all just look the same so why bother? He doubts Norman would bother. "He has bigger things to worry about."

But Birdie does get one striped button-down shirt that he says is "okay, maybe a little loud for a person like Norman." It's gray and has black, blue, and light green stripes. He's not wild about the colors, but I'm pretty sure it's the one thing that keeps him from crying right there in the middle of the store, no matter how much he's doing it for "Norman."

As we walk through the mall toward the parking lot at the other end, in the window of Scare Monkey, I spot Band-Aids that look like real strips of bacon. I point to them and whisper to Birdie, "A first-class find, for sure," and smile a little.

He doesn't smile back, but he stares at them as we walk by. Then I see him looking around, just a bit at first, then more and more intently as we pass by different shops. And that's when I know I've got him playing the best game Mama ever made up.

Nobody could ever come up with games the way Mama did. Our favorite was something we called the First-Class Quest of the North Pine Shopping Center. Sometimes Mama and I would call it "The Quest," but Birdie would always insist that we use the full name.

The game was all about finding the most interesting thing or person. A first-class find. We always finished the game at the Vietnamese restaurant. First, we'd spend thirty minutes walking in and out the shops like the tiny Asian market and the dollar store and the Bubbles Pop Laundromat and the Happy Hair Store, even the parking lot. We'd stay together and weren't allowed to talk to each other. Then, when time was up, we'd go to Phô Tasty Bowl and after we ordered, one by one we had to say our top three best finds. Mama would draw a map, like a reverse treasure map. Each spot where we found something interesting she'd put an X along with a couple words to describe it, like "Wasabi Kit-Kats" or "baby with detergent in laundry basket" or "press-on-fruit nails." Then we'd make our case for why our find was the best. The one with the first-class find was allowed to choose our dessert and get something from the quarter toy machine, which usually had little plastic ninjas or little plastic cats.

At some point, I think maybe two or three years ago, Birdie started drawing the map and I started writing down everyone's interesting thing, along with each person's points for why it was the best, and Mama would watch us with glisteny eyes.

This game probably seems stupid, but Mama got really sarcastic-silly, saying things like, "Guys, I don't think you've considered the repercussions for planet Earth if we didn't have light-up rainbow wigs with attached unicorn horns. The consequences could be . . . *devastating.*"

Then Birdie would mime devastating by throwing his head back with his hand across his forehead.

And there was something about walking around silently for thirty minutes and playing this secret game that no one knew about that made us feel indestructible.

The last time we played the game, about a month before Mama was gone, Birdie won with a ring that had a tiny ballerina on it under a clear plastic dome. "The tiny ballerina dances on a tiny spring when you move your finger," Birdie said. "And it has a tiny pink foil skirt. Everything is tiny tiny tiny and cute cute cute. And just . . . perfect."

Maybe it wasn't the greatest or most interesting thing, but somehow Mama and I knew that Birdie had won this one. I think it was his face as he described it. He gazed down at his hand like he could see the ring on his finger, like he could see the tiny tiny tiny pink foil skirt.

He never did get the ring, but it didn't matter. We left the shopping center like we always did, stomachs full of hot Vietnamese broth and minty spring rolls, feeling like we had the best family in the universe.

We're leaving the crowded mall when Birdie stumbles over one of the big store bags and a man almost runs into him. Now that it's almost dinnertime, the mall is crowded. The man says, "Watch it!" and then looks up at Patrick, who walks over to Birdie. A kid about Birdie's age stands nearby and I'm almost certain I've seen him before.

"Patrick," says the man. "Last place I'd think to find you."

Patrick takes the large bag from Birdie's hand. He doesn't smile. "Ross."

The kid stares at Birdie. I finally recognize him and his dad, Ross, Janet's mom's friend. It's Teddy, a student in Birdie's class who used to bother Birdie when we first moved here. Teddy tugs on his dad's shirt and whispers something to him. Ross looks over at Birdie and then at Patrick and says, "Clothes shopping, old friend?"

"Just a few things," Patrick answers. "We'll see you later."

Patrick tries to turn Birdie away, but Ross continues. "My son tells me that this kid is a distraction in class. Makes it hard for Teddy to concentrate."

Patrick puts his free hand on his belt and frowns at Ross as he says in a low voice, "I hope that won't be the case in the future."

Ross kind of laughs. "I hope you aren't serious right now, with this kid standing here, wearing *that*. It isn't Halloween and even if it was, it still wouldn't be right. You need to straighten that boy out quick. I'm talking to you, Patrick."

Birdie steps closer to me and I grab his hand.

"There's nothing to talk about," says Patrick. "So why don't you go on your way."

Ross laughs again and then smirks. "What's going on, man? What's your problem these days?" He shakes his head. "What am I saying? Even when we were in school you always thought you were better than everybody."

"The boy just needs some direction, so let it go."

"You think you can put different clothes on that kid and have it change anything? And if he continues to bother my son, there's going to be a problem and I will deal with it as I see fit."

Teddy stares at us.

Patrick takes Birdie by the arm and starts walking toward his truck. Birdie doesn't let go of my hand, so I follow.

As we walk away, Ross calls out, "Hope you had fun shopping, *ladies.*" He laughs, but it's not the kind of laugh that makes you want to join along.

We get in the truck and Patrick drives quickly out of the parking lot. My heart is still pounding and I still have Birdie's hand in mine when we turn onto the highway.

I keep thinking Patrick's going to say something like *Don't listen to Ross* or *That guy is an idiot*, but he doesn't.

It's almost dark when Patrick pulls over into a run-down gas station with a small house next to it. It's more of a shack, really, with a bright ordering window where a customer stands looking up at a menu. There's a light-up sign that says THE SWEET POTATO SHOP.

"I'll be right back."

Patrick goes up to the ordering window and gets in line. He talks with a guy in an apron who's sitting out front.

"I don't want to wear those Norman clothes, Jack. Even if they are my size," Birdie says.

"I know." If only we hadn't run into Ross and Teddy. It was too much. It was too real.

"Mama would be so mad if she knew I had to wear clothes like that every day."

There's a sign next to one of the chairs that says SWEET

POTATO LAYER CAKE, SWEET POTATO CHEESECAKE, SWEET POTATO COBBLER, SWEET POTATO PIE, SWEET POTATO COOKIES.

I hear Birdie sniffling and look over, but I can't see his face. "Mama hated sweet potatoes," he says. He wipes his nose on his sleeve.

"It was yams she hated. And she'd always get annoyed when people would confuse the two."

"Yeah well, what's the difference?"

"I can't remember exactly, but I think yams have really rough brown skin. And they're not as sweet. Something like that."

Birdie shrugs. "Who cares."

I sigh. I know there's no point in saying anything else.

When we get home, Duke barks and turns around in a circle. I've never seen him so energetic. Patrick pets him and scratches him behind the ears. He whispers, "I know, boy. I know."

I know, boy. I've been gone all day. They are the worst.

I offer to help Birdie with his shopping bags, but he ignores me and drags them upstairs.

Patrick watches him and then goes into the kitchen and opens the Sweet Potato Shop bag.

"I bought one of everything since I didn't know what you guys wanted." On the table is a big slice of layer cake, a small cheesecake, a miniature cobbler in a foil tin, a slice of pie, and a package of cookies.

He grabs some paper plates and forks. He cuts himself a big piece of the cake and a piece of pie, sticks a fork in the cake, and then stands there with the plate in his hands.

"I don't want him wearing the other clothes anymore. Make sure he wears the new stuff," he says. "That's why I bought them. They fit fine."

Thinking about those stupid clothes in plain "boy colors" makes my whole body itch and feel hot.

"And from now on, I want to know where you guys are at all times. It's no longer a suggestion. You let me know when you're going somewhere other than school."

I just want this horrible Wolf Day to be over.

"Do you understand?" he says, a little louder.

I nod, staring at all the dark orange desserts.

He grabs a cookie from the package and holds it out. Then he says, "Your mama would throw the biggest fit for these cookies. We couldn't drive that stretch of the highway without Dad stopping for some. We'd drive fifteen minutes out of the way just to keep her from seeing the Sweet Potato Shop. She'd stomp up those stairs and slam her bedroom door if we didn't stop." He doesn't smile as he talks.

He stares at the cookie for a few moments and then puts it back into the package.

"There's nowhere else for you guys to go. I hope you can understand that. I need everyone to understand that." He looks at the wall as he says this. It seems like he's still trying to convince himself.

Him and Duke disappear outside, probably into that stupid silo shed.

The clock ticks.

I could make toast, but honestly, I don't think even a million slices of toast would help in this shoebox house.

I eat through part of the cake and part of the pie and a bit of the cobbler. I stick my fork in the cheesecake. I don't eat the cookies.

Why did he buy them anyway? Just to tell his dumb story?

And then I realize what he said. She'd stomp up *those stairs*.

Of course. This must be Mama's old house. The one her and Patrick and Uncle Carl grew up in. And their oldest brother, who I think passed away when she was really young.

And now that I think about it, the picture in Uncle Carl's drawer was taken right here, in this kitchen, against the wall with the ticking clock.

No wonder she left this place.

**Observation # 780: Mama in a Shoebox

Which room did she sleep in?

Did she learn how to build a fire in the wood-burning stove?

Did she help plant the trees?

Did she watch Patrick through the blinds?

Did she learn how to make bread in the kitchen?

With a mom, a dad, and three brothers, was it ever quiet enough
to hear the ticking clock?

Did she sit on the back of the couch and imagine a yard with
rosebushes and a little fig tree?

CHAPTER 8

THE PROPOSAL

The next morning, it's Wednesday and Patrick says we have to go to school. When Birdie finally comes down to the kitchen in his new jeans, plain gray T-shirt, and black sweatshirt, he announces that he has an apology to make to Norman.

"Even he wouldn't wear these clothes!" he says.

I hand him a piece of toast with peanut butter. "Do they fit okay?" I ask.

"If you wore an Alexander McQueen gown to school, would that fit okay?" He takes his mad cap out of his backpack and puts it on in a huff. "I doubt it!"

When Patrick comes down, he takes one look at the mad cap, shakes his head, and points upstairs.

Patrick brings me to school first, saying that he wants to speak to Birdie's teacher again.

Birdie rolls his eyes at this and then spends the drive tugging on the collar of his shirt until Patrick says to stop.

I spend the entire day writing and doodling in my notebook. In English class, I stare at the board behind Mr. Belling's shiny head, pretending to pay attention to his lesson on alliteration. Without looking down, I draw a hundred Honey Bunny Buns, an entire page covered in swirls.

After class, I leave immediately and don't stop at my locker even though I know that my project partner, Krysten, is hoping to talk to me. I practically run to the Quesadilla Ship, hoping she won't follow.

The whole time I'm jogging, all I can think about is my old friend Marguerite and my heart pounds with anxiety.

I've never had a lot of friends and to be honest, even having a best friend like Janet is kind of a new experience for me. I did have one in third grade, mostly because of Mama. Mama was obsessed with first ladies, especially Jackie Kennedy and Lady Bird Johnson. There was this girl in my class, Marguerite, who knew a lot about the United States presidents and their families—especially their pets. She was the first person to ask if Birdie and me were named after first ladies and I almost couldn't believe that she'd guessed on her own.

Then she said her absolute favorite president was John Quincy Adams, who had silkworms and an alligator as pets. A close second was Theodore Roosevelt, who had lots of pets, but she really emphasized his hyena.

We ate lunch together every day after that because Marguerite wanted someone she could talk to about presidential pets and weird presidential family life and all the other presidential facts she knew. And even though the friendship was really Marguerite's doing, it was nice to invite someone over to my house who thought all of Mama's ideas were good ones.

Marguerite also really liked Miss Luck Duck, our lamp in the shape of a woman with the head of a duck, something that weirded a lot of people out. Maybe because it was so big and we kept it by the front door. Marguerite said that with the long dress and bonnet, Miss Luck Duck looked a lot like Lady Louisa Adams, the wife of John Quincy Adams (sixth president of the United States). I remember thinking Marguerite was the best best friend I could hope for.

But then, in fifth grade, Marguerite started playing soccer, and then started inviting Allison, the team's star forward, to our hangouts. Allison asked a lot of questions about Mama and her ideas and ways of doing things, especially when Mama didn't feel like coming out of her room. One time, Marguerite and Allison even came with us on our Wolf Day adventures, but Allison left halfway through because she didn't want to go to the Mission Homeless Center and serve hot meals and give out the friendship bracelets we'd made.

Then Marguerite stopped having fun too, I guess, and pretty soon the three of us were eating together at school lunch but only two of us were hanging out on the weekends and after soccer games.

I had tried to ask Marguerite what was wrong, but the words were having a hard time coming out and in the end, all I said was, "You don't have to pretend to like me, like a jerk." Her mouth opened into a small O and then I walked away. That was the last time we talked.

When Birdie and me left Portland with Patrick, I never told Marguerite I was leaving. To this day I wonder if Marguerite's favorite presidents are still Adams and Roosevelt and if she ever thinks of Birdie and me and Mama.

On my way to the Quesadilla Ship, I pass by Snip 'n' Shine and get Janet's attention through the window. She leans the broom against the wall and comes outside.

"I heard you got nabbed," Janet says. "Are you guys okay? I called yesterday but no one answered and I still don't know about leaving messages on Patrick's phone. You really need to get a cell phone."

"Yeah, I don't think that's happening anytime soon."

"Is Patrick mad?"

"I don't know. I guess. How did he find out, anyway?"

"Dude. The school called Patrick and Carl when you guys didn't show up. And Patrick heard from the librarian or something about you guys looking at bus schedules. Carl told me. Anyway, rookie mistakes. Next time you run away you really need to involve me in the planning. I know about these things."

From the back of the store, Cherylene calls for Janet. Janet sighs and says, "Listen. I get wanting to leave. I'll try calling tonight, okay? Or you call me?"

I nod and she says quickly, "Sorry it didn't work out!" then disappears into the salon.

And with Janet it's that easy.

I cross the street to the Quesadilla Ship when I see Birdie walking to meet me. "Hey," I say.

"Can we get a quesadilla?" he asks. "I don't want to go to Patrick's yet."

"Sure, come on," I say as I head toward Rosie's truck.

Half a block away, Rosie sees us and waves a dishcloth out the ordering window.

"You sneaky squirrels! Get over here!"

"Do you think she knows?" whispers Birdie. "Do you think she's mad?" Birdie can't stand it when people are upset with him.

Before I can answer, Rosie comes out of the truck. "Boy, boy, boy, you should have seen your poor uncle yesterday. You almost gave him a heart attack. He rode all over, asking everyone in town if they'd seen you." She pretends to snap the towel at us.

"We're sorry," Birdie says quickly. His eyes are all glassy and his nose is red. "Really."

Rosie looks at him and then squishes him in a side hug. "Oh, you. Come on, now. Don't cry. You guys hungry?"

She leaves a voicemail for Patrick saying we are hanging out with her and Uncle Carl.

Off in the distance, two hot-air balloons float in the cold blue sky like tiny colorful lightbulbs. Mama would have loved a hot-air balloon ride.

"Rosie, would you ever go up in one of those things?"

"A balloon? Absolutely." She scatters different kinds of cheeses on the tortillas. "In fact," she continues, "I rode one for my thirteenth birthday. It was just me and my dad. I hardly got any time with my dad just on his own and we went up into that big balloon and looked out on the miles and miles of green countryside. You know, we barely said a word to each other. We just grinned like idiots the entire time. It was one of the most joyous days of my life."

Rosie keeps her back to me. She clears her throat. "My dad's having to go into the hospital to get treatment every couple of weeks. But the silver lining," she says, "is that now he calls me all the time. When he's bored, stuck at the hospital, sometimes at three o'clock in the morning. You take what you can get. Hopefully we get along as well when I'm there in person!"

She turns around, two half quesadillas in her hands, each with a sour cream and guacamole heart. Her eyes are wide and kind of glassy like Birdie's were earlier. She's smiling big, though.

"I'd ride a hot-air balloon again in a heartbeat if I had

someone to do it with." Her face is all glowy and I kind of wish I could just stand at the ordering window forever.

But new customers arrive, so we take our quesadillas to Uncle Carl's apartment and he opens the door before we even knock.

He takes my plate and goes over to the counter and cuts off a piece for himself. "Now, I'm only doing this because it's what I deserve after what you put me through yesterday."

"I'm sorry," I say. "We didn't mean to worry you. It just seemed like something we had to do . . . we just . . . we miss . . ."

Uncle Carl waves at us while shaking his head and says, "I know, I know, okay?" He waves his hand again like he just wants to forget about it. He goes to the coffeepot.

Birdie wipes his mouth, which is covered in sour cream, and says, "We probably would have come back to visit. Honest."

Uncle Carl frowns as he pours himself a cup of coffee. "Well, the old man is doing a great job, isn't he? Let's count how many times you ran away when you lived with me. How do you count zero on your fingers?" He plops himself down on the couch, takes a long drink of coffee, and then fans himself with a magazine. "If it hadn't been for my Rosie, I would have lost my head."

Suddenly my eyes are burning. Everything has turned out wrong. Again.

"You should have seen Rosie in action," says Uncle Carl. "She kept me from losing it. She even kept me hydrated as I rode around trying to find you two monkeys. Said I had to keep my electrolytes up."

Right then, Rosie's glowy face pops into my head and I suddenly know exactly what we need. What Uncle Carl needs. Maybe what we all need.

Uncle Carl needs Rosie. For real.

"Hey, Uncle Carl. You have a plan for your next proposal to Rosie?"

He squints at me with suspicion. "Not exactly. Why?"

"I just had an idea."

I tell him about Rosie's hot-air balloon ride with her dad. I tell him it might show how serious he is about marrying her if he proposed up in the sky in a balloon.

"And I could sew you a bow tie so that you look super fancy," says Birdie.

Uncle Carl rubs the back of his neck. I can see him imaging the scenario. Maybe this can be my gift to him. An apology gift. And if she says yes, then maybe he could be reliable enough for us to live with him again. We could all be together. It's perfect.

He gets up and goes back to the coffeepot even though I think his mug is still full. "You ever not have a bunch of crazy ideas in that head of yours?"

"What?" I say. "It could work."

He sighs. "Jackie-O, that woman could be with anyone."

"Yeah, but she hangs around *you*. She parks her truck in front of the Lock and Key! In front of *your* apartment! She could park it anywhere."

"Yeah," says Birdie. "She could park it by the high school and make serious money."

Uncle Carl rubs the back of his neck again, looking at Birdie. Suddenly, he stands up straight and points. "What the heck are you wearing?"

Birdie frowns and picks up a magazine from the table.

"Oh my God, the goat did this, didn't he?" Uncle Carl asks.

"I don't want to talk about it!" Birdie announces. "In fact . . ." He reaches down into his backpack and pulls out his outlawed mad cap. He puts it on and goes back to the women's magazine, his knee bouncing up and down with agitation.

"I swear that old man is clueless. He doesn't know anything about people. He spends too much time with that damn dog! You watch—you thought I went crazy after Marlboro passed away, you wait until that dog kicks the bucket and then we'll see who *really* goes to pieces."

"Uncle Carl, really, you shouldn't give up on Rosie so easily," I say, steering him back. "Give her a chance to say no at least. Like a *real no*, not just an eye roll. You have to at least give it a shot."

He takes a drink of coffee and then sighs. "Well, you two nosy mind readers might as well know that I've been saving some money the last few months. And that maybe I've been looking into a *certain* kind of jewelry that many say might symbolize a *certain* kind of commitment."

Birdie can't help himself. His eyes light up like lightbulbs. "Oh my gosh, your top secret mission is to buy an engagement ring?"

Uncle Carl touches his nose and nods. "So perhaps a trip to Paraby Jewelers might work. *Just to look.* I'm no fool. I know you have to shop around for things like rings."

He winks at me and I smile at him. He's never actually proposed with a ring before.

"Yes!" Birdie hops up from the futon. "Can we please please please go to the mall?"

Uncle Carl looks at me as he takes another long drink. I'm expecting him to say something about not having the money just yet, but he says, "I don't know. I'm not sure if you two knuckleheads can be trusted on a bus anymore." I see him trying to hide his smile and that's when I know we're in.

At the mall, we walk into the jeweler's and it's like everything is made of light and crystal. The counters shine, the jewelry shines, the clerks shine. Even the one giving us a dirty look seems to sparkle.

Birdie's eyes are ablaze. "Wow," he whispers.

Uncle Carl gazes around, scratching under his chin. He keeps a buffer space between him and the glass and doesn't look at anything too close. I look down and see that some of the jewelry doesn't even have the prices marked. And the ones that do are way too expensive. There's no way Uncle Carl can afford anything in this store. I tug on his sleeve.

"You know, Uncle Carl. Maybe diamonds aren't the way to go. Kids in Africa die getting those diamonds. Even Mama didn't like to wear diamonds because of those kids." I glance at Birdie and raise my eyebrows, hoping he'll get the idea.

"Oh. Yeah, that's right, Uncle Carl," says Birdie. "There are better gems. I've read about it. Diamond is so, so last year."

"Really?" Uncle Carl says, looking around. "Man, kids these days know too much. I never knew anything about anything when I was your age."

"Let's look over there." I point to another display with rings of all colors.

Birdie goes over and presses his nose up against the glass, his eyes open wide, probably thinking about all those rings on his own fingers. His breath makes a cloud on the display.

"Please don't touch the glass," says the man in the suit behind the counter. Now his arms are folded. He probably thinks we're going to steal something. "Is there anything at all I can help you with? I'm not sure we have anything . . . in your price range."

Uncle Carl's head jerks back in surprise and he folds his own arms like a mirror image of the clerk.

"*Excuse me,* buddy," says Uncle Carl, bowing his head in a funny way with a smirk on his face. "Maybe my sister was right. Maybe we don't want your child slave labor rings." Then he takes each of our hands and we walk out.

We get to the Royal Chinese Buffet, where they have Chinese zodiac placemats.

Uncle Carl's finger traces the chart. "Jack, you're a sheep. Gentle, introverted, responsible."

"I'm a dog," says Birdie. "Honest and loyal and a true friend."

"Rosie is a rabbit, which is noble, lovely, and elegant," I say.

"Dang, these placemats are good! If that doesn't describe Rosie, I don't know what does. And lookie here: Your mama was a dragon! 'Dragons are eccentric and complicated with a passionate nature.' Well, that's her all right."

My heart buzzes listening to someone else describe Mama. *Complicated and passionate.* I look at Uncle Carl, but he keeps his face pointed down at the mat as he continues to read. "And I'm a snake: 'Perceptive and intense with a tendency toward physical beauty.'"

Birdie looks up at Uncle Carl and the three of us laugh.

Uncle Carl sticks two not-very-Chinese breadsticks into his upper lip and grins, crossing his eyes. He looks like a walrus. "Physical beauty," he says.

I laugh again and take a bite of my sweet and sour pork.

"At school tomorrow, I can use the computer to get some more information about the hot-air balloon rides. Like ticket information and stuff."

"And I will make you a fancy bow tie," says Birdie. "Something dapper. Maybe even suspenders!"

Uncle Carl picks his teeth with a toothpick and looks over at the buffet like maybe he's contemplating a fifth plate of food. "Well, I hate to throw a wrench into your plans, but I was actually thinking of proposing in less than two weeks. I need a ring before she leaves."

"Why? Isn't she coming back?" I ask, my heart suddenly beating a little faster.

"Well, sure, as far as I know. But she doesn't know how long she'll have to stay, with her dad's health and all." He sighs and shrugs his shoulders.

"Well then, we better get organized. You are in charge of the ring," I say. "You can find a ring somewhere else. That clerk was a jerk. Maybe online? And Birdie will work on clothes. I'll find out about the balloon ride. We can meet again tomorrow after school. It will be the most romantic proposal ever. A top secret mission proposal."

Uncle Carl smiles at me and nods. He says, "Deal," and I

can see his mind is going a mile a minute. "What about a ruby? Rosie's birthstone is a ruby."

As soon as he says it, it totally makes sense. Rosie will love a ring with red.

"And hey, listen guys. No more top secret run-away-on-a-bus kind of plans, okay? I mean, I know I'm not the world's most perfect uncle . . ."

My eyes burn again and I don't want to ruin our meal with crying, so I just say that our only top secret plan is his proposal, nothing else.

If we can just help him make the proposal super special, I know Rosie will say yes. Because Birdie's right. She could totally make more money if she parked her truck by the high school. But she doesn't.

On our way out of the mall, Birdie eyes the gumball machines and Uncle Carl takes a quarter from his pocket and puts it in and out pops a plastic capsule. Inside is an adjustable ring that has a cupcake on it. Birdie smiles as he puts it on his finger. "A first-class find," he whispers. Then he holds my hand and swings his arm, which he hasn't done in a long time. Uncle Carl smiles down at us.

Then the bus comes and it almost feels like a Wolf Day as we ride it back to town.

**Observation #781: Birdie's New Clothes

Birdie walks around like a rain cloud now.
His face is a storm.
His clothes are black, blue, gray, dark green.

But when he puts the cupcake ring on his finger,
it's like a rainbow appearing in the sky.
You don't see the rain clouds anymore.
You look at the rainbow and smile.

CHAPTER 9

SUSPENSION

I've been avoiding Krysten ever since the Tuesday bus failure, I don't know why. But she corners me at my locker the next day after school.

"Hey, Jack. You got a minute to talk about the poetry project?"

I say "Umm . . ." as I grab my books and close my locker door. I really need to get to the school library so I can research the balloon ride. I'm not ready to see Ms. Perkins at the regular library yet.

"We could go to the Quesadilla Ship and get something to eat first. I saw you there yesterday. Maybe my mom can drive us and then drive you home after we've made some plans for the project. I'd really like to get started. I love poetry."

"I have to go to the school library."

"That's okay. I'll walk with you. I have time to kill before my mom comes. So, have you thought about who you want to research for the project?"

"Umm . . ." I hate that I get like this around people at school. I pick up the pace as we weave our way through students heading in the opposite direction, toward the parking lot.

"Do you have a favorite poet?" she continues. Out of the corner of my eye, I can see the easy, open smile on her face.

"Elizabeth Bishop?" I don't know why Mama's favorite poet pops out of my mouth.

"Nice, a female poet. I don't know about her. What's her poetry like? Can you recite something?"

I shake my head. "She was my mama's favorite, not mine. I don't know a whole lot about her . . . But I do have one of her books." As soon as I say this, I realize that it's not true. That book is gone, just like almost every other book I used to own.

"Oh, good. Maybe bring it with you next time we meet."

I nod, even though there's no way I can do that.

Krysten says hi to every teacher we pass, and about ten other students. When we get to the library she asks the librarian how her dog is doing after its hip surgery.

While she's busy, I go to an open computer and find the website for White Mountain Balloon Rides. I print out all the pages I think Uncle Carl might need, including one about special anniversary or birthday rides.

When I finish, I go to wave bye to Krysten, but she follows

me out. "So you're friends with Rosie, the owner of the Quesadilla Ship?" she asks.

I nod because I'm not sure if friend is the right word. I would love to call her Aunt Rosie, my soon-to-be-aunt Rosie, my very first aunt in the whole world.

"She's so cool," says Krysten. "I love her pepperoni quesadilla. It's genius. It's like a quesadilla and a pizza had a baby."

I can't help but laugh. "That's exactly how Rosie describes it," I say.

The ice between us isn't exactly broken. But Mama used to say that when making new friends, all you needed was one tiny little crack. And then there was enough space for a friendship. Mama was like a professional at making friends. I think she made a new friend every day of her life.

When we get to the school gate, Krysten gives me her phone number. I tell her I don't have a cell phone, so I can't text her, but she just shrugs. "Call, text, mail, or send a messenger pigeon. I don't care."

We agree to meet at the regular library on Saturday. "I'll do some research, but I think your idea is going to be great. Find your book if you can. Maybe your mom has more?"

Then she's waving at me and getting into her mom's mint-green car.

I wave back and watch them go, wondering how on earth she just did that. How did she get me talking about Mama when I barely know her?

I head to Uncle Carl's, my hand in my pocket, squeezing Krysten's phone number tight.

When I get to the apartment, Uncle Carl is rushing from his room to the kitchen, and I can smell something burning. Birdie isn't here yet.

Uncle Carl opens what looks like a toaster oven.

"That's new," I say.

"Let me tell you, it says right on the box that this contraption can bake a cake, but this is the third time I've tried and look at it."

The cake is a dark brown blackish color.

"What's the cake for?"

"Well, I remember seeing on some show years ago a wedding proposal where the ring was baked into a cake. Rosie loves strawberry cake. I wonder if they allow cakes up in the balloon."

"I don't know if you need a cake, Uncle Carl. But here, I brought the info from the website." I pull out the papers I printed at school and walk over to him. "Maybe it will say somewhere in this."

He glances at them as he washes cake batter off a giant bowl. "Jeez, I might as well be paying for actual airplane tickets. Isn't it just a basket, a balloon, and a whole lot of hot air?"

The phone rings and he ignores it because he hates talking on the phone.

He reads from the printout. "'Sunset balloon ride for two with champagne landing.' Now that sounds romantic to me."

"I wish we could go with you," I say, knowing there isn't enough money for two more tickets. "But maybe we can have the cake ready for when you land. A landing party."

The phone keeps ringing and Uncle Carl smiles. "A landing party. I like that. We could have a celebration of sorts right there."

The call goes to voicemail. Out of the machine comes Patrick's voice. "Carl. Pick up. I'm trying to find Jack. Rosie said Jack was with you two. Tell her to get home now." There's a pause that seems to go on for minutes. Then he says, "Birdie was suspended." And then a click.

Uncle Carl and I stare at each other.

And then I'm throwing my backpack on and going through the door. Uncle Carl calls out, "Don't you want to call to let him know you're on your way?"

But I'm already down the stairs, sprinting along the sidewalk, my feet making slapping sounds with every step.

As I pass the ramshackle deli on the edge of town, I see Janet coming out with her skateboard under her arm.

"Hey Jacko. Marathon train much?"

"No. Um, something happened to Birdie and I have to get home fast."

She looks at me for a second and then back at the deli, where some high school girls come out, showing each other their phones and laughing. She puts her skateboard under her foot and takes a cigarette out and holds it between her fingers. She says, "Actually, I just heard Birdie tried to kiss a boy in the bathroom or something. Is he okay? Do you want some soda or a chip? You don't look so good." She holds the bag out for me.

"What are you talking about?"

"Teddy Garner. He was at the Stop-and-Go telling anyone who will listen that your brother is gay and tried to kiss him."

"That doesn't make sense."

"Don't worry, Jack. He's known to cause trouble. You know Teddy is a grade A idiot. He can't help it. It's genetic. Look at his dad. I can't believe my mom hangs out with that guy. Ross is a bully and now he's raising *more* bullies. Hey seriously, you look a little pale. Take a drink of soda."

I shake my head. "I really need to go."

"Okay. Well, let me know what happens."

I nod and hitch my backpack up so I can run. "I'll call you later." Then I'm off speeding toward the highway.

Inside, Patrick's house is dark and quiet. None of the curtains are open.

It's not that late, but with all the curtains closed it feels like night. Upstairs, in the hall, there's light underneath both of their doors.

I wait by Birdie's.

You know those anxious moments when your body stops and all you can hear is your heart beating like it climbed right up your neck into your ear?

"Knock, knock," I whisper.

His bed creaks, but he doesn't say anything.

"Knock, knock," I say again.

He doesn't answer.

"Are you okay, Birdie? I'm going to start dinner. Come down if you want."

Still nothing.

I drop my bag in my bedroom and it hits the floor with a thud, and I go back downstairs to boil water for spaghetti.

Just when I think that maybe neither of them are coming down, Patrick shows up, followed closely by Duke. I fix him a bowl of spaghetti without waiting for him to ask, mostly because it gives me something to do. We eat for a while before Patrick finally says something.

"You hear about Birdie?"

"Yeah."

"You talk to him yet about that boy at school?"

There are two pieces of pasta left in my bowl. I push them around, wondering what he knows. "No. I haven't seen him yet. What happened?"

"He's suspended tomorrow."

I set my fork down. "What for?"

"Birdie was in some kind of fight in the boys' bathroom. He refuses to talk about it with me or anyone, but both him and the other student are suspended. The school has a zero-tolerance policy for violence."

"Birdie doesn't start fights. And Janet said that Teddy is known for causing trouble."

His fork stops midway to his mouth. "It doesn't matter what Janet says. Birdie needs to learn how to blend in." His voice is low and gravelly. "You don't live at my brother's anymore. Birdie can't be running around however he wants. Dressing however he wants." He takes his bite of food. "It makes him a target. And running away won't solve anything."

"But he's not doing anything wrong!"

"That is not up for discussion." Patrick looks at me over his fork of spaghetti. "I have a job in the next county tomorrow morning that I can't skip. You'll have to stay home with him. I'll call your school and let them know you'll be out. I'll be back around lunchtime." He takes a drink of his water and wipes his mouth. "I want you to make sure he stays inside the house. No wandering around. No bus ride stunts. No visits to Carl's place."

"Like forever?"

"We'll talk about it later."

The last noodle left in the bowl is always kind of sad-looking. I chop it into tiny pieces with my fork.

Patrick eats his last bite and goes to the sink. "You two will adjust." He rinses his bowl and cup and adds some soap to a sponge. "You can't be missing from school or getting in trouble. I know Carl let you do all kinds of things, but those days are over. That wasn't good for any of you." He puts his bowl and cup into the drying rack and dries his hands. "Thank you for the spaghetti."

And then he's gone.

I remember when I was younger, when Birdie was still a baby, I'd asked Mama if she had any brothers or sisters. "Like I have Birdie," I said to her. "Don't you have a Birdie?"

She looked at me with sad eyes and then picked me up and said, "Sure. I have Birdies." I felt safe in her tight, tight hug. "It's just . . . right now those Birdies of mine, well, they have an opinion about everything and we don't get along real well. They've got loud mouths."

"Sometimes I don't like it when Birdie cries at night and wakes me up. He's got a loud mouth too." She hugged me tighter.

I never asked about her siblings again, but ever since living with Patrick, I wonder: Can you be loud without saying anything at all?

**Observation #782: Honey Bunny Bun Magic

Now I know how easily Honey Bunny Buns can disappear.

Like a magic trick,

6 Honey Bunny Buns

become 1.

Except these don't disappear into a silk top hat.

& Uncle Carl isn't here to pull more from his sleeve.

& we aren't there to assist him in his greatest feat yet:

A marriage proposal that ends with yes.

CHAPTER 10

WHEN TO USE THE MICROBLASTER

The next morning, I sleep in since I'm not going to school and I'm not sure Birdie will be ready to talk. I lie there for a long time wondering if Uncle Carl will be able to buy the balloon tickets on his own. He's not exactly good at using the Internet and he avoids talking on the phone at all costs because he says when you're talking into a microphone, who knows who—or what—could be listening.

On my way downstairs, I see Birdie's door is wide-open. The blanket on his bed is pulled straight and perfectly smooth. The pillow doesn't even look like it's been slept on.

Downstairs, Duke lies on the couch by the front door. He'll probably be there all morning waiting for Patrick to come back.

The leftover spaghetti is gone from the fridge. I grab an

apple and that's when I hear a strange sound coming from the backyard.

Birdie's on the patio with a giant orange water gun that's almost as big as he is. He's aiming toward empty soda cans on a rusty bench at the far end of the yard. I'm surprised he's wearing his puffy purple jacket.

"Hit any yet?" I ask.

He turns toward me. I gasp, finally seeing his face properly. He's got a scab on his lip and a purple half-moon underneath his right eye and a puffy eyelid. "Oh, Birdie."

"Thanks for saving some spaghetti," he says, going to the hose for a refill. Like an outlaw, he's stuffed another water gun in the front waist of his pants. He turns off the water, replaces the water cap, and goes back to the end of the patio and continues shooting. He still doesn't hit anything.

"What's the one tucked in your waist?" I ask.

"That's my MicroBlaster. For a last-resort shot." He shoots the water again and hits a can.

I watch him, sticking my hands into my hoodie pockets. The air is cold, flowing down from the mountain that already has some early snow. Before moving here, I used to think that California was always warm. I had no idea that it would get colder than Portland.

"Patrick says I need to defend myself." He doesn't stop shooting. "He wants to teach me how to fight."

"I'm not sure water guns is what he had in mind."

"I know, but this is as far as I go. I'm not punching Teddy Garner no matter what Patrick says."

"Is that who punched you? Teddy Garner?"

"He didn't punch me. He elbowed me. After pushing me to the ground."

"Was it because of something you were wearing?"

"No. I was wearing the stupid clothes Patrick bought."

He aims and hits the bench.

"Did you try to kiss him?" The question is out before I realize what I've said.

Birdie is out of water again but he silently pulls the trigger over and over with nothing coming out. Finally he goes to the hose for another refill.

"At lunchtime, I was working on Uncle Carl's bow tie and suspenders design for the proposal. I had my notebook and the Alexander McQueen book out and Teddy saw me. He followed me into the bathroom and tried to steal my book. I had to hit him to keep him away." He looks over at me, his purple eye squinting a little. "Then he knocked me to the ground, and elbowed me in the face. He put my book in the toilet. I kicked him to try and make him stop, and pulled his hair, but then someone else came into the bathroom and Teddy ran out. I pulled the book out of the toilet, but it's ruined, Jack."

"Don't worry, we'll wash it off and dry it out. Teddy is a jerk. I knew he was lying."

He focuses on refilling the gun without spilling.

"I can't believe Janet's mom hangs around with Teddy's dad," I say.

"Yeah well, Teddy said that him and his dad couldn't stop laughing at the *gay outfit* I was wearing at the mall. They laughed the whole way home."

"Janet's right. That kid is a grade A idiot."

"He hasn't bothered me since last school year but since seeing him at the mall, he's worse than ever. Anyway, I have to keep practicing. I want to show Patrick that I can shoot when he gets back from work."

"Where did those guns come from anyway?"

"I found them in a box by the side of the house."

"Patrick seems really upset. You probably shouldn't be wearing your purple jacket."

He stops shooting and sighs heavily. Like an old-man sigh. Except he's only nine years old.

Then, without warning, Birdie sprays me with the rest of the freezing water. I can barely make a sound before he's dropped the gun and is off, running toward the side gate.

I'm startled, but my feet are running too, chasing him into the trees, and onto the road. He's faster than I expect, but I pump my legs, my track pants swishing with every stride.

After crossing the empty street, Birdie runs through some thorny buckbrush and his jacket gets caught. I almost reach him when he pulls out the MicroBlaster. The cold water hits me in the face. "Last-resort shot!" he shouts. Then the bush lets him go and he weaves through the plants toward the reserve. I stay in the brush, breathing heavy, my right eye burning from getting hit with water, my arms scratched from the thorns.

Despite my track pants, I am totally winded and have a stitch in my side. So I decide to walk, not run, the rest of the way.

When I get there, I don't see Birdie, but I know he's in the pallet fort. It isn't exactly his fort since the wooden shipping pallets were already here when we first explored the reserve. But they had collapsed, and I helped Birdie stand them back up and later he added a bunch of branches to the top, which made it look like a beaver dam.

I stomp loudly as I approach, deciding that if he really wants to get away, he'll hear me and then he'll have time to leave. I'm hoping not to get sprayed again.

I'm almost there when the MicroBlaster is tossed out of the fort. "I'll give you one chance to shoot me in the face. It's only fair," he says.

I creep past the gun to the entrance, which is just a gap between the pallets. He sits inside on the dirt. He moves over, letting me share the space.

"Your eye is really red," he says.

"Yeah? It's kind of burning." I rub it a little, but that only makes it feel worse.

"Teddy called me gay, Jack."

"Do you know what that is?"

"I know what gay is. It's like when boys like boys, okay?"

I nod.

He says, "It's just . . ." and then stops.

"Mama always understood," I whisper.

"Yeah."

A gust of wind blows and the fort's branches scrape against each other.

Birdie gathers his knees to his chest and puts his head down. "I want to go back to Uncle Carl's."

I wipe my eyes and take a deep breath and try to smile. "That's why we have to help him propose, Birdie. Just think. We'd be able to live with him again. Him *and* Rosie. Maybe they'd move into a new apartment, like the ones over by the park, and we'd get our own room." The sting in my eye is almost gone, but I can't help but rub it again. "Rosie makes Uncle Carl better."

I scoot closer and lean my bent knees toward his. "And Mama used to love ceremonies."

He nods. "She would love the hot-air balloon idea."

"Absolutely."

"But what about Patrick?" asks Birdie, his knee knocking against the inside of his fort. "He doesn't want us going anywhere."

"It doesn't matter," I say. "Patrick can't keep us from our family, right? We'll go early, before Patrick gets up."

"Maybe we can also look for my bag. It got all dirty and

a little ripped in the fight and Patrick took it away and gave me one of his old ugly backpacks. I said I could fix it, but he took it anyway."

"Your bag with the ice cream cones all over it?"

"Yes." He kicks the dirt. That was a birthday present from me and Mama two years ago.

"I'll talk to Patrick about it, okay? I'll get it back."

Birdie suddenly sits up straight, almost hitting his head. "Oh my gosh! Duke! Did you leave the back door open? Do you think he got out?"

"Not likely. I doubt he'll move from his post in the living room until Patrick gets back."

"I tried to bribe him with some of the spaghetti and he didn't even sniff it. He'll never like me."

"Well, I hope you ate some of the spaghetti. It wasn't there to try to make Duke like you."

"I ate . . . most of it."

I sigh. He's the most picky eater I know. But there's one thing he never refuses. "How about some green eggs? I brought the blue dye from Uncle Carl's."

"Really?" he says. "But it's not my birthday."

"Well, maybe we need to eat green eggs more often."

His smile stretches wide and I can't help it; mine does too.

...

Mama told me that when I was four, she'd read me the Dr. Seuss book *Green Eggs and Ham* and immediately afterward I demanded to know what green eggs actually tasted like. "Aren't they yucky?" I guess I asked. Mama said absolutely not! And then she made me some to prove that they were delicious.

She tried and tried to make the ham green, but it always came out mostly brown, with dark green splotches all over that looked like mold. The eggs, on the other hand, were always this perfect peppy green. So we decided to forget all about the stupid ham and just focus on the perfect green eggs.

So the birthday green eggs started when Birdie was three. He was still trying to figure out how to string words together because he was kind of late to talk, and Mama had asked him what he wanted for his birthday. He jumped up and down and screamed, "Green eggs! Green eggs! I want green eggs!" And then he did this little exuberant dance with his hips moving around in a circle like there was an invisible hula hoop, and Mama and I looked at each other and just broke up laughing and so did Birdie. It was so unlike the quiet Birdie we were used to.

So when my birthday came, I copied his dance and shout because I thought it was cute and from then on we always made green eggs on our birthdays. And every once in a while, Mama made them for no reason and it was like Santa showing up at your house in July.

CHAPTER 11

GIFTS

On the way back to Patrick's house from the reserve, I tell Birdie about the hot-air balloon information I found online for Uncle Carl.

"The ride includes a champagne toast, a *commemorative* flight certificate, and a unique souvenir gift package."

"Ooh. What kind of souvenir?"

"I'm not sure. Something romantic. You can reserve tickets online, but you know how Uncle Carl is with the Internet, so he'll have to call."

"But there's no way he'll call on his own," says Birdie.

"Well, that's why I was hoping to see him today. I can coach him through it. I'd do it for him, but I don't have a way to pay." I kick a pinecone into the road. "And now Patrick said he'll be home around lunchtime. There's no way he's going to let us go over there."

"Maybe we should try calling?"

"I did last night. His voicemail never picked up. He probably unplugged his phone again."

"So our plan is doomed."

"No, it's not. You're going to keep working on the bow tie. I'll keep calling Uncle Carl when Patrick isn't around. Then, tomorrow, before Patrick gets up, we'll head to town. I'll leave a note so Patrick can't get mad that we left. You're technically only suspended today."

"I bet he'll still be mad, though. And I hope he's not early today. It's already eleven."

But when we return, the house is empty, except for Duke, who's still on the couch.

Birdie scratches him behind the collar and Duke raises an eyebrow, but not much else. "I'll work on Uncle Carl's bow tie today after green eggs. Do you think Duke would let me put a bow tie on him? He'd look so cute!"

"I doubt *he'd* notice, but Patrick would. And speaking of Patrick, you should really change out of that jacket before he gets home."

Birdie sighs. "I know."

I'm about to start on the green eggs when there's an engine rumble from outside. Patrick is back.

Birdie looks at me surprised and then runs upstairs.

I get some water from the fridge and start to head up too, when Patrick comes in.

"I need to get the backyard in order," he says right away. "I think it's best if you guys start helping on the weekends." He pauses, but I don't know what he's looking for me to say, and he continues, "I have to get some tools from the garage. Meet me in the backyard in fifteen minutes."

Upstairs, I tell Birdie.

"But what about our green eggs? And how am I supposed to sew if Patrick's making us work in the yard?"

"We'll figure it out. Maybe we can make them at Uncle Carl's."

"Oh no! I forgot to take Uncle Carl's measurements for the bow tie."

"You can get them tomorrow." Though I have no idea how Patrick will react to us being gone in the morning. What if he finds us before we get to town?

When we go outside, we find Patrick chain-sawing a pile of large branches he pruned earlier in the week. We wait for him to see us because the noise is so loud. After a minute, the chain saw cuts out and there's Patrick standing there with a bandanna over his face, staring at us.

Then he comes over with the chain saw, hands me two sets of gloves from his pocket, and tells us to put all the other branches into a big pile. The gloves are huge, which he seems to realize as soon as he gives them to me. Then he puts his bandanna back up and goes to the other side of the yard and continues cutting.

We work for almost an hour moving the branches and raking leaves. Patrick finally stops the chain saw for good and the silence that follows is wide and hollow.

I think Patrick notices it too, because he starts whistling, but stops after a little while.

He has us gather rocks and other stones and a bunch of old bricks. We stack them into a giant pile on the side of the house. He carries all of the large ones and we get into a rhythm where none of us is ever in the same part of the yard at the same time.

Then suddenly, Patrick breaks the silence. "All of these bricks are from an old outdoor oven my dad built when I was ten. But Dad didn't always know what he was doing with the impulsive projects he'd start, and the oven got unstable and fell apart. But not before we got to make a pizza once."

My mind races trying to decide what to say. I steal a glance, trying to see if maybe there is actually a smile on Patrick's face, but his face is the same as it ever is: old, hard to read, and topped with a hat pulled low.

I can't stand the quiet, so I say the only thing I can think of. "What kind of pizza?"

Patrick stops and then says, "Pepperoni and mushrooms. My mom's favorite."

Mama's favorite too. One of the few times she'd eat meat was on a pepperoni and mushroom pizza.

I can feel this thought swimming around in my chest,

ready to come out of my mouth. But I can't. I can't talk to Patrick about Mama.

So I keep my mouth closed.

After we are done with the rock and brick piles, Patrick has us sort through a bunch of wood to find good pieces to use as kindling for fires. But we only work for another fifteen minutes because suddenly Patrick comes over to us and tells us that we're done.

"I'm going out," he says. "I'll be back in less than an hour."

Then he turns around and goes inside the house.

"What is going on with him?" asks Birdie after a couple minutes. "Are we supposed to continue with the wood?"

"I don't know."

We hear Patrick's truck start and then disappear.

We're washing up inside when the phone rings. I let it go to voicemail because I'm still nervous about answering Patrick's phone.

But then I hear Janet's voice blaring on the message: "Good afternoon! This message is for Jack Royland. I'd like to speak to her if phone calls are allowed at the asylum. If she could be so kind as to use the phone and call her dear best friend, I'd be in your eternal debt. Ciao!"

I don't get to the phone before she hangs up, but I call her right back and after I say hello she immediately says, "Please don't erase that message. Please have Patrick listen to it and tell me what his face looks like when he does."

"He's not here right now, but he'll be back in a bit."

"Okay, whatever, whatever. I'm like two minutes from your house. I'm going to stop by, okay?"

"Stop by?"

"Yes. I have something for Birdie—be there soon!" And then she hangs up.

I go outside and here she is, jogging up to Patrick's fence.

"Please tell me Birdie is here and not in some dungeon somewhere serving out his sentence."

"He's washing up," I say. "Patrick had us doing yard work."

"Hard labor punishment, huh? You got roped into it too, then?"

"I don't think we were doing it as a punishment. Patrick was helping."

"Well, why would he be doing that now? I've honestly never seen him do anything to his yard other than maybe cut the hedge in the spring."

"I don't know," I say.

We head upstairs and I go to tell her about moving the bricks when she's like, "Wow. Look at these bare walls. Talk about stark."

When we get to Birdie's room, his books and binders are on the floor, and he's busy putting them back on the shelves one by one in order of color.

"Birdie, my man," Janet says, looking around the room. "I heard about your debacle."

Birdie shrugs, looking down at his Book of Fabulous.

Janet looks over at me and I shrug too. She soldiers on. "Anyway, I thought I'd come by with a gift—actually, two gifts—to maybe lighten the sting a bit." She pauses. "Although in my opinion, you shouldn't give two thoughts to a person like Teddy Garner. However, I understand you don't have a hardened exterior like mine yet. But give it time. Anyway, your gifts!"

She hands Birdie a brown paper lunch bag and he opens it up.

"Also, they might jazz up this new prison uniform that Patrick has you wearing," says Janet.

He pulls out a headband and a pair of sunglasses. The headband is simple. It's made of bright red wire and it's in the shape of cat ears. The sunglasses are white, with thick round frames. The lenses are a reflective sky blue.

"I got those from the thrift store ages ago. I kept meaning to give them to you, but never had the chance. I guess I was holding on to them until the right time."

He just holds them in his hands.

"Well, come on, now," she says. "Put them on. Patrick isn't here."

Birdie does and she brings him over to the mirror attached to his dresser.

"Perfecto!" she says. "Dang, am I good or what? Why am I doing hair? I should be a stylist to the stars."

Birdie laughs.

Janet turns back toward me. "Listen, I also came by to tell you that I'm heading out of town with my mom. We're going to go visit her sister in Utah even though she's always called my aunt a self-absorbed cow. But I guess I have a new cousin or something and my mom is insistent on us going now."

I nod. But I feel a little bead of abandonment roll around inside me.

This must have been what she felt like when she caught us leaving. But I guess probably worse.

Janet says she better go before the warden returns and then she kind of pushes the back of Birdie's head, messing up his hair. Birdie just keeps smiling into the mirror.

He looks like Audrey Hepburn.

All at once, I feel this tidal wave of joy wash over the room.

The first tidal wave of joy I ever felt came after Birdie got his favorite purple jacket when he was seven.

Mama found the puffy jacket with its tiny hearts and stars during one of her thrift-store visits. The thing Birdie doesn't know is that Mama had bought it for me. But when she came home, Birdie found it on top of one of the bags and picked it up. He hugged it to his face even though we hadn't washed it yet.

Mama and me stood in the kitchen and I said, "I thought you said the purple jacket was mine."

"I know, but look at him, Jackie."

Mama could always tell when I was glowering, even if she wasn't looking right at me. She put her arm around me and said, "I'll get you another."

She squeezed me tighter and said, "Imagine all those dark feelings inside of you being swallowed up by Birdie's joy, his love for the jacket. Joy can do that, you know. Even someone else's. It can swallow up the bad feelings because you know that joy spreads like a tidal wave."

I watched Birdie as he put it on, watched him straighten it and pull the shooting-star zipper up and down. It was way too big on him, but he didn't care. Purple was and still is his favorite color, plus anything "sparkly and amazing" like shooting stars.

"Whoosh," whispered Mama as she moved her hand in front of me like a wave. As I watched Birdie in the jacket, and imagined the giant tidal wave, I could feel the dark, selfish feeling disappear. Down, down, down it shrank until it was at the bottom of the ocean.

Patrick comes back exactly an hour after he left and he has a big jug of liquid garden fertilizer, two bags of compost, and a giant pizza with him. I watch from my window as he puts the fertilizer and the compost near the garage and then comes inside.

I want to write about the pizza in my notebook, but Birdie comes to my door. The headband and sunglasses are gone.

"Patrick brought home a pizza," he says.

"You saw it?"

"I smelled it."

"What kind of pizza, I wonder."

"I'm guessing pepperoni and mushroom," he says. "But it smells so good."

Downstairs Duke barks. "Even the dog is excited," I say.

"Should we go down or wait?"

I breathe in the smell. "Go downstairs."

When we get to the kitchen, Patrick is nowhere to be seen. I'm just snagging a look at the pizza when he comes in from outside. I instantly let go of the lid and hop back.

"I hope you guys eat pepperoni," he says.

We look at each other for a second, then he goes upstairs.

I grab a slice and so does Birdie. I stick my nose close to the cheesy heat, breathing deeply. It's been more than six months since I've had pizza that smells this good. Uncle Carl would sometimes buy the frozen ones, but they just don't compare.

Birdie does the same, closing his eyes as he breathes in. "I probably would have eaten it even if there were mushrooms."

"Yeah. Me too."

"Maybe even anchovies and monkey brains."

"Gross."

"Pizza is the best thing in the world."

As I take my first bite, the salty savory amazingness that is cheese and pepperoni and sauce hits my tongue and I think that maybe pizza can solve every problem on the planet. Like if we just had enough pizza it would be all right.

After finishing the first slice, I pause and take a long drink of Sprite, which is another new thing Patrick brought home. I take a second slice from the box.

Patrick comes down and doesn't say anything, but he seems to move about the room with lightness, which is also new.

"Don't eat those frozen pizzas from Grocery Plus," Patrick finally says. "If you're going to eat pizza, you have to get it from Vincent's over the hill. It's the only pizza worthy of being called pizza in fifty miles."

His voice is kind of serious, but he's tipped his hat back a little and I can see his bushy eyebrows.

I think that this might be the perfect time to ask Patrick about going to the library to meet Krysten tomorrow for our project and then visiting Uncle Carl, but I just can't get my mouth to form the words. I don't want to change the air in the room. So I keep silently chewing, along with everyone else.

True, it isn't green eggs, and it is a long way off from being a tidal wave of joy, but it is better than nothing.

It is definitely better than nothing.

**Observation #783: Inner Colors

Birdie is the color of a cloud, but one with secret rainbows like the cupcake ring & the cat ears headband & the giant round sunglasses.

Patrick used to be black. Or white. Something clear-cut, plain & obvious.
But now he looks gray.

What color am I?

CHAPTER 12

CRACKS IN THE ICE

I wake up thinking of two things: green eggs and Uncle Carl.

The sun is just beginning to rise when I find Birdie downstairs on the couch. He's wrapped in a blanket with a novel open on his lap. He has the stupid plain black sweatshirt on. Across the room, in a small bed by the wood-burning stove, Duke is sleeping.

"Patrick is outside," Birdie says without looking up. "He gets up early even on a Saturday."

"I know. I saw him doing something in the silo shed."

"So our plan is ruined." Birdie sighs. "No Uncle Carl's now."

I peek out the window. The light is still on in the shed. "Have you eaten breakfast yet? Leftover pizza?"

"No, but I did try to get Duke to come onto the couch,"

says Birdie. "It's like he's hibernating or something, because I scratched him behind the ears and he still didn't move."

"I'm surprised he's not outside with Patrick."

"He was, but then I overheard Patrick at the back door telling Duke to go inside and get warm. He walked right over to his bed and went to sleep." Birdie tugs at the collar of the new sweatshirt.

"Guess what? I came to make good on a promise." I hold up the little bottle of blue food dye.

"Really? What about Patrick?"

"What about him? He never said we couldn't scramble some eggs."

We go into the kitchen and while I get everything together, Birdie goes to the back door and looks out the window. "I think Patrick is making a garden. He's got a big bag of flower bulbs. And you should see this thing he has."

I go over to the window, and when I do, some kind of machine Patrick holds blasts on. He pushes it along the yard and it turns the dirt over as he walks.

"I think it's a tiller," I say. "I guess he is making a garden. I saw him take some plants out of the shed."

I scramble the eggs and then add three drops of blue food coloring. I mix it all together until it's a perfect peppy green. I keep thinking Birdie is going to watch me work, but he just stays at the window spying on Patrick.

When the eggs are finished, Birdie comes over and breathes deeply.

"They're perfect," we say at the same time.

We sit down to eat and for a moment, I wonder if we should say or do anything, like a prayer. But I have no idea how to do something like that, so I hold out my fork and say, "Cheers!" and we clink forks and dig in.

They *are* perfect—salty, buttery green eggs.

All of a sudden, I realize now how worried I was that they weren't going to turn out right, even though I've made scrambled eggs about a thousand times.

Birdie eats while smiling and humming quietly. It's the first I've seen him eat this way in a long time. Even last night with the pizza, it was more like he couldn't believe our luck and was worried that maybe it would just suddenly disappear. Honey Bunny Buns are the only thing I see him eat at Patrick's and still stay relaxed. Which suddenly reminds me.

"Oh yeah, I have some bad news," I say. "So you remember that I promised you the rest of my Honey Bunny Buns when we were at the mall with Patrick getting your new clothes? Well, I kind of ate them all. Except one."

Birdie taps his fork on the plate.

"But I still have one," I say, playfully elbowing him. "It's all yours. I'll go get it."

"No, it's okay, Jack. You can have it."

"But I promised, Birdie. You should take it."

"Yeah, but . . ." He stands up from his chair and tugs on his collar again. "You need them too."

He only has one bite of egg left. He leaves his toast on the table and brings his plate into the living room.

Ten seconds later, I hear, "He did it!"

I stand up, but Birdie runs over to my plate, steals a small bit of egg, and then disappears into the living room again. "Come look!"

I follow and what I find is Duke sitting up in his bed, licking Birdie's hand. "He loves it! He loves green eggs!"

Somehow, Birdie convinces me to donate the rest of my eggs to Duke. He lies under the table at our feet, just like he does with Patrick, and Birdie drops eggs to him, one little piece at a time.

I make extra pieces of toast and Birdie tells me about the bow tie he's making for Uncle Carl.

I'm in the middle of wondering how I can get Patrick to let us go to Uncle Carl's when the back door suddenly opens and Patrick comes in. He looks surprised to see us and glances at our plates and then at the large bowl with raw green egg streaking down the sides and the dirty pan.

"What is that?" he asks.

Duke stands up and walks out from underneath the table. Patrick frowns at him as he appears.

"It's egg? Scrambled egg?" I say, sounding uncertain, and I hope he doesn't think I'm lying.

"Why is it green?"

I don't know how to explain it, about me and Mama and Birdie's little dance and birthdays. "Um, Dr. Seuss?"

Patrick's covered in dirt and shoves his gloves into his back pocket and goes to the sink to wash up. "Why aren't you in bed?" he says to Duke.

"He likes the green eggs," Birdie suddenly says. "Duke ate them right up. Mama used to make them for us. But Jack knows how too."

Patrick turns the water off and dries his hands.

"That dog will eat anything," he says. He goes to the fridge and grabs the last two slices of pizza. "Make sure to clean up the mess. And I'll need your help again in the yard later . . . Come on, Duke." Him and the dog and the pizza go out the front door.

I guess there is the pizza Patrick and there is the green eggs Patrick. We probably shouldn't confuse the two.

After we've cleaned up, we hang out in Birdie's room and now it's my turn to watch Patrick at the window. There's no way to sneak out without him knowing. Especially if he's expecting us to help in the yard.

Birdie puts his sunglasses and headband on and fixes them in the mirror. "We have to do something, Jack. We have to help Uncle Carl get those balloon tickets."

"I'm going to ask Patrick if I can go to town," I say. "I had already agreed to meet a classmate at the library for a project. I was thinking of canceling on her, but I'm going to go. Because then I'll figure out a way to visit Uncle Carl."

Birdie studies me in the mirror. "Are you sure? What if Patrick finds out?"

"He won't. It will be quick."

Birdie puts the glasses and headband away in a drawer. He's back to grays, blacks, and blues. But he's smiling.

I find Patrick in the garage polishing some kind of metal pipe with an old rag.

I tell him I have to meet a friend at the library. "It's for a school project. For English class."

"Why don't you meet her during school?"

"Because it's homework."

He twists the pipe and squints, looking off toward town and then down at the ground where Duke lies. The dog lifts his head at me, which is a first. But I don't have any green eggs, so he goes back to his nap.

"Who's this friend?"

"Her name is Krysten. I had already agreed to meet her before Birdie was suspended."

He puts the tool down and picks up another and begins polishing again.

There's no way I can mention seeing Uncle Carl. I know he'll say no.

Finally he says, "I'll drive you."

A half an hour later, Patrick is dropping me off in front of the library. "Should I come pick you up? Or can you walk back?"

I know what he's really asking. He wants to know if he can trust me to not go "wandering around."

I say I can walk and he says okay.

I don't wait for him to pull away from the curb before I hurry inside. If I can finish up with Krysten, I'll still have time to visit Uncle Carl.

Ms. Perkins sits behind the reference desk helping a gray-haired man.

I hope she won't notice me. I still haven't talked to her since the bus trip.

Krysten is already at a table, reading a book and taking notes. She waves me over and as soon as I see the Elizabeth Bishop books, I remember that I was supposed to bring my book. The book that I don't have anymore.

"I forgot that I lost that Elizabeth Bishop book," I say right away.

"Oh—okay," she says, surprised. I don't think I've ever been the first to speak. "No worries, though. As you can see, the library has some." Her eyes kind of sparkle as they roam over all the books on the table. "This woman is fascinating."

"Yeah?"

"An unmarried woman! A lesbian!" I look around at the couple of heads that have turned our way. I think there are a lot of reasons why Krysten stands out in this town. "And she won the Pulitzer and the National Book Award! You really know how to pick 'em!"

I have no idea what she is talking about, but I can feel the grin on my face. Krysten has one of those smiles, where it's hard not to smile back.

"Um, do you think Mr. Belling will let us pick her?" I ask, looking down at a black-and-white photograph on the back of one of the books. "She wasn't on his list of suggested poets."

"He already said okay. I asked him yesterday, when you weren't at school."

She stops talking then, I guess waiting for me to talk about why I was absent. *My brother was suspended* is what I want to say. But I can't.

"Did you already check all these books out?" I ask.

"Yes, but you can borrow any of them." She continues to look at me with her kind, blue-framed eyes. "Especially if you don't have anything of your own."

"I used to have one. Really. But we had to move in with my uncle Carl and there wasn't space to bring all my books and that was one I left behind. To be honest, I never really read it. I kind of regret that now."

She nods slowly.

I can't believe I just said all that.

"That sounds awful," she says. "I don't know what I would do if I couldn't keep my books. Even when we moved here from Sacramento, when I was in the second grade, I insisted on bringing all my books with me. I think my mom only let me because she felt bad that she was taking me away from my friends and the city to live in a small town."

"Yeah, talk about Nowhere, Northern California, right?"

She chuckles and says, "Seriously."

I don't even know why I'm trying to joke around. Maybe it's just Krysten herself, who goes to my same school, who isn't a tornado, but more like a clear blue sky, the kind of sky that stretches on forever and makes you grin.

"We only moved here because my mom grew up here and got a job at the clinic. She's a gynecologist. She also serves a couple of the nearby Native American reservations."

"And you said you *still* feel like the new girl even after five years?"

"Yeah. But maybe that's because there's only one other black family in like a hundred miles. It's like being a human island."

I had no idea she felt this way. She always seems so connected at school.

She looks down at an Elizabeth Bishop biography. "I think that's why my dad stays in Japan."

"Your dad lives in Japan? Are your parents divorced?"

"No. It's just a complicated job situation he couldn't get out of. He's supposed to move back next year, but I want to visit him first. Maybe this summer."

"My mom always wanted to go to Japan," I say.

"How come you don't live with her anymore?"

"She passed away almost a year ago."

All of a sudden I have this feeling of being on a roller coaster and I'm coming over the top and gravity is pulling me down down down and I'm going incredibly fast, and there's absolutely no way to stop it.

"We wanted to scatter her ashes in Japan," I keep going. "But there was no time or money. So we had to scatter them at a lake near our old house up in Portland. But I kept a tiny bit of her ashes so I can go someday and eat fresh soba noodles by the sea just like she always wanted to and scatter them there. I have them in an old Skittles bag."

I haven't thought of this since I stood on the shore of the lake, shoving the last few Skittles in my mouth, and secretly replacing them with a pinch of the ashes. Neither Birdie nor Mrs. Spater saw. I did it without thinking, and I still have the Skittles bag, taped shut, inside a plastic bag, that's inside another small pouch, which I have hidden in an old pair of socks. I shoved it in there ten and a half months ago and haven't looked at it since.

"I think that's a great idea," says Krysten. "We scattered

part of my grandfather's ashes in San Francisco over the summer and the other part in Atlanta, Georgia, which is where he's from. I like the idea that he's in more than one place. It's almost like he has special powers now."

Krysten is probably the only person in the world who sees nothing wrong with keeping a bit of your mom's ashes in a Skittles bag. She spins her pencil along her fingers.

"I'm sorry about your grandpa," I finally say.

"Oh, thank you. Sorry to hear about your mom."

I nod at her. "Well, it's nice to finally meet another island."

"It is. And hey, we're an archipelago now," Krysten says. "A chain of islands."

On my way out of the library, I forget to check for Ms. Perkins. She catches me outside, in front of the doors.

"Jack!" she says. "I haven't seen you in a while." Her eyes are serious. "We were all very worried for you and Birdie during your bus ride. And I hear he's been in a bit of trouble at school."

"He was suspended for fighting," I say, not wanting to explain everything in such a public place.

"I can't imagine Birdie fighting."

In a flash, my eyes start to sting. "I know, neither can I."

"I saw you working with Krysten. That girl knows her stuff, but let me know if you need anything. All right?"

I nod and she shoos me off in her normal Ms. Perkins

fashion, acting like I was the one who interrupted her. But I smile as I watch her march back into the library.

I run into Uncle Carl coming out of the Stop-and-Go in a hurry, coffee and an unlit cigarette in his hands.

"Uncle Carl!" I yell.

"Jackie-O! You won't believe it!" He puts the cigarette behind his ear and takes a long drink from his mug. He sees me looking at the cup and says, "From Juan as a special de-stressor."

"De-stressor?"

"Things have gotten intense, this proposal."

I start to apologize for not coming sooner, but he just holds up his hand. "No explanation needed. I know you live with the goat. Anyway, I got the balloon tickets. It's all set. One week from today, me and Rosie will be high in the sky!"

"Oh my gosh, really?"

"*Really*, really. Except now I have a problem—the ring. There's just no money for one and I'm going to have to do something drastic to get it."

"Drastic?" I say.

"Well, let's just say an opportunity has come my way, and I think I better take it, for my Rosie."

"An opportunity? Uncle Carl, what are you talking about?" My voice sounds weird—higher than normal.

But he holds up his hand again to stop me. "No way. If I think about it or talk about it too much, I'll freak myself out and it won't happen. If it hadn't been for Juan, that exact thing would have happened with the balloon tickets. No. I'm on my way to meet the guy now and that's that."

"What guy?"

"Never mind, Jackie-O. You can't help with this part. Sometimes something drastic is what needs to be done and I have to do this myself. But come by tomorrow! I'll need your help with the ring! And we can finish planning the landing party. The last pieces to this Rosie puzzle." He downs the rest of his coffee and straps the empty mug to the rack behind his bicycle seat.

"But Uncle Carl, I might not be able to—"

But Uncle Carl cuts me off. "It's a plan! See you tomorrow! Wish me luck!"

Then he gets on his bike and pedals off around the corner, headed for whatever drastic thing he feels he needs to do.

**Observation #784: Islands

Maybe everyone is an island, even if we can't see the water all around.

B/c if Krysten is an island, then so is Janet. A neon-colored island in an ocean of small-town boredom.

If Janet is an island, then so is Rosie. A compassionate & smiley island in a sea of double-continental responsibilities.

And that means Uncle Carl is one too. & Ms. Perkins & Mrs. Spater. What oceans do they swim in?

Drastic ones? Busy ones? Lonely ones?

Of course that means Mama was an island, the brightest island floating in a dark & ordinary ocean.

& maybe the most obvious island is Patrick, the uncle who put himself out to sea.

CHAPTER 13

A DRASTIC THING

Birdie crawls onto my bed Sunday morning and says, "I'm worried about Uncle Carl's drastic thing."

"Birdie," I say with my eyes closed. "It's six thirty. Please go back to sleep. We don't have to be up for another hour."

"Is that all you can think about? Sleep? Aren't you worried?"

"Yes, but there's nothing we can do about it now. Especially from under a warm blanket with my eyes closed."

"Patrick's already up." Birdie leans toward my ear and whispers, "Again. Now we can't sneak out."

I sit up, rubbing my eyes. "Is that still the plan? Sneaking out?"

"Well, how else are we going to go help Uncle Carl? I don't want our plan to go up in smoke, you know."

"I'm going to ask Patrick for a ride again."

He looks at me with excited eyes. "You think he'll actually let us go?"

"I think he'll let *me* go."

"That isn't fair." He tugs at his sweatshirt collar again.

"Birdie, nothing about living here is fair." I spit the words out before I can stop myself.

Birdie slides off my bed and walks toward the door. "You don't have to tell *me* that."

"You want my Honey Bunny Bun?" I call after him as he leaves my room.

"No. I'm going to go make some toast!"

He doesn't ask if I want any.

At eight o'clock we go into the backyard. Patrick comes from the side of the house and hands me two pairs of gloves. These ones are smaller and brand-new.

"Those should fit better," he says as he looks out over the backyard. "Today you guys are going to carry more stones. We're going to mark out some garden beds."

Patrick shows us where he's tilled up a bunch of dirt. We're supposed to lay a stone border down to make four garden beds. He also wants stones around the four smaller trees—apple, apricot, and two cherry—which he says have been there for forty years.

I want to ask if they grow any fruit, but Patrick says, "Well, let's get to it," and then he goes to the other side of the yard where the tiller is. It bursts on with a bang and the opportunity for questions is gone.

We work for two hours and when Patrick turns off the tiller for good and goes inside, we sit on the old bench.

"When are you going to ask Patrick for a ride?" Birdie asks.

"Soon." Approaching Patrick is like getting close to a wild animal—no sudden movements and the timing has to be just right or he'll bolt. So I change the subject. "Did Patrick ever talk to you about learning how to fight?"

"No. I'm pretty sure he's only said like five sentences to me since we moved in."

I wish I could say that this isn't true, but he's probably right.

"At least the garden looks good," says Birdie. "I like the dark dirt and the light-colored stones together."

"But I bet we're gonna have to come out here and water a lot," I say. "I miss Portland rain."

"Yeah, and even with all that rain, it still felt sunnier than here."

Patrick comes out with a mesh sack of flower bulbs in one hand and a plate in another. "A little snack," he says as he sets the plate down between us. It has some of his thickly sliced homemade bread with something white smeared on top. It almost looks like cream cheese or butter, but not as smooth.

"It's cheese," says Patrick. "Just a soft house cheese I make sometimes. Goes well with the bread with a little honey on top. It's not strong tasting." He holds up his slice of bread and cheese to show us. He doesn't smile, but his hat is pushed back again and his eyebrows go up and down like Uncle Carl's do sometimes when he's excited.

Then he looks out onto the garden and takes a bite.

I do too.

It's creamy and soft, and saltier than cream cheese. It's delicious.

Birdie tentatively takes a bite.

A minute later, all three of us are quietly eating, looking out onto the garden.

Birdie is right. The nearly black dirt sparkles under the sun, and the contrast with the stones and bricks makes the yard look like the beginnings of an actual garden. The sun is warm and it feels like a good day.

"Patrick?" I say, after finishing the first piece of bread. "Birdie and me want to go see Uncle Carl. Could you please drive us?"

He doesn't say anything. He doesn't look at us. He looks down at the flower bulbs.

"It would just be for a couple hours," I add. "Not long. We just haven't seen him in a while."

Suddenly, I remember the long stretches of time we didn't see Patrick when we lived with Uncle Carl. Days, weeks, even. Mostly only when he came to help Rosie with the Quesadilla Ship's engine trouble. Only twice did he come to Uncle Carl's apartment.

We never asked Uncle Carl if we could see Patrick.

I wonder if Patrick thinks of that time.

"All right," Patrick suddenly says, crumpling up his napkin. "But I'm picking you up before dinner."

Patrick doesn't come in with us. He just drops us off at the curb and watches us walk up the stairs.

Uncle Carl answers the door after one knock, which totally surprises me.

"I'm not doing so hot," he says. "Have a giant headache. Things aren't going well. I've been hoodwinked!" He puts out his cigarette and pours himself some coffee.

"Maybe you should drink water," I say. As we walk in, I immediately see what's wrong. Marlboro is gone.

He sees me looking at the empty spot on his coffee table.

"Yeah," he says. "It's almost too horrible to even talk about. I don't know what to do." He's pacing around and picks up his pack of cigarettes. "I go to sell Marlboro to this dude, this animal collector. I met up with him yesterday to show some pictures of her. The guy says my Marlboro has some kind of rare print on her back. Says she's practically a celebrity dragon and that he'll pay top dollar for her. And I must be dang crazy because I think this is a great idea! Great plan! He gets Marlboro, I get cash, and Rosie gets the ring of her dreams! It should have been that easy." He sits down, lights another cigarette, and puts his head in his hands.

He doesn't usually smoke when we are here.

"What happened, Uncle Carl?"

"This morning I go to meet him, right? A ways out of town . . ." He continues pacing and puffing away. "And that guy took my Marlboro *and* the money. Marlboro is *gone!*"

"Call the police!" I say.

"I did! That's what I was doing right before you guys got here."

"They'll get her back," says Birdie. "That's what the police is for."

"They didn't even know what a bearded dragon was! And I talked to my buddy Rhett at the sheriff station and he just said that they'll take the report but finding something like a stolen taxidermied lizard is going to be difficult." He fans himself with a magazine. "And I'm proposing in less than a week! Isn't stress the number one killer in America? Or number two? Right behind Big Macs or something?" He looks at his cigarette and then is like, "Oh jeez, sorry, guys!" He smashes it on his ashtray and then gets up and starts pacing again.

"It's okay," I say. "You've still got the balloon tickets. If you want, I'll make a strawberry cake for when you land. It will still knock her socks off and maybe she doesn't even want a ring in the first place."

He picks up his cigarettes again and hits the pack in his hand. "I'm going down to the Stop-and-Go real quick," he says. "Maybe Juan knows something." And then he's gone and we're left standing in his apartment, not any closer to a finished proposal plan.

"I'm gonna go change," says Birdie, taking off the black jacket and heading into the bathroom with his backpack.

I say, "What do you mean?" but the door closes and when he comes back out he's got his old clothes on—his leggings with the rainbow knees, a thin leopard-print skirt, and his purple jacket. And the purple eye shadow.

"Uncle Carl still not back?" he asks, getting out his bow tie supplies and his Alexander McQueen book, which we secretly dried out Friday night with the bathroom space heater. Already Birdie's eyes are bright and his shoulders relaxed.

"He'll be back soon," I say. "We'll figure this out."

Birdie looks perfect in his clothes.

Ten minutes later, Uncle Carl is back. And he doesn't look any better despite having a free cup of coffee in his hand. "Juan reminded me that we only lose what we cling to," he says, sitting on the couch. He puts his head in his hands and mumbles, "I cling, I lose."

Birdie nods and pats him on the back.

I think this is the first time Juan hasn't been able to calm Uncle Carl down. And he can't go to Rosie, so I'm not sure what will help. Birdie says, "Don't worry, Uncle Carl. You also have a bow tie. Let's try it on, maybe?" Uncle Carl sits there, slowly sipping his coffee.

I go to the bathroom to splash water on my face.

When I come back out, Birdie's like, "So, it turns out that Duke's neck is a lot wider than Uncle Carl's."

"This kid!" says Uncle Carl. "He thinks I have the neck of a basset hound!"

Birdie puts his hair up into a bun. "I can fix it. Patrick wouldn't let us come over here, so I had to use *someone* as a model."

Uncle Carl lies back on the couch with his arms stretched out and his eyes closed. "So you pick a dog!"

I have to steer him back to normal. "Uncle Carl, what can we do for the landing party besides a cake? Maybe party balloons? Ones with hearts or something?"

He doesn't move. "Glow sticks. In the brown bag. My buddy who works at the Shasta Dam gave them to me."

"Glow sticks?" Birdie says.

"I don't know," groans Uncle Carl. "I saw this thing on the TV where someone spelled out 'I LOVE YOU' on the beach with them. But I don't even know how many we have. Maybe there's not enough to do that." He flaps his arms around. "Don't ask me. I obviously don't know what a good idea is!"

"It's okay," I say. "It's a *great* idea. It's a sunset balloon ride, right? Don't worry. I'll count them."

I dump the glow sticks onto the floor. There are two different kinds and most of them are individually wrapped.

"And mark my words, Mr. Bird," says Uncle Carl, sitting up. "I'm going to talk to that goat about your new clothes. It's ridiculous. Shows you what a clam knows about style!"

I say, "And you have to change out of those before Patrick comes back, okay, Birdie?"

"I will." He rolls his eyes.

"Don't worry about the kid," Uncle Carl says, lying back down. "He's gotta do what he's gotta do. And he can do that here."

Birdie smiles as he leans over his sewing. It almost feels like we are back here for good.

No amount of pizza or homemade bread and cheese can replace Birdie being able to be himself. It just can't.

The phone goes off and I jump. Uncle Carl lets it go to voicemail, but no one leaves a message.

I inspect the two different kinds of glow sticks. One package says SAFETY LIGHT STICK 12 HOUR ORANGE GLOW and the other says 6" GREEN LIGHT STICK.

Uncle Carl gets up and paces around again. He's decided he's going to report the animal collector/thief to the police in San Francisco and Sacramento because surely the thief would have to go to a big city to sell her.

But then he lies back down and says he can't face making

another phone call today. He closes his eyes and tells Birdie to wake him up when he needs a human neck.

I was going to finish counting the rest of the glow stick packages, but instead shove the two in my hand into my pocket and say, "I'm going to go get some quesadillas for us to eat. That will pep us up." Plus I need some air to clear my head because my mind is starting to ask the question I don't want it to ask: What happens if Rosie says no?

When I get down to the Quesadilla Ship, there's a long line of people, including a group of seven who are all dressed with green hats that say *Lisa & Fargo Get Hitched*.

"Can you lend me a hand, love?" Rosie asks. "There's this whole Lisa and Fargo group going to the balloons, and I need that block of cheese grated."

I feel this surge of hope because hot-air balloons and getting hitched! It's something that people do! Hot-air balloons *are* romantic!

Rosie's phone rings and she sighs and picks up, the whole time flinging cheese and onion and tortillas around. "Okay, okay, but where is Linda, Mum? The *nurse. Linda.* Where is she?" She sighs again. "*Right now? Okay.*"

She hangs up. "I need to go. My mum needs me. But look at this queue." She looks over at the line. There are probably almost twenty people out there. "I can't afford to lose these customers," she says. "Especially with me having to close up while I'm in England. How did I become a one-woman show?"

That's when I see it: the answer.

This will be the thing that makes her realize Uncle Carl is *the one*. Maybe he won't need a ring at all.

"What about Uncle Carl?" I say. "I bet me and Uncle Carl could do these orders. We've both helped you before."

"I don't know, love." She plates three more quesadillas and adds sour cream and salsa. "It's a lot, running this joint. Even for a short while."

"But you have all the recipes posted up and I've made a ton of quesadillas and also Uncle Carl has helped you before. I even remember how to do the money."

Her cell phone starts to ring again. She looks at it and then puts it back in her pocket. "Okay," she says. "But only if he's okay with it."

There's a quesadilla almost burning.

She nods up toward Uncle Carl's apartment. "Go on, then. Go get him."

I smile, hop out of the Quesadilla Ship, and run upstairs.

"Rosie needs help," I say as soon as I go through the door.

Uncle Carl jumps up before I can even explain. Birdie shrieks about messing up the bow tie, which is back around Uncle Carl's neck. I tell them about the long line of people and Rosie needing to go to her mom.

Uncle Carl doesn't hesitate. "Sorry, Mr. Bird. But my Rosie needs me."

"That's okay. I want to brainstorm anyway. It's time for my muse to visit." He closes his eyes and holds his hands to his temples. I give him a look because where does he come up with these things? But Uncle Carl is calling to me from the doorway.

We run down to the truck and see Rosie frantically flipping quesadillas. "You sure you can do this? I won't be long," she says.

"We can do it, Rosie!" I say, stepping inside the truck.

Uncle Carl glances anxiously at the people in line and starts looking unsure. But again I get a burst of confidence when I see those green *Lisa & Fargo Get Hitched* hats. I don't even know who Lisa and Fargo are, but I'm so happy for them.

"We can do it," I say again. "Go help your mom. We are the Unstoppable Spatula Crew!"

She laughs nervously and Uncle Carl begins to sweat, but I just smile and kind of puff out my chest, hoping to look older and taller. I think she's about to change her mind, but then her phone rings again and she steps out of the truck. "Okay. I'm on my way, Mum. Just stay right there. No, don't go anywhere." She glances back at me and I give her a thumbs-up. She nods and hops in her car and drives away.

I pick up an apron and hand it to Uncle Carl. "Let's make some quesadillas!"

Uncle Carl and I work perfectly, side by side in the Quesadilla Ship. I chant, "We are the Unstoppable Spatula Crew, making cheesy treats for you! We'll get you through the queue!"

Uncle Carl laughs.

I've plated sixteen specialty quesadillas when I start to think I might have the hang of this.

Only two orders are left when I hear Uncle Carl yelp.

I turn around and he shouts, "Get back!" just as he throws a giant cup of water on the burning skillet.

You know when time seems to slow down to nothing, when everything is happening around you and you're caught in a bubble? Your brain is working like mad, but the rest of your body won't respond fast enough, like trying to swim in a pool of honey? I see the fire rising up from the pan and I know one thing immediately: This is a grease fire.

When I was seven, there was a fireman who visited our classroom. I remember he looked really impressed when I asked him how to safely put out a small fire. Well, that's when I first learned about grease fires.

If you don't know anything about grease fires, you should. Because everyone thinks, *Oh, you need water to put out fires.* But that isn't always true, no matter what the cartoons say.

And when I see Uncle Carl pouring that big cup of water, my brain lights up with facts about grease coming from cheese, and water repelling grease, and grease spreading like an explosion, and that's exactly what happens. What was one small fire is now six, lighting up the stove and surrounding countertop. Uncle Carl pushes me away, but I lean toward the stove to try to turn off the burners. Uncle Carl keeps shouting to *get out! get out!* and then he waves a towel around and brings it down on the burning stove and counter. But I know if the stove isn't turned off, the truck will be lost.

So I press forward and that's when the fire finds the small bowl of sesame oil and it leaps up to the ceiling, doubling the amount of heat. Smoke pours out of the window and I can see that it's reached the point that the fireman had called "the point of no return."

Everything is happening so fast and so slow at the same time. I can hear shouts and maybe the distant siren of a fire truck. Uncle Carl is frantic, his face all twisted up, curse words like I've never heard before coming out of his mouth. "I've got to stop this!" he yells, and I'm trying to get him out and suddenly Birdie is there stepping through the door, yanking on my arm and now there is a stranger pulling my arm too, and Birdie is shouting my name.

It's only when the fire makes a leap from the wall to Uncle Carl's shirt that he bounces back toward the door. We tumble out, Uncle Carl rolls on the grass, and I land on top of Birdie and the Stop-and-Go employee who'd been trying to pull me out.

Someone shouts, "Is there a fire extinguisher?" and then someone else yells, "The fire truck is on the way!" and then there's a small *pow!* as something else in the grease-laden kitchen explodes. I cover my eyes and cough as more and more smoke pours out of the ordering window.

We get up and move away from the truck. I look over at

Uncle Carl and he's covered in black sweat, his eyes open and chest heaving up and down.

At some point my brain registers the amount of heat coming off burning metal.

Suddenly, Uncle Carl is running back toward the truck. He's too far away for me to do anything. I think I'm yelling, but the fire and the crackling and popping is all so loud I can't hear myself.

Then out of nowhere, Patrick is there, wrestling his brother back.

They almost look like they're dancing as Patrick pulls Uncle Carl farther from the blaze.

"Let me go!" shouts Uncle Carl. "I can save the truck. I can fix this!"

Patrick holds on.

"Let. Me. Go!" yells Uncle Carl.

There's another pop just as the fire truck appears and the firefighters jump into action.

The tree above the truck is on fire.

Water streams out of a fire hose.

"I could have saved it," says Uncle Carl.

"You would have been killed," says Patrick.

"Yeah? What's it to you, huh?"

Uncle Carl twists out of Patrick's grip and stares at him, breathing hard. He curses, tugging on the twisted Quesadilla Ship apron.

Right when I start to feel light-headed, I hear Rosie's voice.
It sounds really far off, like she's running down the street.
Then she's there, next to a fireman who's trying to calm her
down.

"Oh my God, oh my God, oh my God!" she says. "What
happened? Oh my God!"

She looks over and sees Uncle Carl and runs up to him
and kind of grabs his shirt and is asking him what happened.
At first she's just kind of confused and stunned, but then she
gets madder and madder when Uncle Carl doesn't say anything other than I'm sorry. At one point, he starts to say that it
was an accident, but she yells and tugs on his shirt and I've
never seen her face look so mad and sad and lost.

Patrick steps in between them and Rosie backs away,
shaking her head like she can't believe what's happening.

"You really don't understand why I always say no? You
look at that truck and tell me why I always say no!" She puts
her hand to her head and stares at her poor burning truck.

All I want to say is I'm sorry. I'm sorry. I'm sorry. But nothing
comes out no matter how hard I try to speak. Rosie looks at
me a second and just shakes her head and walks away.

Uncle Carl stumbles back toward his apartment, the
Quesadilla Ship apron hanging loose around his neck.
Patrick goes to follow him, but then stops when Birdie lets
out a cry of pain from a paramedic cleaning a giant scratch
he has along his arm. "Birdie—?"

"My arm's fine!" Birdie jumps to his feet.

"I really should finish wrapping that," says the paramedic, but Patrick waves him off.

"I'll take care of it," Patrick says, looking over at me. "Let's go. Now."

Birdie's purple eye shadow is smudged. His skirt has a grass stain, I guess from when we fell out of the truck. Patrick looks around at groups of people who have gathered.

"Can I at least get my things from Uncle Carl's?" says Birdie as Patrick leads him away.

"Don't worry about that," says Patrick. "Get in the truck."

"But Uncle Carl's apartment is right here." Patrick's truck is parked haphazardly along the wrong side of the street.

"Get in. *Now.*" Patrick's voice is low and serious.

Birdie jerks the door open and sits down with crossed arms and no seat belt.

I look back at the Quesadilla Ship. The fire's out, but smoke rises from the black hole that had been the middle of the roof. I get in and buckle up Birdie and me.

As we drive away, I see Ms. Perkins standing on the sidewalk with a bunch of others. She raises her hand in a melancholy wave and I remember saying goodbye to Mrs. Spater all over again.

**Observation #785: The Quesadilla Ship

The Quesadilla Ship was a lime-green food truck decorated with planets, stars & asteroids & nebulas, all painted by some student from the community college over the hill. It had a short nose & a tall door, which was black with white splatter paint to look like the Milky Way Galaxy. I guess quesadillas remind Rosie of UFOs.

There was some rust, but Rosie always said it just added to the space effect.

Inside there was a huge griddle & a big rack of spices & a spot next to that where Rosie kept specialty oils like sesame for the Asian fusion quesadillas & her homemade jalapeño oil for her Some Like It Hot quesadillas.

It's hard to believe that something as big & loud & perfect as the Quesadilla Ship can just disappear. It seems like once something is that big & important, it has to be there for good.

One moment, you're days away from the best wedding proposal ever & a new place to live, a new future &

the next, everything's gone up in smoke.

CHAPTER 14

ISLANDS ON THE LAKE

It's five a.m. and I've been awake for more than an hour, my brain heavy with images of fire, Rosie's angry face, and Uncle Carl's apron hanging loose around his neck as he retreated to his apartment.

There's a knock on my door.

"Jack?" Patrick says through the door. "Are you awake?"

I open the door and a light over the staircase puts everything in shadow. The cold hallway air makes me glad for the space heaters that appeared in our bedrooms a couple days ago.

"Wake up your brother," he says. "We're going to Lake Moser. And dress warmly. We leave in thirty minutes."

...

Turns out, there was a small boat hitched to Patrick's truck. So I guess we are going boating.

Now that we're here, the sky is just beginning to lighten. The entire lake is surrounded by trees—almost to the water— except for a small parking lot near a dock and restrooms. We get out of the truck while Patrick gets the boat ready, making quick but deliberate movements as he takes off the tarp. He doesn't look any happier than us to be out here.

Birdie walks over to a bench and puts the hood of his new black jacket up.

"Why are we here?" Birdie asks. "It's so cold. And it's a Monday."

"You'd rather be at school?" I ask.

"No. But I thought that was the big problem with us living at Carl's. We were skipping too much school."

"I don't think that was the only problem."

I think of last night, when I secretly tried to call Uncle Carl and the phone just rang and rang. The answering machine never even picked up. Which means Uncle Carl unplugged his phone again.

"I'm just saying we need to help Uncle Carl and Rosie. We have to tell her that the fire was an accident. She'll under- stand once we explain and then she won't be mad." He tugs on the collar of his jacket. "And I hate this stupid jacket. I'm never doing Norman another favor again!"

I'm about to say that I think Rosie's feelings are more

complicated than that when Patrick yells, "Okay, guys! Let's go!"

Without saying another word, Birdie turns and walks down toward the water. I go too.

The boat is small, just a rowboat with a motor, really, and it's wobblier than I'm expecting. I grip Patrick's hand tight so that I don't fall when I step inside. His arm is completely still. We both help Birdie into the boat, and then Patrick's inside too, and suddenly the small motor roars to life and we are on our way, moving slowly across the water.

We ride for a while before Patrick cuts the engine. Cold silence follows. Hills of black-looking trees tower around us and there's the big mountain, covered in snow, looming in the distance. I'm glad I wore my hat and jacket and I hate to say it, but I'm also glad that Birdie's in the new clothes. Leggings and his purple jacket wouldn't cut it out here on the water. He's got a real pair of jeans on, along with a thickly lined jacket and warm hat that goes over his ears.

The boat slowly turns. Patrick takes a thermos out of his bag.

"Hot chocolate. You guys drink that?" He holds the thermos out and says, "You can share. Take it."

So I do and I offer it to Birdie, but he shakes his head. I take a drink because I feel like my nose might fall off if I don't take a small sip. As soon as I do, it reminds me of the hot chocolate Birdie and me bought at the bus station.

What a simple thing a bus ride seems now. It was just Birdie and me trying to get home.

But home is gone. We could go there, and the duplex might still be there, but there would be other people living there. Some other older lady, maybe. Next to some other family.

And now the Quesadilla Ship is gone too.

Patrick sips his coffee and looks out onto the lake.

Birdie hunches into a black-and-navy-blue ball and seems to sleep.

I drink the hot chocolate, feeling a little guilty, like I shouldn't be enjoying it, but the heat goes straight into the center of me and radiates out. I hold the thermos cup under my nose like Uncle Carl does with his coffee in the mornings.

I wonder if Uncle Carl will ever plug his phone in again.

Suddenly, Patrick's head shoots up. "Look!" he whispers, pointing to the sky.

It's a bird, a big one, its wings are outstretched and it circles once, twice above us and then flies toward the other side of the lake before swooping down near the water and then into the trees. Its white head surprises me. I know exactly what kind of bird it is, even though I've never seen one in real life until today.

"A bald eagle," I say, still looking at the trees where it disappeared.

Patrick nods.

He gets his fishing rods out. I look behind me at Birdie to see his reaction to the eagle, but he's still curled up on the seat with his eyes closed.

Patrick casts the two fishing lines into the water on either side of the boat and hands me one. I don't know what to do with it, so I just sit there, holding it like he does. I look into the trees, which are now turning from black to dark green from the rising sun. Maybe the eagle will come out again.

It reminds me of the first Wolf Day, and that one wild eye and how I stared at the darkness for a long time after it disappeared hoping to see it again.

"Shouldn't we be in school today?" I ask.

Patrick reels his line in even though it was only out for like two minutes. "Yes, I would prefer you be in school. But it was important to get out of town today. Get some space from everything."

"You mean space from Uncle Carl?"

He sighs and casts his line out again. "Carl needs some time alone. And it's not good to be around him right now."

"Are you sure he doesn't need our help?"

"He doesn't need our help, no. It's not your job to fix him and I want you and your brother to stay away. And, look, it's not that big of a town. People talk. It's best for us to not be in the middle of all that at the moment."

I'm about to remind him that he said running away doesn't solve anything when I feel the fishing rod twitch. I look down at it and it twitches again and again. Finally

Patrick turns around and all he says is, "Reel it in, not too fast."

And so I do, and then out pops this spotted yellow fish about as long as a ruler.

"A brown trout," says Patrick, leaning over to help me with the line.

Birdie sits up and rubs his eyes. "You caught a fish?" he asks.

"I caught a fish," I say, and I suddenly think of the poem Mama used to recite by Elizabeth Bishop called "The Fish." She liked to say a couple lines of it when we were out at a seafood restaurant and would always do it like she was reading Dr. Seuss even though the lines didn't rhyme and the poem was actually pretty solemn. The waiters and waitresses always looked confused, which made the whole thing kind of embarrassing but also funny.

I don't remember the words to the poem, but I do remember that the fish is freed at the end and I ask Patrick if we can throw the fish back. He nods and undoes it from the line and holds it out to me and I take it from him with both hands without even thinking. It's slick, cold, and weightier than it looks. I hold it for a moment and then lower my hands into the water. The fish slides back in and quickly disappears. All of a sudden I have that rushing, roller-coaster feeling like I had with Krysten at the library, and before I can stop, my mouth opens and speaks.

"Have you fished your whole life?"

Patrick kind of chuckles and then shakes his head. Maybe it's what some people call *scoffing*.

"It was my mama who loved to fish," he says, still looking down at the water where the trout swam away. "She'd come out to this lake on her own because Dad didn't like the water and she knew she could be alone out here. She'd bring her coffee and whiskey and these rods. Sometimes me and Carl and our older brother, George, would go with her, but we knew she preferred to be on her own out here. She always came back with something for dinner."

"You learned how to fish from her, then?"

"The very basics. I try to come out here on her birthday. I don't really like to fish. It's a whole lot of waiting around for hardly anything to show for it, but it seems like a good thing to do for her."

"Is today her birthday?"

"No, but I didn't go this year on her birthday, so maybe I'm just making up for that."

He reels in his own line, fiddles with the hook and bait, and then casts it out again.

"Did she ever teach my mama to fish?"

"No. But your mama—she grew up separate from us boys."

"Because she was a girl?"

Patrick pauses for a second and then says, "Maybe. But I think mostly because she was fifteen years younger than us. So she was separate and always did her own thing."

I know that he is telling the truth. Even though I didn't know Mama way back then, I could see how she was completely alien from her family.

Patrick continues, "Her and Carl were sometimes close. But even then, Beth was always going to do what she wanted, and it was me who was expected to pick up the slack when she screwed up or disappeared with friends or some guy."

He opens his tackle box and the tingly roller-coaster feeling begins to heat up, starting at my toes. Patrick closes the box hard and says, "Just like Carl now—that fire should not have happened. He screws up and now there are pieces to pick up, problems to fix. Neither of them ever seemed to care that I'm the one who has to deal with it. "

My whole body flushes mad and hot, the roller coaster replaced with a runaway freight train.

I set the rod down and turn away from him with my arms crossed. Birdie is still hunched over with his hood up, but from this angle I can see that he is awake, silently listening to the truth of what we are to Patrick.

**Observation #786: A Wild Animal

A wild animal got into Patrick's backyard. It ruined the garden.

- The rock borders destroyed.
- The piles of good kindling & burn wood scattered.
- The beds dug up.
- Flower bulbs lay in wet dirt, looking like the small moldy onions Mama would throw away after forgetting about them in the bottom of our cupboard.

   This morning, Birdie said: Did you see the garden? It's destroyed. I think a wild animal got in & dug everything up.
   I said maybe it was a coyote looking for an old buried rat.

   What I didn't tell him was that after he had gone to bed last night, I went down to get a glass of water & I saw Patrick from the window. He sat on a stump for a long time, frozen.

   Then, he exploded in movement, throwing rocks, branches, tools. He slammed the shovel down on the dirt again & again & all of a sudden I remembered Mama doing the same to her own garden once and I got confused, so I took my glass of water back up to the bedroom & shut the door & crawled into bed.

CHAPTER 15

PICKING UP THE PIECES

Yesterday on the boat, Patrick never did say anything else about Birdie and me being problems to fix. He just told me to reel in my line and then he turned the boat's engine on and steered us back to the dock. He spent the rest of the day in the silo shed until the middle of the night when I saw him destroying the garden.

As he drives us to school, I sneak three looks at him: one at his face in shadow from his hat pulled low, one at his knuckles gripped tight on the steering wheel, and one at his shoulders tensed under his ears. When we get to my school, he only says one thing to me: "No going to Carl's. You come right back to the house after school."

And it's the perfect excuse to avoid hanging out with Krysten, who tries to catch my eye all through class. I know she knows about the fire because of how much she loved Rosie's truck. But I can't face her right now. She'll ask too many questions. Give too much advice.

Still, she follows me out to the parking lot as I speed off, but before she can say anything, I call out over my shoulder, "Sorry. Can't talk today. My uncle wants me back right away."

"Okay, but are you all right?"

"I'm fine. I have to get my brother and go home." I walk through the school gate hoping she won't follow since she has to wait for her mom.

She stays at the gate, but calls out in a loud voice, "I'll call you! Maybe there's something we can do for Rosie and her truck! I want to help!"

I say *archipelago, archipelago* over and over in my head, but it doesn't help. The anxiety of having to answer her questions about the fire, and Uncle Carl and Rosie and Patrick, is too much.

I know she's supposed to be my friend, but how do I add a friend to this kind of life?

Archipelago. Archipelago. Archipelago.

I stop and turn around just before crossing the street. "All right!" I yell to her. "Call me later. But I have to go. Bye!"

She nods and I turn and head toward town.

When I get there, Birdie is already at our meeting place, which is no longer the Quesadilla Ship. Now it's just a giant asphalt hole. Birdie sits on the curb looking tiny in the truckless spot and I notice he doesn't have a backpack. He has a plastic grocery bag instead.

"What happened?" I ask.

"Stupid Norman backpack didn't help anything!" he shouts when he sees me. He stands up and starts walking toward the highway. "Norman and his ugly clothes are becoming a problem."

"Why?"

He shoves the grocery bag at me as we walk and inside is Patrick's black backpack with pink paint dumped on it.

"Teddy and his friend Mario did it. I guess they saw me in my outfit at the Quesadilla Ship fire. They said they knew I didn't like wearing plain colors. So they added the pink for me."

"Did you tell your teacher?"

"Mrs. Cross-Hams? Yeah, right. Don't you remember that things always get worse when she's involved?" He walks quickly and looks back toward town as we cross to the other side of the highway.

We walk along in silence and when we're about to turn down Patrick's street, I hear a skateboard and Janet's voice cuts through the silence of the neighborhood.

"Hey dudes! Hold up!" And suddenly there she is. "Seriously, I leave town for two seconds and all hell breaks loose."

"I thought you were in Utah visiting your aunt," I say.

"Yeah, and I'm back now. But who cares about that, seriously, what happened to the Ship?"

"There was an accident," I say, almost whispering as I think of that first pop and the fire that rose out of the pan.

"No kidding, I can't believe it. Rosie must be so mad. I swear sometimes it seems like nothing can go right in this town." She puts a hand on Birdie's shoulder. "Mr. Bird, where are your sunglasses? I'm disappointed. And really, you guys kind of look like zombies. Why don't you guys come to the trailer? I have a leftover pizza and you can tell me what happened to the Ship."

Across the street is Patrick's house. The driveway is empty, which means Patrick is still at work. Birdie looks up at me and for once he looks excited at the prospect of going to Janet's.

And to be honest, Patrick's shoebox is the last place I want to be. A place where we are just someone's problem. Someone's slack to pick up.

Anyway, who wants to live in a house with a yard all wrecked? It looks worse than it did before he started.

I don't care about Patrick's rule to go straight home. I have only one question for Janet.

"What kind of pizza?"

We spend the next hour eating warmed-up pizza, playing checkers, and talking about the fire.

"It's the one crazy thing to happen here and of course I miss it by a couple hours."

"It wasn't entertainment," I say. "It was horrible."

"Of course! I'm not saying it wasn't. But you know how it gets here. Like, no one talks about anything except when snow might fall and how long it's been since it rained. Boring. Have you talked to Rosie?"

"No. She hasn't answered any of our calls. Neither has Uncle Carl."

Janet rolls her eyes. "No surprise there, I guess."

I ignore her jab at Uncle Carl because I know she's right and it makes me mad and sad at the same time. Because I want Uncle Carl to be reliable. I want him to be better.

It seems like Janet's trailer is the only place on Earth Birdie and me can just *exist*.

"So you got back Sunday night?" I ask. "Short trip."

"Yeah, not short enough." She gets up and throws her pizza crusts into the trash can, then flicks a pack of cigarettes sitting on the counter. "And look who forgot her cigarettes again, wherever she is." She takes one out but doesn't light it. "We got home Sunday night and she immediately disappeared with Ross and hasn't been seen since. Typical."

It was Tuesday afternoon. "You haven't heard from your mom since Sunday night?"

She shakes her head and looks at a lighter, which she spins on the kitchen counter.

Before I can ask her how she feels about it, she looks up at Birdie and says, "You have any more trouble with Teddy?"

Birdie sighs and tells her about his backpack.

She says, "Some kids take after their parents too much, Mr. Bird. It's hard."

He nods at her.

That's when I realize Teddy got worse after we ran into him and Ross at the mall—after Patrick did nothing to stop Ross from saying all those things. And Teddy watched.

"Don't pay attention to *anyone* like that," Janet continues. "And don't worry. I have a backpack you can use. I'll get it."

Janet disappears into her room and when she comes out, she has her old backpack in her hands. It's black and covered in white stars.

"It's not as colorful as your old one, but at least you won't have to use a backpack covered in paint or a plastic bag for school."

Birdie nods and says, "Thank you," as he zips the small front pocket open and closed.

I wonder if Birdie has made the connection between Ross and Teddy and Patrick at the mall.

The wind suddenly picks up outside and the trailer windows rattle. But in here, the little heater glows red and warm.

Birdie picks his last piece of pizza apart, which is how he eats pizza.

Janet stays surprisingly quiet and just looks at him with curious eyes the entire time.

"So, Birdie," Janet says, breaking the silence. "Do you think you're gay?" I'm too shocked to say anything.

"I don't know," says Birdie in a small voice.

"Do you want to be boyfriends with girls or boys?"

"I don't want to be boyfriends with anybody."

"Janet," I say, "this has nothing to do with being boy-friends with anyone. And I've already talked to him about that."

"Okay, okay," she says, waving her hands at me. She turns back to Birdie. "So, do you feel like you're a girl, then? Have you ever heard of the word *transgender*?"

"Janet!" I say, smacking her leg. I don't know exactly what it means, but I also don't know if I'm ready to have this all swirling around. It was a lot easier with Uncle Carl and Rosie. They didn't ask questions.

"I don't know," says Birdie, shrugging. "Everyone says I'm a boy."

"But what about on the inside? Do you feel like you're a girl on the inside?"

Birdie shrugs for the millionth time. "I don't know. Sometimes I wish I was a girl because then it would make everything easier. But I don't know what my mind is." He looks down at his shoes again. "Is it bad that I don't know?"

For a few seconds, no one says anything. Probably because we don't know if he's supposed to know.

We don't really know anything.

Mama would have known exactly what to say.

But she isn't here.

All I know is that Birdie is fine just the way he is.

"No," I say firmly. I look at him until he makes eye contact with me. "It's not bad that you don't know, okay? You're perfect just the way you are."

The silence takes over again and I wonder if what I just said is actually true because sometimes it feels like you *have* to know the answer. Because what does it mean if he doesn't know? If you aren't a boy and you aren't a girl—then what are you?

But then I think, what if he *does* know? What if he knows he's a girl but he just can't say it? What if he's too scared?

"Where did you hear about all this?" I ask Janet.

"*The Ellen Show*." Janet laughs then, her cackle filling the small space of the trailer living room, making me feel lighter again. "I can find some information online for you guys, maybe."

I sit quietly because it's all so much, and I worry that it's all too much for Birdie. But he just has this small smile on his face and his feet swing off the tall kitchen chair. He's looking in, as Mama used to say. He's looking in, and he's happy. After everything that's happened, he still doesn't really care what other people think.

It's here in Janet's cluttered trailer with cold pizza and the smell of old cigarette smoke that the ground feels totally solid. The walls are close and safe and the air is warm, like this is our own haven, which is a word I looked up in the dictionary after Rosie first invited us to the Quesadilla Ship and gave us warm plates of food. A haven—a place of shelter and safety, a refuge.

I look over, and now Birdie's laughing about something Janet's said that I missed.

Their laughter builds as Janet combs Birdie's hair into two pigtails and then adds a bunch of tiny rose clips. She wraps a red feather boa from her mom's room around his neck. They sit huddled together as Birdie shows her his Sudoku puzzle book and tries unsuccessfully to teach her the mystery of numbers one through nine.

I sit and watch them, and get my observation notebook out.

**Observation #787: Tornado Sounds

Nothing fits better in the ear than your best friend's voice.

...

After an impromptu fashion show, more pizza, and two more games of checkers, I get up and use the bathroom. I'm washing my hands when from outside comes a screech of truck brakes, tires crunching gravel, and then a yell. I'm out of the bathroom immediately and Janet is there with Birdie.

"Get in my room and don't come out," she says, pushing us back while looking toward the front door.

There's more yelling outside, words that I don't quite understand, and shouts, and Janet's lazy dog, Lucky, starts barking. It is late, I realize. Patrick is probably off work by now.

I can't see anything out Janet's window, but I hear a truck or car door open and close and Janet yells, "Mom!"

Then a man shouts, "You think I care about that? Wow. I always knew you'd do something like this! Well, we're here now, Kathy, so where is it? I drove you all the way back, so get my money."

Now Janet's shouting, telling him to leave or she'll call the cops, and Janet's mom is yelling too, but I can't understand her, and at one point I think I hear Janet's phone ringing, but it sounds like it's stuck in the couch. "You owe me! I know you have it. You can't just use four hundred bucks and then expect to not pay it back!" The man's voice is louder now, and I step outside Janet's room to try and get a better look through the front window. I see a truck with the driver's-side door open, the headlights beaming, lighting the swirling dust from the gravel road as it floats up and around a man in jeans. It's Ross.

"You're out of your mind," Janet's mom says, pointing at Ross. Her skin is darker than Janet's, but under the harsh fluorescent porch light and the truck headlights, it glows almost white. She turns toward Janet and says, "Janni, get back inside." But Janet doesn't move.

Ross says, "You know I'm not leaving until I have it." Janet's mom tells him that the money isn't here and Lucky keeps barking like a maniac. Janet yells again and there is more gravel crunching.

"You get! Me and your mom are talking!" yells Ross, and Janet screams at him and there is more gravel crunching crunching crunching underfoot.

And then I'm opening the front door to help Janet, but as soon as I see Ross, recognition flashes across his face.

Ross looks up at me and says, "What in the—? What are you doing here?"

He steps toward the door and Janet says she's calling the police.

And that's when I see Ross look next to me and I know that Birdie has followed me out of Janet's room.

Ross kind of laughs and I can tell that maybe he's not quite solid on his feet. "And what's that gay boy doing here? This place is a freak show!"

Janet rushes into the trailer and closes the door behind her, locking us in. Ross starts yelling at Kathy for the kinds of friends she and Janet have and what is happening to this town, and he continues to swear at her and tells her to stop crying.

Janet's also cursing because she can't find her phone to call the police and that's when a second truck drives up and everything goes real quiet. I back into Janet's room, pushing Birdie behind me and closing the door, worried about who's in that other truck, hoping they don't also want something that Janet's mom can't give. And I'm praying they don't know Birdie and me and I can't believe I was stupid enough to show Ross my face.

I hear the second door squeak open and Janet goes outside.

Ross says, "Well, of course it's you! Still haven't straightened out that gay boy, I see."

Then, in his booming mountain voice, I hear Patrick yell, "Birdie! Jack!"

I burst out of the room, holding Birdie's hand tight, and open the front door.

There's Patrick, his hat pulled low like normal, his flannel shirt tucked into his jeans. He looks exactly like he should.

"Seriously, *Patty*," says Ross. "What is wrong with you? You know Teddy can barely concentrate in school because of that freakish kid?"

"Stop, Ross," says Patrick. "Just stop talking."

"Who are *you* to tell me that?" He points at Patrick and scowls.

"Just go home. It's late and this is not the place. You need to sleep."

"Don't tell me what I need!" Ross slaps the side of his truck. "You're just making excuses for that little gay boy and you know it."

Suddenly, Patrick slams the door to his truck closed and takes a couple steps forward. It happens in a flash, almost in a single motion. It's the quickest I've ever seen Patrick move. "Don't call him that again. You don't address that boy by anything but *his name: Birdie*. He doesn't need your fixing or anyone's. Now get in your truck and leave." Patrick's voice is the lowest I've ever heard it. "*Or I will call the police.*"

Ross goes to say something, but then stops and cuts the air with his hand. "Screw all of you!" he yells as he stomps across the yard. He gets into his truck and peels out, leaving more dust in his wake.

After his taillights have disappeared, Patrick looks over at us and says, "Birdie! Jack! Come here."

Holding hands, we run outside.

I try to get Janet to come with us back to Patrick's house, but she waves me off, saying she has to stay and help her mom. Even Patrick tries to get her to come, but she just shakes her head.

As we get into Patrick's truck, I watch Janet walk toward

the trailer with her mom—side by side, conjoined twins disappearing in the dark.

Patrick doesn't say anything until we walk into the house. Birdie and me start up the stairs and Patrick says, "Let's meet in the kitchen."

We wait at the table while Patrick makes a fire in the wood-burning stove. Duke sits by Birdie's feet.

Patrick comes in and he's silent as he boils water and gets the bread down from the shelf. He makes three mugs of hot chocolate and tops some sliced bread with his homemade cheese and honey. He sets everything in front of us at the table.

He sits down and says, "Well, don't let it get cold."

I think that Patrick is going to tell us that it's not safe at Janet's. That now we aren't allowed there, either.

Or maybe he's going to lecture us about not coming straight home after school.

"I want to make this absolutely clear," says Patrick in his serious mountain voice. "You guys are not problems to be fixed or issues to be solved. You're not slack. You're a couple of kids who have had a hard time, but you belong here. In this house. I'm sorry if I wasn't clear about that before."

He looks at the bread and rubs his neck. Then he takes a piece and eats.

I also take one

So does Birdie.

"Ross is not a good person to be around. Don't listen to anything he says, because it's usually nonsense. This is not the first time he's stumbled around and caused himself and others trouble and it probably won't be the last. But he doesn't know what he's talking about, so don't pay it any mind." He finishes his hot chocolate and looks at Birdie. "Okay, Birdie?"

"Okay," Birdie says back in a small voice.

Patrick nods. "Don't stay up too late." He picks up his mug and a slice of bread. "Good night."

Him and Duke walk out the front door.

Birdie and me watch him go and then take our hot chocolate and bread into the living room.

I wonder what could be in that shed that would make Patrick want to be out there in the cold instead of in here with the fire.

I think about Rosie and her truck.

I think about Janet and her mom and their tiny trailer heater.

I think about Mama and how she'd say that when toast and poetry and notebook writing don't help, warm mugs and a fire could at least give you a chance to close your eyes and breathe.

**Observation #788: Patrick's Truck

A red & tan Chevrolet pickup truck.
By the doors in shiny letters it says SILVERADO 20.
The motor rumbles like it's bringing a far-off thunderstorm.

But it must have some sort of magic too.
Because how did it know to show up at Janet's trailer?

CHAPTER 16

An Enigma

Before the sun is fully up, I find Patrick standing in the living room without his shoes on, looking out the large front window, which isn't curtained for once and the dawn light comes through. The house is completely silent, like it hasn't realized that anyone is awake yet.

From the top of the stairs I can see the steam from his coffee rising into his face as he takes slow sips. Without his hat, the scalp on the very top of his head shows through his thinning hair and all of a sudden I feel like it's probably wrong to spy on him—even though it wasn't like I'd planned to spy. I want him to put his hat back on, but I don't see it anywhere.

I should go to my room, but I'm afraid if I move the floor will creak and he will notice me. So I hold real still and wait until he goes back to the kitchen.

When he comes out, he has his work boots and hat on. He leaves through the front door. When I hear his engine start, I creep downstairs and watch his truck pull out of the driveway and disappear down the road. I guess Birdie and me are walking to school today.

Mama used to say that imagining yourself in someone else's shoes can help with feeling the tidal wave of joy.

So I try to imagine being Patrick, having his shoebox life to himself and then suddenly sharing his life with two kids he doesn't know or understand and didn't ask for.

Through my own socks I feel the heat in the carpet where Patrick was standing. I bring my hand up like I'm drinking an imaginary cup of coffee, like I actually like living in a shoebox, but maybe I might like to open the curtains now too.

What I feel next still isn't a tidal wave of joy, but it's something. Something smaller, but also maybe deeper.

For the first time I wonder what it's meant to Patrick to lose his sister.

I'm surprised when Patrick backs into the driveway an hour later. Birdie and me are about to walk to school, but Patrick says he'll drive us. "Get in the truck," he says as he runs up the stairs. "I've got breakfast. I'll be just a minute."

Inside Patrick's truck the heater is going and there is a box of donuts and two coffee cups sitting on the dashboard.

They're filled with hot chocolate. A travel mug with coffee sits in the cup holder.

"I don't think I've ever met an adult who likes hot chocolate as much as Patrick," says Birdie.

"I don't think he normally drinks it. He just thinks that we like it," I say.

"And he's actually right for once." He holds the steaming cup in his hands. "Hot chocolate at night. Hot chocolate in the morning. He's onto something."

Patrick gets in with Duke and pulls out of the driveway and says, "Take your pick of donuts. I wasn't sure what you guys like, so I got a mix. I'll take the extras to the guys at the job I'm going to."

I pick a maple bar and Birdie grabs the chocolate twist. Patrick takes a chocolate old-fashioned and he tilts his hat back a little before taking a bite.

We are all quiet but this time it's only because of the donuts. I'm halfway through my maple bar when I say, "Can I please go see Janet after school? I need to check on her."

Patrick doesn't answer right away and I'm sort of regretting asking him. But for some reason, this time, it felt like the right thing to do.

"After last night," he says, "you should understand why it isn't okay for you guys to be wandering around. Why I think it's important to blend in."

"I won't wander around and I won't stay long," I say,

pressing ahead as the roller-coaster feeling returns. "But she's my best friend and I need to make sure she's okay. And she won't tell me the truth over the phone. I know it—"

"You can go to Janet's," Patrick interrupts in a firm voice. "But *no side trips*. Absolutely no going to Carl's. You go straight there and don't stay after dark. And you go right home if you get there and see Ross."

"I will," I say, but I'm still holding my breath, thinking he might take it back.

But Patrick just nods to himself and then finishes his last bite.

In English class, we split into partners to work on our poet project. The second we get seated, Krysten looks me straight in the eye and is like, "Jack. The Quesadilla Ship. I wanted to tell you yesterday. I am *so* sorry."

Her eyes are wide and sincere.

"Yeah," I say, looking down at my notebook as my breath catches, imagining the flames and heat again, the smell of burning plastic. It's been three days since the fire and I've called Rosie seven times, but it always goes straight to voicemail. I've called Uncle Carl three times, but it just rings and rings. I wonder if he'll ever plug the phone in without me or Rosie or Birdie there to encourage him. He's never left it unplugged for so long.

"I called you last night," Krysten whispers.

"Oh, I was . . . at a friend's house." She nods and I continue, "And I'm pretty sure my uncle just lets every number he doesn't know go straight to the message machine. Sorry."

"It's okay. I just wanted to make sure you were all right."

"I'm okay."

Other than everything being worse than it ever was.

"At least her truck isn't lost, right? The future is bright for quesadilla-pizza babies! That was really great of your uncle to help Rosie, by the way."

"What do you mean?"

"My mom is friends with Rosie and Rosie told her about it before leaving for England. Your uncle—Patrick?—he helped Rosie salvage the truck. He convinced her he could fix it because I guess her insurance company said it was permanently ruined or something."

"Rosie is in England?"

"Yeah. My mom said she left yesterday. Didn't you know any of this?"

Rosie is gone.

"No, I didn't know," I say. "My uncle Patrick—he doesn't tell us a whole lot."

"Yeah, my mom calls him Mr. Enigma."

"Mr. Enigma?"

"You know, enigma, like a puzzle or a mystery."

I nod, but I can't stop thinking about Rosie's truck.

The Quesadilla Ship might be saved.

And Patrick's helping her save it.

**Observation #789: Enigma in Pants

Maybe Patrick isn't a clam in pants. Maybe he's

- a puzzle
- a conundrum
- an enigma.

B/c how can Patrick defend Birdie in front of Ross,
but still make Birdie wear those Norman clothes?

How can Patrick make us hot chocolate & buy us donuts
& still keep us from seeing the only other family we have?

& how can Patrick say that we aren't slack to be picked up or
problems to be fixed,
when he still disappears into the silo shed?

CHAPTER 17

One Island Next to Another

I have to knock five separate times before Janet finally yells at me to stop the racket.

I'm surprised that after last night the front door is still unlocked like it usually is. I find Janet in bed, her head covered with a blanket, and I realize that maybe she hasn't left this spot in hours, maybe even all day.

She points toward the corner of her room.

"Birdie left that evil number puzzle thing," she says through the blanket. "Where is he, anyway?"

"Patrick's. He said the new clothes were itchy today. Are you going to Snip 'n' Shine? Did you go this morning?"

"Didn't go. And not going."

"Come on, Janet."

"What? All I do there is sweep hair. And fold the towels when Captain Cherylene is feeling particularly generous."

"So now you're just going to go to school and forget Snip 'n' Shine?"

"No, I'm giving that up too. Now let me sleep."

"Have you eaten anything?"

She grunts and I leave her and go into the kitchen. The counters are still a mess, filled with open food containers, the empty pizza box, a fast-food bag, and lots of mugs and half-filled cups and soda cans. I throw everything away and fill the sink with dishes, hot water, and soap. I find an overripe banana and some bread and peanut butter in the fridge. I make us sandwiches and pour Janet a big glass of water. She's still in the same position when I return to her room.

"I made you a sandwich," I say.

"What are you, my mom, now?" she says through the blanket.

I think she's joking, so I laugh. "Yeah, right. Like your mom ever made a sandwich for you."

She uncovers her head and looks me in the eye. "She did. She used to make me cheese and mayonnaise sandwiches when I was a kid." She takes the sandwich from the plate and it's gone in a minute and then she drinks most of the water.

"Hand me the brush," she says, sighing, and I roll my eyes and hand it to her. She divides my hair into two sections down the middle of my head and starts brushing.

I stare at her empty plate. I've never had a cheese and mayonnaise sandwich before.

"My mama would sometimes disappear too," I say. I feel

the brush stop for just a moment. "Sometimes she disappeared into her room. Other times, when she had some grand idea in her head, she'd be gone out of the house."

Janet ties sections of my hair back and starts to braid.

"But she made the best roasted tomato sandwiches and made up the best games."

She finishes one braid and then picks up another portion of hair.

"What happened to her?" Janet asks in a quiet voice.

"There was a car accident," I say. "Black ice on the road. She passed away."

The brush stops. Janet lays it in her lap.

Neither of us says anything and I'm grateful she isn't asking a bunch of questions.

"So my aunt Veronica and her husband live in this giant house that they built on a golf course," Janet says. I can tell she's trying to sound normal, but her voice is sad too. "They have two snot-faced kids and a new baby that poops literally every hour. My mom was uncomfortable the entire time and when she told them how I was working at a salon and how some customers were wanting to try me for their hair, they didn't get it. All my aunt said to my mom was, 'What about college? You're not going to just let her cut hair for a living, are you? Don't you want something better for her?' She had her stupid plastic surgery nose curled up in the air like cutting hair was a job that smelled bad." Janet stands up and walks around. "So we left. On the drive home my mom said

we'd never go back there and I was glad. Rich stuck-up jerks."
I try not to look at her, but from the corner of my eye, I see
her wipe her nose with her sleeve.

My heart beats a few times, pounding hard because I've
never heard Janet sound truly hurt.

"But you know what's horrible?" she says between sniff-
ing. "All I could think was that at least my aunt had gone and
married some rich dude. At least her kids have a real house
and parents who are there and I didn't see any bruises. *A mom
and a dad and a big house.* At least she's done that for her kids."
She looks over at me and her mascara is running all the way
down her face to the end of her chin. "They have every perfect thing and they are still horrible. I just don't get it."

She wipes her face with her sleeve. "I'm sorry," she says.
"I'm sorry for blabbing on like an idiot when your mom has
passed away."

"You aren't blabbing on like an idiot."

She kind of scoffs, but I can tell she's trying to keep herself from crying again.

"No one ever knows what to say," I whisper.

A great surge of sorrow presses on the inside of my head.
But it's okay to feel sadness when you are one island next to
another. We are an archipelago.

"It's like everyone in my family disappears," I say. "Uncle
Carl has disappeared into his apartment. Rosie disappeared
to England. And after everything that's happened, Patrick still
disappears into that stupid silo shed."

"Patrick still won't let you see Carl?"

"No. And I know if I could just go to Uncle Carl's apartment, I could get him to plug his phone back in. I could help him get better."

Janet picks up the brush again.

"You know, I've never seen Patrick like he was last night. He really stood up to Ross. Can you tell him I said thank you?"

"I will."

"And I can try to go to Carl's. He probably won't answer the door for me, but I can at least remind him that you and Birdie need him."

That's when I realize that Janet's right. It's not just that he needs us. We need him.

If that's true of Uncle Carl, is it true of Patrick?

**Observation #790: Grief

Disappearing into apartments.

Disappearing to another country.

Disappearing into silo sheds.

Disappearing with bad boyfriends.

Disappearing under your blankets.

Disappearing inside clothes that itch.

Disappearing into a notebook.

What else does grief look like?

CHAPTER 18

A SMALL WOODEN THING

It's been almost a week since the Quesadilla Ship fire and still no Uncle Carl. And now it's Saturday. Balloon day. Today should have been the day Uncle Carl proposed up in a hot-air balloon and Rosie said yes.

But instead, there will be two empty spots in the balloon basket. A total waste.

I look through three books of Elizabeth Bishop poetry searching for something to recite for the project. Krysten said we should definitely open with a poem and I feel like she's the kind of person who knows what she's talking about when it comes to an effective presentation.

But I've been looking for two hours and there isn't one poem that I really care about. It's hard to care about any of it.

The house phone rings and Patrick answers it and then calls my name.

"Janet's on the phone," he says when I come downstairs. Then he goes back outside to the garden, which he's been slowly putting back together. He hasn't asked Birdie or me to help.

On the phone, Janet talks quickly. "Jacko, I only have a minute because I'm finishing up my break at Snip 'n' Shine, and Cherylene's glaring at me already, but I wanted to tell you that I went to Carl's and he's not doing great. He didn't answer the door, but I know he's in there because he called me a menace and said he'd call the authorities if I didn't stop pounding on his door."

"When was this?"

"Just a few minutes ago. I told him he was an idiot and not because of the fire. I said the fire was an accident and he's an idiot because he's left you and Birdie in Patrick's prison and how could he be so selfish. And then I said that hiding away wasn't going to solve anything and that him and Patrick need to get their problems sorted because this situation wasn't helping anyone, and that until someone discovered a way to a dimension where everything was made of Honey Bunny Buns, he needed to figure out how to live and be a real uncle."

"You said all that?"

"More or less. I tried to lay the guilt on pretty thick."

"Janet, you *are* a menace. An *awesome* menace."

"I know. I was in my element. But I really have to go now

because Cherylene's tapping her nails on the wall and that usually means I'm not moving fast enough and she's about to put me back on sweeping duty."

I tell her thanks and when we hang up, my whole body is on the roller coaster and I immediately go outside and tell Patrick that Birdie and me really need to see Uncle Carl.

But he just sighs and pulls his bandanna out of his pocket and wipes his face. "Jack. I don't know how many times I have to say it: You can't see him right now."

"But you can't keep us from him forever."

"Carl isn't in a state to be contacted."

"I know that, but we have to help him, don't we?"

He puffs his cheeks out. "No, we don't."

"But he's fifty percent of the family we have!"

Patrick takes his gloves off and picks up a mesh sack of tulip bulbs and starts walking to the side of the house. "I'm not discussing Carl right now."

I follow him as he takes huge strides to the front yard.

"You never want to discuss him!"

"Not now, Jack."

He goes to the silo shed and starts fiddling with the lock and I stand next to him. "But you can't keep avoiding him. He needs us. You can't keep buying Birdie and me hot chocolate and pizza and donuts and then just expect us to forget about Uncle Carl. He's our uncle. He's your brother. How can you just disappear on him?"

Patrick drops the shed lock. He turns around to face me. "Enough!" he says in a loud voice.

I stomp inside the house, up the stairs, and into Birdie's room. He's sitting in his window seat with the Alexander McQueen book and his *Book of Fabulous* and I go straight to the drawer where he keeps his mad cap.

"I need this!" I say, grabbing it without asking. Birdie just watches me as I pull it hard onto my head and then go into the other room. I pace around a few times and punch my pillow. Then I jump onto the bed and look out the window.

Patrick is in the silo shed. *Again.*

Twenty minutes later, when Birdie comes in the room with peanut butter and jelly rolled up in tortillas, I don't say anything but I move over so he can sit on my bed.

He knows I don't want the stupid leftover pizza from last night's dinner.

"Patrick's fixing the garden," Birdie says. "But he didn't fix the hole in the back fence, so that wild animal is just going to come back and destroy everything again."

I take a rolled tortilla.

There's the lightest line of purple nail polish on Birdie's pinkie fingernail.

"I *hate* that stupid silo shed," I say.

"Me too," says Birdie.

We finish eating the peanut butter and jelly and I'm about to open the last Honey Bunny Bun for us to share, when there's a screech, a smash of metal, and then yelling from the front yard. Through the blinds, I see Uncle Carl detangling himself from his crashed bicycle.

"These bushes!" Uncle Carl yells. He stumbles across the yard. "What you did ain't right, brother! I should have told you earlier, I should have told you decades ago, but I'm a coward." His words slur a little. "I'm a coward . . . but so are you! You come out here!"

"I'm right here!" yells Patrick, coming out of the silo shed. "What are you doing?"

Uncle Carl laughs like it's the dumbest question he's ever heard.

Birdie and me run downstairs. Then we go through the front door and stop on the front step.

Patrick's telling Uncle Carl to calm down.

Uncle Carl's eyes go all big and he says he'll show him *calm* and then climbs up on the hood of Patrick's truck, yelling at Patrick the whole time, calling him all sorts of mean things. I worry that he'll fall off the truck and am about to rush forward when Patrick yells, "Stop!"

That's when Uncle Carl starts laughing real hard. "Well, well, well," he says. "Look at the state of this place. Mama and Dad would be disappointed you've turned their home into some kind of recluse's spot, Patty. You ever heard of a new coat of paint? Or watering the grass?" He laughs again, slapping his thighs with his hands, but wobbles and puts his arms out to steady himself.

"You get down from there!" yells Patrick.

"Or what? You gonna come get me, big brother? Come on up, old man."

"I don't have time for this."

"You never do, do you?" Uncle Carl spins around once, nearly falling off the hood. "Jeez, you'd think that you were the president of the U-S-of-A with how much time you *don't* have."

Patrick yells again. "Get down from there, I said!" He moves closer to the truck as Uncle Carl tips to the left, then catches himself. When he sees his brother advancing, he crawls to the top of the cab, streaking mud from his shoes on the windshield.

"Come on up, Pattycake! Come get me."

He wobbles some more and I take a couple steps forward. Birdie hangs back. I'm starting to feel this pressure inside my body. After disappearing for a week, this is how he shows up. It would have been better if he'd just stayed home forever.

Uncle Carl starts teasing Patrick and Patrick yells back. But they aren't actually saying anything and no one is listening to me as I shout, "Come on, Uncle Carl, get down!" but he doesn't stop talking and I know he's making it so that him and Patrick go another five years without talking.

"Stop!" I yell. "Why can't everyone just stop!"

But Uncle Carl starts talking. "You couldn't stand that I was finally gonna get my Rosie, huh? You always said she was too good for me. And me and the kids had an awesome plan and now everything is ruined and you couldn't be happier, am I right?"

"You know that's not true, Carl, now get down!"

But now Carl is really upset, saying it is true and everyone knows it, and now Marlboro's gone, and Rosie's gone, and Birdie and me are gone. But Patrick's shouting that he's going to call the police if he doesn't get down and I feel like each of my bones are about to explode, more than two hundred individual bombs ready to go off.

So I pick up a big rock and yell, "You guys ruin everything!" and throw it, as hard as I can, toward the silo shed.

It hits the center of the front window, which shatters instantly. Everything goes quiet. Both Patrick and Uncle Carl look at the shed with open mouths.

"Get down!" I yell again. "You're going to get hurt!"

But saying that turns out to be a bad idea, because then Uncle Carl turns toward me and stomps on the truck's roof, hollering, "What makes you think I'm not already hurt, huh? Any new hurt won't be nothing new. Nothing. New." He slams his foot down to the beat of the last two words. And that's when the wind gusts and he loses his balance and goes tumbling off the truck.

Next thing I know, Patrick has a frown on his face as we hover over Uncle Carl. Birdie joins us and asks if he's okay.

I lean down to get a good look at Uncle Carl's head. When he fell, he partially rolled down the windshield and then plopped to the gravel. His head looks to be in one piece and I think I even hear him snoring.

Suddenly, from the shed, there comes a long creak and then a great crashing sound, like something big just fell from up high.

The door to the shed is still open and something small and round rolls out and stops in front of Patrick's truck.

Everyone stares at it.

I go over and pick it up.

It's a small wooden egg. Just like the one Birdie and me and Mama got from the family with backyard chickens we helped move during a Wolf Day.

No one says anything as I walk to the shed door. As I feel around for the switch, I think of the part in the Bible, at least I think it's the Bible, when God says Let there be light!

And then I see.

It's everything from home.

Mama's old armchair that she usually just sat in front of. The Miss Luck Duck lamp. Our bright green bookcase that we found next to the dumpster behind an old office building. The mannequin that used to hold Mama's and Birdie's sewing projects. Boxes on top of boxes on top of boxes and so many trash bags. And I finally see the big rock I threw, which lies by an open cardboard box on the ground.

My hand around the wooden egg feels numb.

"Miss Luck Duck!" says Birdie, who's suddenly beside me.

"How long has she been in here? And the Tokyo Tower hat rack!" He points to the far wall. "And Mama's chair . . ." His eyes start to move quickly all around the shed; back and forth they dart until his face has morphed into a frown. "I don't understand. Why does Patrick have our stuff?"

I grab his hand and hold up the wooden egg.

"Follow me," I say.

We turn around and walk toward the gate.

"Where are you guys going?" Patrick asks.

"To the reserve!"

Patrick picks Uncle Carl up and Uncle Carl groans, his arm slung across his brother's shoulders.

"Wait a minute, Jack."

"What, now you want to talk?" I say over my shoulder. "Why don't you go inside your silo like you always do!"

He opens his mouth to say something, but doesn't. He hefts Uncle Carl up again and watches us go.

I walk quickly, holding Birdie's hand the entire way. When I don't turn down the road to the reserve, Birdie looks up at me, tugging on my sleeve.

"We're not going to the reserve," I say. "We're taking the bus."

CHAPTER 19

BRIGHT SPOTS IN THE DARK

An hour and a half later, Birdie and me are standing outside a chain-link fence. In the middle of the grass are two big balloons lying sideways. They're attached to baskets and people stand around and a couple of trucks are parked nearby.

Birdie drinks his hot chocolate. It was the last thing we could buy with our money while we waited for the bus. I also offer my last Honey Bunny Bun, which I'd shoved in my jacket pocket after Uncle Carl crashed into the bush.

The balloons get bigger and bigger as huge fans blow waves of air inside them. Two guys keep them from going anywhere as they inflate.

"Patrick's going to be so mad when he finds out we didn't go to the reserve," says Birdie.

"So what?"

"Don't you want to see what else is in the shed? There's like a mountain of bags and boxes in there. I think I even saw Mama's mannequin."

"Yeah," I say. "It was like slipping into another dimension or something."

"Maybe we did," says Birdie.

I take the wooden egg from my pocket and give it to Birdie. He squeezes it and then holds it up to his eyes. "It looks like the real thing. It looks like our wooden egg."

"Yeah. I don't think we're dimension hopping."

Once the balloons are inflated, flames shoot out of some kind of heater, I guess warming the air inside. Within seconds they float up and the baskets sit upright.

"Wow," says Birdie. "They're huge."

I half expect to see Uncle Carl as one of the people waiting to board. But of course he isn't there.

Birdie leans into the fence, putting his eye up to the metal, and I do the same to get a clear view of takeoff. And before I know it, the baskets are up in the air, higher than the trees.

"Why would Patrick keep that stuff in the silo shed and not tell us?"

Because he's selfish and cruel.

But I don't say that.

We watch the balloons for a while as they slowly float higher in the sky. They kind of remind me of the figs from our old tree and I tell Birdie.

"Yeah," he says. "Kind of like upside-down ones."

"You know what? I kind of hated that fig tree."

"Why?"

"Because it hardly ever grew that many figs and it seemed like every year Mama was disappointed and she'd get upset about it."

Birdie nods, still looking up.

I don't realize I'm crying until I start talking again. "I hated it when she got upset. Because then she'd disappear and it didn't matter how many times it happened, I always wondered if she'd come out of her room again."

"She always came out, though," says Birdie. "And you always made really good grilled cheese and ramen and bean burritos when she was hiding in her room."

"But I didn't want to do that, Birdie. I wanted *her* to do that. I always wanted her to not disappear."

"I know," he says. "Me too."

The red, green, and blue of the balloons are hardly visible now that the sun is beginning to set.

"Do you ever wonder," Birdie whispers, "if she'd still be alive if she never came out of her room after that Wolf Day? If she'd stayed inside and left on a different day, maybe a day there wasn't black ice on the road?"

"I don't know," I say.

"Or maybe if we'd never done a Wolf Day, then everything would have been fine, we'd still be home?"

I hope he isn't actually looking for an answer. Because I don't have any.

"Sometimes I hate Wolf Day," he says.

"Don't say that."

"But it's true. Sometimes I hate it."

"I know, Birdie. Me too."

We'd been all over the city on that last Wolf Day. We'd seen a movie and sneaked into a second. We'd been up in the theater projector room with a woman named Reed and then we drove to where they were setting up for a free movie-in-the-park showing that night. Then we were going to go with a caterer to shell a bunch of beans at this organic farm just outside the city and Mama got really excited since it'd always been one of her dreams to live on an organic farm.

But then the farm owner got weird about having kids come help or maybe it was all the questions Mama was asking and her twitchy enthusiasm that she always had a hard time containing. Either way, the farm owner talked to the caterer and the caterer apologized and said that it would be best if we left.

I could tell Mama was disappointed. More than disappointed, which made me nervous. It was already the late afternoon, so we decided to head home. But Mama said we shouldn't drive because it might get in the way of us encountering something new, which was important for Wolf Days. Something new might help make up for the farm disappointment.

I tried to convince her otherwise because I was pretty sure it was a long walk. Even the caterer tried to tell us not to walk. Birdie was tired because he was still getting over a cold. It might be five or ten miles before we could find a bus, the caterer said. But Mama shook her head. We left the car at the farm and started on foot.

But then Mama stopped and turned around. She said, you know what? All I need to do is talk to the farm owner and make it clear we only mean to help, not get in the way. Birdie sniffed and asked about waiting for the wolf. I said maybe we should just go home in the car, but that maybe we could do it by a different route and then the day could still end unexpectedly.

But I already knew there was no changing her mind.

So we went back, and the farm owner and the caterer were near the gate discussing Mama's car. There was some confusion because Mama just walked right past them and into the shed where the beans were being shelled and a bunch of other vegetables were being sorted.

The owner was starting to get mad and the caterer just stood there like she had no idea what she'd done by inviting us here.

At some point I was begging Mama for us to just leave. To

get in the car and go. But she just kept saying, "We say yes to everything! Even to stubborn beans covered in aphids! We say yes to everything on Wolf Day."

I could feel the caterer standing right behind us, stunned.

"Please, Mama, let's just go."

The caterer and the farm owner looked totally weirded out and had no idea what to do. And then Mama started digging around in a couple other bins, one filled with tomatoes and another filled with some kind of leafy vegetable. The farmer and caterer rushed forward.

"Please stop," said the caterer. She turned toward the farmer. "What are we supposed to do? Call the police?"

"Please don't," I said.

The caterer looked at me. "Honey, I don't think I can let you go home with her."

I looked at Mama again. "Please, Mama. Let's just go. If we don't they're going to call the police."

But she ignored us.

The caterer led Birdie and me around the corner to the front porch of a house.

"She's just really, really enthusiastic sometimes," I said.

The caterer nodded with sad eyes.

"Is there anyone you can call? Maybe your dad or a grandma?"

"She'll be fine if you just let her help with the beans. Can't she just help with the beans and then we can go?"

I wasn't crying yet, but I could feel a lump in my throat. I didn't want her to call the police.

A loud crash came from the direction of the shed and then we saw Mama storm off to her car. "Jack! Birdie! We're going! We've said yes enough!"

She got in the car and slammed her door shut and turned on the engine. She stepped on the gas so hard her tires spun on the dirt. "Jack and Birdie, let's go!" she shouted out the window.

"I can't let you drive with her," the caterer said, holding on to my arm. I don't know why, but that kind of freaked me out, like I realized that I had no clue who this woman was.

And that's when Mama again shouted, "Let's go!" and then backed the car out. She peeled out of the gate and disappeared down the street, without us.

The caterer said she'd drive us home, but I called Mrs. Spater, which I didn't want to do because I knew she hated driving and leaned too far forward and cursed at her car and other drivers, and she never said those words other times. Driving would bring it out of her. But she came and got us anyway.

By the time we were home, Mama was in her bedroom. Mrs. Spater looked in on her. When Mrs. Spater came out, she said for us to be quiet and let her sleep, as if we didn't already know that. It'd been a while since it had happened, maybe six months, but we knew what to do when Mama got sad. She once told me that when the world and loneliness became too much she needed to burrow down and that it's best to just leave her alone. I always imagined that she was going down into a rabbit's burrow, like Peter Rabbit, which we'd read together.

Later that night, Mrs. Spater tried to get us to come over to her side of the duplex, but by then, Birdie was sitting in the kitchen cupboard he'd sometimes hide in for fun, except this time he wouldn't come out, not even for Mrs. Spater's lemon pound cake.

So we didn't have lemon pound cake and we didn't wait for the wolf and for whatever reason, Mama didn't come out of her burrow for five days, the longest she'd ever stayed away.

Afterward, for a few days, she tried to make us breakfast and pack our lunches and do normal things, but she wasn't the same and I knew something was wrong when she left a wintry Saturday morning to visit an old boyfriend. It was like her mind was still in her room, in the rabbit burrow under her covers.

The police said there was slippery black ice on the road.

And that's why she never came back.

So in my mind the beginning of the end was that Wolf Day. I could draw a straight line between the two, a long sloping line running down to the end.

The sun is almost set, the sky orange and pink, streaked with clouds. We watch as the balloons hover, the people in the baskets probably enjoying the view, maybe even complimentary champagne.

I take the wooden egg from Birdie, thinking that maybe I'll throw it over the fence and get rid of it for good.

But it's proof that I didn't imagine all of Mama's things in the silo shed.

I shove my hands, along with the egg, deep into my pockets.

I feel the glow sticks right away. I kept meaning to take them out, but then I got used to them being there.

I give one to Birdie. He watches as I open the other one, then crack it and shake. It glows neon green. Birdie does the same and his glows orange.

We sit in the grass and share the Honey Bunny Bun, even though I'm sick of them. We wave the glow sticks as the baskets begin to return to the ground. Birdie throws his into the air and for a moment it looks like a crystal ball as it spins. I toss mine toward him and he catches it and throws his over to me and then we're flipping them back and forth, waving at the people as they slowly land, the wind beginning to pick up. A couple of the people wave back at us and we twirl our glow sticks at them, two bright spots in the dark.

We head back toward the bus stop along the highway and I notice Patrick's Chevy Silverado on the side of the road right away.

He leans against the truck and doesn't move.

Birdie says to me, "Are we in huge trouble?"

"Probably."

"Should we make a run for it?"

"Probably. No stopping until we reach Canada, okay?"

"Except there's no way I can run in these dumb baggy jeans. Stupid Norman clothes haven't solved any of our problems."

"Yeah, maybe you should tell Patrick about that."

"Maybe I will."

When we're about a hundred feet from Patrick's truck, Birdie shouts, "I'm not wearing these Norman clothes anymore! They've made everything worse! Besides, Norman's all better now, so he can shop for his own clothes! I quit!"

Patrick shouts back, "Do you want a ride home?"

"Do we have a choice?" I yell.

When we reach the truck, Patrick shrugs, but his face and voice are serious. "If you want to ride back on the bus in the cold, be my guest."

I don't answer him and Birdie follows me to the passenger side of the truck. We get in.

Duke sits in the back part of the cab and pokes his head forward by Birdie's face. Birdie leans his head against the old dog.

We drive for a few minutes and Patrick blasts the heater and no one says anything at first.

"I'm sorry I didn't tell you guys about the shed," Patrick

says. "I always meant to. But I didn't know what to say. I didn't know how to start that conversation."

"'I saved your mama's stuff' would have worked," I tell him. "'I have secretly hoarded all of your things' also would have done the job." I fold my arms.

"I know," says Patrick.

"I don't think anyone heard me earlier," Birdie interrupts, shouting toward the windshield. "I said I'm not wearing these clothes anymore. So I hope my dresser and everything else is in the shed."

Patrick re-grips the steering wheel. "I heard you, Birdie."

But is he listening? I wonder.

After a while, Patrick tries again, "Look, this is all new for me too. It's my job to keep you guys safe. I'm doing the best I can. But . . ." He stops and lets out a sigh. "But maybe I'm no better at this than my idiot brother."

"It's only because Uncle Carl actually likes us and you don't," I say. "We're pretty sure you even like Duke more than you like us."

He glances over at me and for once he looks totally shocked. "What are you talking about?"

"We know you don't like being around us. And you bring Duke everywhere. You're around him all the time. You're only with us for like two hours in the backyard. That's it."

"That's not true," Patrick says.

"Yes, it is." He doesn't understand. So there's no point in saying anything else.

When we get back to Patrick's house, he parks the truck but leaves the engine and heater running. All three of us look over at the silo shed. I want to know what is in there. I want to open every box, bag, and drawer.

But it's like there are ghosts in the shed. They are friendly ghosts, for the most part, and I do want to meet them. But they are still ghosts and how are we supposed to fit ghosts into this new life?

"Look, it's probably hard for you to understand. But I've been dealing with my own feelings regarding your mama. We had an argument a very long time ago. She needed my help and instead of supporting her, I pushed her away. She left, never returned, and it was my fault."

I want to know what the argument was about, but something tells me that's not the important question right now.

"So what are your feelings toward us?" Birdie suddenly asks.

Patrick pushes his hat up and sighs.

"At first they were tied up with your mama. I was mad at her. And I was mad at myself because you two reminded me that I'd made a big mistake." He rubs his jaw. "But I guess now, I just want to get to know you guys."

A light comes on in the house.

"Okay. Well, I'm Jack, and this is Birdie," I say.

Duke nudges the back of Patrick's neck. "And I'm Patrick, Beth's brother. Your uncle."

**Observation #798: Silo Shed

Birdie was sort of right about the silo shed: It's a grain bin, not a silo (according to Patrick)

- 18-foot diameter
- 3 windows (1 still broken)
- 1 large door with a padlock
- Made of corrugated metal

The silo shed looks like a spaceship, especially when it's lit up at night, its cone roof seeming to hover in the trees & bushes. In a way, it's like something from outer space, from some other place.

Wherever Mama is.

CHAPTER 20

WHAT HOPE LOOKS LIKE

In the morning, me, Patrick, and Birdie go out to the shed and begin bringing everything inside the house. Uncle Carl is still asleep upstairs in an extra room that's always been locked.

No one talks as we go back and forth between the house and the silo shed, and part of me wishes that Patrick would leave us alone to do this. Because as I carry the boxes and bags, I see a piece of fabric sticking out, or the handle of a mug, or the cover of a book, and I know exactly what it is, and all I want to do is feel the weight of it in my hands and know it's real.

But rain is supposed to come soon and Patrick said we should get everything inside if we want to look through it.

We work for an hour and then take a break before deciding

what to do with the shelves, chairs, three dressers, and two small tables.

Patrick goes into the kitchen and Birdie and me sit in the middle of the bags and boxes looking around. Birdie notices a box of old magazine clippings and rushes over to it. I try to decide what to open first.

For just a moment, I feel like I'm drowning, which seems so stupid because all I've been wishing for is to have a piece of home and now I have it. I have it times a thousand.

Patrick comes back into the living room with two cups of coffee and looks around at all the stuff with a tired face. He says, "I'll leave you guys to it," and then goes upstairs.

Last night he had asked us if we wanted to look through the silo shed right then, but it was dark and cold and windy, and we were tired. And I couldn't help thinking of ghosts even though I don't believe in them, but mostly I didn't want to go through everything with Patrick standing over us.

Birdie kneels down beside me, holding a Ziploc bag and a picture of him and Mama and me from when he was a toddler. The bag has a bunch of magnets, along with more pictures and old flyers, and a sketch of a *Breakfast at Tiffany's* Audrey Hepburn that Birdie did when he was seven. There's also an A+ book report I wrote in fifth grade on a book called *The One and Only Ivan*. My teacher had written: *You have a very special eye! Keep looking, keep watching, keep listening. It's a gift.* Mama teared up when she read that and I didn't understand it at the time, but I think it was because she was proud.

"This is the stuff from our fridge," says Birdie. "I can't believe Patrick kept all of it."

I put everything back inside the bag to sort through later, but keep the picture of us three out on the coffee table.

After picking through three boxes, I find a bunch of my books and there, at the bottom, sits *The Complete Poems 1927–1979* by Elizabeth Bishop. The light orange cover is battered, and inside, in pencil, it says $4.75, which is what Mama must have paid at some used bookstore.

Below that, she wrote on a sticky note: *To Jack, Find your favorite! Love, Mama.*

Birdie and me comb through the stuff for another hour and a half and then Uncle Carl and Patrick come downstairs.

"Holy smokes, Patty, you weren't kidding," Uncle Carl says.

Patrick brings Uncle Carl a fresh mug of coffee and a cup of water and then says he'll get started on breakfast. Uncle Carl asks if he needs help, but Patrick just waves his hand and says to hang out with us.

Uncle Carl's eyes roam all around, still in shock, until they stop on the couch.

"Miss Luck Duck!" he shouts.

"You know Miss Luck Duck?" Birdie asks.

Uncle Carl walks over to our favorite lamp and picks her up. "Of course. Dad—your grandpa—gave it to our mama as a Valentine's Day gift. Oh, must have been fifty years ago now."

"That is fifty years old?" I ask.

"At least. She used to sit in this window right here, on a little table." He points to a small window by the front door.

And it turns out that isn't the only thing of Mama's that used to belong in this house. The painting of the fat cat in a tuxedo and the banana clock and even Mama's favorite vintage Nestlé mug all came from here. But there were also lots of things that Uncle Carl didn't recognize, like our cheeseburger pillows and Tokyo Tower hat rack, and we told him how good Mama was at sewing and hunting for treasures at thrift shops and garage sales. I said that she always tried to be smart with her money, and only buy the most special and unique things, but that it was sometimes hard for her to hold back when she was really excited about something.

"But she always made everything seem magical, even some stained old jacket from the secondhand store." I hold up a black jacket of Mama's that has a giant embroidered tiger head on the back.

"I should have done more to help her, especially since she had the two of you to look after," says Uncle Carl. He picks up a basket of pinecones, which we'd collected from our old backyard two winters ago. "Patrick used to send her money for you guys. I knew he did that and I never offered to contribute." He sets the basket down and takes a couple long drinks of water. He sniffs and says, "I'm sorry, guys."

"It's okay, Uncle Carl. At least you visited us on your motorcycle," I say. "And then you let us live with you."

"Yeah, and all those Honey Bunny Buns," says Birdie.

Uncle Carl tries to smile and shrugs. Then he goes into the bathroom.

For breakfast, Patrick makes eggs and cheese, bacon and sausage, apple slices, and grilled buttered bread. There is hot chocolate for us and more coffee for him and Uncle Carl.

We don't talk a lot, but as Patrick sets up Mama's old record player, he tells Uncle Carl that he really needs to plug his phone in or charge his cell because Rosie has been trying to get ahold of him.

"Other than these kids," Patrick says, "that woman is the absolute best thing to ever have happened to you. You're a plain idiot if you let her go."

Uncle Carl pushes his eggs around and mumbles that he doesn't think he deserves Rosie. Patrick just shakes his head and says, "So you really *are* an idiot." And then he clicks the speaker on.

We all go quiet as we listen to the crackling piano music playing from one of Mama's thrift-store jazz records.

Later that day, Patrick drops Birdie and me at the library before bringing Uncle Carl home so he can shower and change and plug his phone in. Birdie has the damaged Alexander McQueen book in his backpack.

As we walk to the entrance, Birdie stops and asks, "Am I the only one like me?"

"I don't know," I answer truthfully. "Janet doesn't think so. Don't you trust her?"

"With my hair, sure." He smiles a little, but then furrows his brow. "I think Patrick still doesn't get it."

"Listen. You get to decide who you are. Not me. Not anyone else. And you let me know if someone ever calls you names, okay? I will be here no matter what. And I think Patrick will be too. You are so brave, Birdie." Then I give him a hug and he's kind of stiff like a mummy, but I hold on tight until he hugs back. "And if you want to know if there is anyone else like you, then I'll help you find out. And in turn, you can help me."

He pulls back a little. "Help you with what?"

"Everything. Doing my clothes and hair right. Being unique and amazing, which you're so good at. I mean, I'm not looking to start wearing dresses or anything, but I think I'm going to need your help once I hit high school. Maybe by then I'll be ready for something new."

"I hope so," he says, looking me up and down and then cracking up. "I'll whip you into shape."

I wrap my arm around his neck and rub my knuckles into his head. He squeals and twists away and then we walk into the library.

Ms. Perkins spots us right away and when we show her

the book, she is not happy. She's got her hands on her wide lady hips.

"This was an expensive book," she says. "Full-color photographs, et cetera."

Birdie and me don't say a thing.

"There is a replacement fee and a nonrefundable five-dollar processing fee. The replacement fee is the price of the book. Let me look it up." She starts typing on the computer and then she says, "Haven't seen you two at the library for a while."

Birdie glances over at me, I guess maybe wondering what to say.

I clear my throat. "We were dealing with some . . . family stuff."

She looks at us with an eyebrow raised and then goes back to the computer screen. "Well, looks like you're in luck. The fees were paid a couple days ago."

Birdie and me look at each other and then back at Ms. Perkins. "Don't look at me," she says. "I'm just reading what I see on the screen."

"Who paid the fees?"

She makes a couple of clicks and says, "Patrick Royland."

Birdie and me look at each other. "Our uncle?"

She nods. "Looks like it." Then she closes the book and slides it back across the counter.

Patrick paid the fees?

"But what will happen to the book? Will you fix it?" asks Birdie.

"Birdie, this book has been *irreparably damaged*. Have you looked at it with seeing eyes? I can't have a book with wrinkled, torn, and stained pages on a library shelf. Not here."

"So you're just going to throw it *away*?" Birdie's voice is a click higher than normal.

"Don't get in a panic inside this library. What you do with the book is your business." She moves from around the counter to straighten a few books on her display. "The fees have been paid. The book is yours now."

Birdie stands there frozen and I take the book from the counter.

Then he runs up and gives her a big hug. She doesn't exactly hug him back, but pats him on the shoulder and says, "This library and its books are for all kinds of people who respect knowledge. I think there is knowledge in that book for you. And others too. You take good care of it."

Birdie carries the book in his arms the whole walk home and despite the overcast sky that looks like it's going to rain, his face is bright bright bright like the sun.

That afternoon, we continue sorting through boxes and bags while eating lunch, and Patrick comes in through the front door. In his arms is a bag of organic fertilizer and three old pillowcases. "I'll be out back planting for a while before the rain." He shuffles the bags in his hands, trying to get a better grip. "So, if you want to help, you can. I'll also be doing the roses next weekend."

By now I know that there are flower bulbs in those old pillowcases. He dug them out of our garden back home, along with a few clippings of Mama's rosebushes, and brought them here. Mama's tulip, daffodil, and hyacinth bulbs, to be exact.

But I wonder if Patrick would rather work alone.

Planting Mama's bulbs in the new garden seems like one of those important but maybe private things to do. A grieving kind of thing.

He looks around at the piles of books and boxes of dishes and bags of clothing and everything else crowding the living room. "Maybe Carl is right," he says gruffly. "Maybe the house needs a little life again."

Patrick heads to the backyard, and a moment later, Birdie suddenly stands up. He holds Mama's gold-and-blue sequined purse above his head. "Yes! Found it!"

"Have you been looking for that the entire time?"

"I've been looking for everything," says Birdie. "But this one makes me really happy." He hugs the purse and I wonder if Patrick is really ready for all this stuff to be here.

But then I realize maybe Patrick wasn't talking about all the things bringing life into the house. Maybe he was talking about the people.

...

That night, I pace around my room, trying to memorize Elizabeth Bishop's poem "The Fish." Krysten called me earlier and said that this coming week we should decide which poem to recite so that way we have enough time to practice it. I'd like to surprise her by reciting some of this one at school tomorrow. I know she likes over-the-top gestures like that.

I've got about a third of it down when there's a knock on my door and Patrick peeks his head into my room.

"I have a couple things for you," he says after I open the door wide. "The first is this." He places a little black book on my bed that says *Diary* on the front in faded gold script letters. "This was your mama's. She was your age when she kept it, I think, based on the first date. I found it in one of the drawers and thought you should have it."

I look at it, but don't move.

"I haven't read it, and you don't have to either if you don't want to, but I think you should decide what happens to it. Especially since you're so much like her with the writing and all."

"Mama used to call me a little spy," I say.

"Well, I don't know if that's what you are, but I've seen you with your notebook. And it always reminds me of your mama." He takes a breath and continues. "Anyway, I thought you might also like to have this."

It's a photo album. It has a worn, dark green leather cover. Outside, it starts to rain.

"You know, your mama was so happy when you finally came along. I guess you know that things weren't stable with your and Birdie's dad, but that didn't affect how she felt about you. She tried her best. I know that sometimes it wasn't good enough. But she was alone and I'm sorry for that." He taps once on the outside of the album. "She was something, that girl. A firecracker, Mama used to call her." He smiles a little and opens the album up and we look at a few pictures. There are lots with Uncle Carl and Patrick with long hair, like the pictures in Uncle Carl's junk drawer. There's even one of Patrick holding Mama when she was a baby. Patrick must have been at least my age.

"This hasn't been easy," he says, "with your mama gone. I don't know what to feel or think."

The *ping ping ping* of the rain on the silo shed reminds me of Portland with Mama.

"Your mama and me, we were just too different to get along. Had too many fights. And our oldest brother, George, just spoiled her rotten and gave Carl and me a hard time. Then George died and I hated how your mama talked about the war when it was something he'd just died for. But I said a lot of things I regret." He lets out a breath. "Anyway. What's done is done. But you and Birdie, you're lucky to have what you have. It's how siblings should be."

I turn to the last page and there's a picture of Mama holding a baby.

"You don't remember me, but I was there when that picture was taken of you and your mama. I should have been more supportive."

Patrick already seems to be on the verge of tears or maybe just running away, so I resist the urge to say anything about the money Uncle Carl mentioned. I finally let out my own breath I realize I've been holding.

Patrick knew Mama for a lot longer than I did. It's strange to think that he has his own memories.

In the picture, Mama's face is tired but happy, her cheeks all red like she just ran a marathon.

"Sometimes I'm so mad at her," I whisper. "Everything she did was perfect and amazing and magical. Almost always, it was that way. But then sometimes . . . it wasn't. Sometimes she was sad."

"Jack, you're allowed to be mad at her. It doesn't mean you don't love her. And it doesn't mean she wasn't a good mother."

"But why couldn't she just do what she was supposed to do? Do the things that made her better?"

"There's no answer to that, Jack. Only your mama knows that."

In the next room, Birdie laughs and commands Duke to sits so he can measure his neck again. Then he goes quiet as the rain pounds down and for a few moments, we all listen.

"I'm trying to be okay without any answers," Patrick says. "That's what you guys have taught me. That life continues to go on. And I need to be here and not let it pass by. I hope we can help each other be okay. All of us."

I nod and then look back down at the photo. Even though she's tired, Mama looks perfect to me.

I say, "All three of us. Plus Uncle Carl and Rosie."

"Yeah. Them too."

He taps the album twice and then heads toward the door. But just before leaving he says, "Jack. You're not a spy. You're a protector. So you keep watching. It's what we need. And I'll keep watching too."

**Observation #799: Someones

Everyone in the world has lost someone.
Sometimes that someone is a mother.
Sometimes they are a sister.
Sometimes they are a grandfather.
I guess sometimes they are a bearded dragon.
Sometimes they are a teacher, a next-door neighbor, a friend.
The world is full of someones to lose.

But the world is also full of someones to win.
Someone who talks and also listens.
Someone on your level.
Someone in your corner.
Someone to connect with.
Someone quietly looking out for you.
Maybe even loudly too.

EPILOGUE

Journal Entry No. 1, December 13

Dear Journal,

You know that feeling at the beginning of the school year, when you're nervous, but also excited?

That's the feeling I had when we arrived at the lake.

I thought I'd be sad because Mama had now been gone a year. But I knew that this day wasn't just about me or Birdie. It wasn't a Wolf Day. It was something more.

Birdie was there and so were Patrick and Duke, both wearing bow ties custom made by Birdie, and Uncle Carl and Rosie were holding hands. And when we walked over to the dock, Krysten's mom pulled up with Krysten and Janet. They kind of hung back a little and didn't say anything the whole time, but I liked knowing they were there.

We didn't have a plan. Instead, we stood on the edge of

the dock and listened to the water move with the wind. Birdie wore his ice cream backpack (which Patrick fixed and gave back to him, right after talking to Mrs. Cross-Hams.) He also wore his favorite purple jacket, his milk-and-cookies charm necklace, his cupcake ring, and a new pair of jeans with rhinestones along the pockets.

Uncle Carl was the first to say something. He held out a cup of coffee from the Stop-and-Go. "This one's for you, Sis. Special from Juan." Then he poured the whole cup into the lake.

Uncle Carl told me that him and Juan fought together in the war and that Juan had stayed behind to protect Uncle Carl, and then got injured. So Uncle Carl carried Juan three miles through the jungle to camp and that because of that, Juan said when they got back home, he'd take over his parents' store like they wanted, and Uncle Carl could have free coffee for the rest of his life. Uncle Carl said that Juan was the only person on earth who truly knew the real him—pre-war, at war, and after. Uncle Carl keeps a bunch of pictures on his fridge now, including one of him and Juan in Vietnam, with big goofy smiles on their sweaty faces. Uncle Carl put the junk-drawer picture of Mama into a frame he got from Rosie. He keeps it on the coffee table where Marlboro used to be.

At the lake, Birdie spoke next. "It's hard without you, Mama."

To be honest, I didn't hear everything Birdie said because so many memories flooded in and it was hard to concentrate with so much sadness at once. Birdie's purple nail polish flashed as he sprinkled a pinch of gold glitter into the wind. Then, on the end of the dock, he placed a collage he'd made, using a painted rock to keep it from blowing away. He ended by saying that she shouldn't worry because Rosie was continuing his sewing machine lessons.

Patrick cleared his throat right after that and said, "Beth, as you can see, you have a couple of good kids." He took his hat off and rubbed his neck and kind of laughed. "I'll do the best I can, even if I'm not as fun—or sparkly—as you. But send me some help, okay? I'll need it. I'm sorry it's taken me so long to say that." He paused. "Jack and Birdie will be okay with me. They'll be fine. Actually, I think we'll be more than fine."

I waited before saying anything to make sure Patrick was done. Then I said: "Mama, you are a dragon! And so is your brother Patrick! That's something I've learned here. I miss you and your games, and so many things from our life, but I am also ready for this new one." I took the Skittles bag out of my pocket and let the pinch of ashes go without a second thought. "Like Patrick said, we'll be more than fine. There will probably be some really hard days, but Birdie and me have so many people around us here. There are lots of people looking out, not just me. And guess what? We're even going to plant a fig tree in the front yard. So we'll have the figs you always loved. And I guess Grandma loved them too, Patrick said. Yeah, we'll be okay."

The best part of the day was that Mama *was* still there. She sent us a Wolf Day to let us know. It happened when we were at the Sweet Potato Shop after the lake and two couples drove up in a shiny black car. They were talking loudly and one of them was on their cell phone. They were lost, trying to make their way to the balloons. Uncle Carl and Patrick took turns trying to tell them how to get there. And then it turned out that there were two other couples who were supposed to go up in the hot-air balloon with them. But they got food poisoning from some bad stir fry at the mall, which meant they had four extra tickets and did we want them?

There were a lot of questions and then Patrick said, fine, let the kids go! But the balloon people said there had to be a guardian.

Birdie and me begged and begged Patrick. He said Uncle Carl and Rosie should take us, but Rosie shook her head and said she'd have her own balloon ride someday soon.

And so, after a lot of sighing and rubbing his neck, Patrick said, "Oh, all right. You knuckleheads win."

And Birdie danced around chanting, "Knuckleheads win! Knuckleheads win!"

The view from the balloon was unlike anything I've ever seen. And when I looked around at Uncle Carl, Patrick, and

Birdie, I saw that we were all experiencing our own feelings as we stood together in the basket.

Writing this now, I realize maybe that's what Wolf Day is really about—not some spontaneous adventure, but something else entirely.

Turning islands to archipelagos.

– Jack

ACKNOWLEDGMENTS

Writing a book is like climbing a mountain. It's hard work, yet enjoyable, and you come out the other side exhausted, but feeling accomplished and maybe a hair wiser too. Writing this book was a lot like hiking to the top of Half Dome in Yosemite National Park in California. On the way, I kept thinking I was nearing the peak and every time I arrived at a crest, there was another peak to climb.

As this is my first book, there are a lot of people to publicly thank.

The first has to be my editor, Kathy Dawson. Like all great editors she has a talented eye, a nose for details, an instinct for story. What you don't know is how great of a writing companion she is. How patient she is when I drift off the trail into the bush. She knows how to wait for me, how best to help direct my wanderings. Thanks just doesn't cut it so I'm not gonna try.

Along with her, I have to thank all the incredible people at Kathy Dawson Books/Penguin Young Readers—especially Rosie Ahmed and Regina Castillo—who have poured hours and hours of love and work into this book. I'm so thankful to be a part of this publishing family.

And before there was Penguin, there was Susan Hawk!— my agent, my unwavering cheerleader and the voice of kindness, wisdom, and practicality. *Thank you for taking a chance on me and this book.* Her early enthusiasm provided the steam to truly put myself out there and her professional savvy made this book into an actual career.

I owe a great debt to early readers of my writing, including Laura Irmer, Paula Turk, Theresa Alvarado, Cate Nuanez, James Nuanez, and Marieke Nijkamp. Additionally, I must thank my incredible and weird family. The ridiculous amount of support that I have received from them—siblings, parents, grandparents, in-laws, aunts, uncles, close friends—and especially those who help wrangle my toddler—is lovely, overwhelming, and something I will value forever.

I have huge appreciation for my dear grammy, for the love, shelter, electricity, water, and internet she's given me and my family. These are the real-life things that make novel-writing possible.

As you may have seen, this book is dedicated to my parents—Mom, Brad, Dad, and Theresa. They show me what a loving, unconventional family can look like. Their unwavering support for all the wacky things I've wanted to accomplish has helped turn my dreams into reality.

Super thanks to my cats, Linux and Computer, premium lap and back warmers, loud meowers, and the best reasons to get up from the desk to stretch my wrists and rest my eyes after a long writing session.

I absolutely must recognize my young son. This book was

written and sold before he came along, but the editing that brought it alive happened after he made me a mom. Though it became harder to write after he arrived, he gave me a reason to continue and continue well. He gave me a deeper understanding of Mama, a kinder eye toward her. The book would not be as good without him.

For my husband there aren't words that fully convey my appreciation for all the support, companionship, leadership, love, wisdom, and comfort he has given me since we were just kids in high school. He read all the troublesome early drafts. He lent his keen eye and ear for voice and character authenticity. He hustled hard, worked full-time, commuted long hours, then took care of our son, all so I could meet deadlines. He was with me at the top of Half Dome and I'm so glad to have him here with me at the top of this mountain.

Lastly, I want to recognize all the amazing and coura- geous gender non-conforming kids and adults who have shown, posted, recorded, written, told, and lived their sto- ries. Although Birdie was not inspired by anyone specific, his voice grew clearer in my head the more I opened my mind to all the awesome people who are like him. I've watched, read, and listened to countless stories, but wanted to specifi- cally recognize C. J. and Lori Duron and Jacob Tobia—their public vulnerability and authenticity has truly shaped how I see the world.

OPPORTUNITIES

in

Technical Writing Careers

OPPORTUNITIES

in

Technical Writing Careers

REVISED EDITION

JAY R. GOULD
WAYNE A. LOSANO

New York   Chicago   San Francisco   Lisbon   London   Madrid   Mexico City
Milan   New Delhi   San Juan   Seoul   Singapore   Sydney   Toronto

The **McGraw·Hill** *Companies*

Library of Congress Cataloging-in-Publication Data

Gould, Jay Reid.
    Opportunities in technical writing careers / by Jay R. Gould and Wayne A.
Losano.
        p.   cm.
    Includes bibliographical references.
    ISBN 0-07-149311-5 (alk. paper)
    1. Technical writing—Vocational guidance.   I. Losano, Wayne A.   II. Title.

    T11.G663   2008
    808'.0666—dc22   2008005170

1 2 3 4 5 6 7 8 9 10 11 12 13 14 15 16 17 18 19 20   DOC/DOC   0 9 8

ISBN   978-0-07-149311-6
MHID   0-07-149311-5

Interior design by Rattray Design

McGraw-Hill books are available at special quantity discounts to use as premiums and
sales promotions or for use in corporate training programs. To contact a representative,
please visit the Contact Us pages at www.mhprofessional.com.

This book is printed on acid-free paper.

Contents

1. The Field of Technical Writing   1

What is technical writing? Need for technical writers. Sharing your knowledge. Making a name for yourself. Job titles. Areas of specialization. Disastrous effects of bad technical writing. Examples of good technical writing. Where to find jobs. Qualities necessary for success. Problems faced by technical writers.

2. Training for Technical Writers   23

Background you'll need. Differences between technical writing and technical editing. Courses in technical writing. Applying to university programs. In-company training. Society for Technical Communication. Additional training options. Words of advice. Education costs.

3. Getting Started   45

Employment outlook. Researching the field.
Researching the jobs. Sample job titles. Letters of
application. Résumés. Salaries.

4. Duties of the Technical Writer   55

Technical presses. Promotional writing. Technical
advertising. News releases. Public relations.
Instruction manuals. Proposals. Research and
development. Government-sponsored activities. Trade
journals and house organs. Special projects. Technical
reports. Audiovisual scriptwriting. Technical
translation. Document coordination. Technical
editors. Sample job advertisements. Large vs. small
companies. Opportunities for advancement.
Importance of teamwork. Final words.

5. Employers of Technical Writers   95

Industrial companies. Research groups. Government
agencies. Journals and magazines. Support companies.
Higher education. Teaching technical writing.
Consulting and freelance writing. Summer
employment. Working overseas.

6. Related Fields and Growing Trends   117

Medical writing. American Medical Writers
Association. Business writing. International
Association of Business Communicators. Trends in

professional education. Global information. Machine
translation. Computer documentation. Looking ahead.

Appendix: Professional Associations 135
Recommended Reading 145

1

THE FIELD OF
TECHNICAL WRITING

DIFFERENT FORMS OF writing have been used to relay information since ancient times. People have communicated facts, lore, data, news, science, wisdom, and entertainment in writing using methods ranging from ancient cave drawings and hieroglyphics to the latest bestseller, computer manual, or blog.

Writing can be broadly classified into two categories: fiction and nonfiction. The novelists, short-story writers, poets, screenwriters, and playwrights who produce fiction manipulate words and language to create scenes, moods, and effects so readers can feel as though they are unobserved, passive participants to the events described. Nonfiction writers present facts and data in a variety of formats, including magazine and newspaper articles, books (textbooks, biographies, how-tos, self-help, travel guides, and more), booklets, reports, brochures, memoirs, manuals, journals, newsletters, advertising copy, and even the text inside the pages of the phone book.

What Is Technical Writing?

Technical writers write, edit, and prepare publications in many fields of technology, science, engineering, and medicine, including articles for technical and scientific journals, both in print and online. The publications may be technical reports, instruction manuals, articles, papers, proposals, brochures, and booklets and even speeches for technical meetings and conferences.

Technical writers must remain objective and factual about the subject matter they are dealing with. Their sole function is to write dispassionately about facts and objects and to relate useful, relevant, reliable information that readers can understand. The language they use must be simple and direct and contain a minimum of nonfunctional descriptive adjectives. Their verbs must be in the active rather than the passive voice to eliminate any doubt about what the writing means or implies.

Any writing that requires familiarity with (or willingness to learn about) a technical field would be considered technical writing. Writing about museum conservation is technical writing as much as writing user manuals for a software product or a troubleshooting guide for a broken tractor. Technical writing is a useful communication tool whenever information of a technical nature must be transmitted.

Need for Technical Writers

The twentieth century saw a sharp rise in the amount of nonfiction material produced, largely because of the nearly continuous advances and developments in technology, which shows no signs of slowing down. Thanks to this rapid and abundant increase, there is a growing demand for technical writers.

In the early days of technical writing, people with scientific and technical backgrounds were given writing assignments for which they weren't prepared or qualified. Not surprisingly, much of the writing they produced was often very poorly composed, stilted, and boring. This in no way reflects on the intelligence or education level of the writers, but represents the difficulty of merging technical knowledge with writing skills to produce an acceptable product. It is not unusual for highly educated technicians to produce poor-quality writing because their training and experience have not focused on verbal and written skills. On the other hand, writers with no scientific background had difficulty understanding how to present and interpret scientific data and subject matter so that the reader would be properly informed.

The need for technical writers arose because these situations almost always guaranteed poor results. Managers were often less concerned with the quality of the writing than with simply having the work done. Sometimes the writing was so poor that readers failed to derive any usable information from it. For example, if the assignment was a construction manual for a process or a use manual for a piece of equipment, the results could be disastrous and detrimental to business.

Sharing Your Knowledge

Technical writers have another important function: to teach others about their profession. One technical writing graduate who works for the Federal Energy Regulatory Commission has led instructional seminars in technical writing for her colleagues.

This writer has the potential to go far because she has jumped into a new area and demonstrated her ability to explain, describe, and illustrate. These characteristics will help her immeasurably in preparing training programs.

Making a Name for Yourself

Will you become famous as a technical writer? It's highly unlikely. In fact, technical writers are often, by necessity, anonymous authors who don't get to see their byline attached to their work. (The exceptions to this rule of anonymity are people who write scientific or technical articles for newspapers, magazines, and scholarly publications under their own names or who write popular how-to guides.)

If you're wondering why most technical writers don't have a byline, think about the last time you tried to assemble a new barbecue grill or program a home entertainment system. Even the most effectively written instruction manual may leave some users frustrated, wishing they could lodge a complaint directly with the person who wrote the instruction manual. That's reason enough for the writer's anonymity!

But that aside, most employers who produce technical material want to reach their audience with concise and easy-to-understand language and to promote their product or train their audience in its use. No writing stars are required or encouraged.

With that said, you can still build a name for yourself through your list of credits. Every assignment you complete becomes another item to add to your résumé, and in some cases you might even be able to keep a sample of your work and create a professional portfolio to show to new clients. Word of mouth and employer and client references and recommendations also will help you to become known in your area of specialization.

Job Titles

Although the term *technical writer* is the most common job title used, there are other titles as well as ranks.

Assistant technical writer
Associate technical writer
Consulting technical writer
Copyeditor
Copywriter
Corporate technical writer
Course developer
Curriculum designer
Curriculum planner
Documentation contractor
Documentation specialist
Education specialist
Information systems writer
Instructional designer
Junior technical writer
Knowledge analyst
Lead technical writer
Senior technical writer
Software technical writer
Technical communicator
Technical editor
Technical intern

Technical translator
Trainer

Areas of Specialization

The areas in which a technical writer can work are vast and varied, but most specialize in just one, sometimes two, areas. For example, a medical writer wouldn't be expected to be knowledgeable about software or the environment, just as an advertising writer wouldn't necessarily be familiar with agriculture.

This list of fields that need technical writers is just a guide. Your own research will no doubt help you add to it.

Advertising
Agriculture
Architecture
Armed forces
Computer system documentation
Corporate communications
Education
Electronics
Engineering
Entertainment
Environment
Film and documentaries
Finance and banking
Government
Graphics design
Information development
Instructional design

Insurance
Investments
Journalism
Manual writing
Manufacturing
Market research
Mechanics
Medicine
Multimedia specialist
Pharmaceuticals
Proposal writing
Public relations
Publication management and design
Publicity
Research firms
Sales
Science
Telecommunications
Video production
Web page authoring and site design

The different specializations and the type of writing that technical writers do in various areas will be covered in greater depth in Chapter 4.

Disastrous Effects of Bad Technical Writing

Technical writing should never confuse the reader. The example that follows is a piece of writing that proved to be dangerously ineffective. (This letter is part of the public record.)

Babcock & Wilcox Company
IR Generation Group

TO: Manager, Plant Integration, Three Mile Island
FROM: Manager, Plan Performance Services, Babcock & Wilcox
Subject: Operator Interruption of High Pressure Injection (HPI)
References: Two titles listed

References 1 and 2 (attached) recommend a change in Babcock and Wilcox's philosophy for HPI system use during low-pressure transits. Basically they recommend leaving the HPI pumps on, once HPI has been indicated, until it can be determined that the hot leg temperature is more than 50°F below Tsat for the reactor cooling system (RCS) pressure. Nuclear Service believes that this mode can cause the RCS (including the pressurizer) to be solid. The pressure reliefs will lift, with a water surge through the discharge piping into the quench tank. We believe the following incidents should be evaluated:

1. If the pressurizer goes solid with one or more HPI pumps continuing to operate, would there be a pressure spike before the relief valves open, which could cause damage to the RCS?
2. What damage would the water surge through the relief valve discharge piping and quench tank cause?

To date, the Nuclear Service has not notified our operating plants to change HPI policy consistent with References 1 and 2 because of the above-stated questions. Yet the references suggest the possibility of uncovering the core if present HPI policy is continued. We request that Integration resolve the issue of how the HPI system should be used. We are available to help as needed.

Signature

Did you actually read all that? Probably not—and neither did the plant manager at Three Mile Island. Babcock & Wilcox Company's intention for the above letter was to warn Three Mile Island managers that they could uncover the reactor's core (and thus possibly have a nuclear meltdown) if certain operating procedures were not changed. As you may recall, a nuclear meltdown is exactly what happened. How would you revise that letter?

Examples of Good Technical Writing

Advances in technology and science are leading to more variety in technical writing. As new terminology, theories, instruments, processes, and machinery are developed, others are discarded—an ongoing process that makes relatively new equipment and procedures obsolete almost before the packing crates are opened. Scientists in every field are constantly striving to make new discoveries, which means that technical writers must replace old paragraphs with new ones at a feverish pace. Several examples of scientific writing are cited below.

Example One

The velvet background on a painting of Elvis looks black because it reflects so little light. But getting a surface to reflect no light at all is surprisingly difficult. Now researchers have created a virtually reflection-free surface by coating it with filaments only a few billionths of a meter thick.

Improved antireflective surfaces might have many uses. For example, they could eliminate light-wasting reflections in fiber-optic telecommunications, or the surfaces could brighten low-power light-emitting diode (LED) lamps.

Applied to a clear surface, the coating would make a lens absorb more light, increasing its transparency. On an opaque surface, the filaments would make a silicon solar cell, for example, almost perfectly absorbing. . . .

Light rebounds when it strikes the boundary between two materials that have different "refractive indices"—measures of how fast light travels through the substances. For example, sunlight bounces off the surface of a pond because light travels more slowly in water than in air. The greater the difference between the refractive indices of any two materials, the more light is reflected.[1]

Example one is the beginning of an article that appeared in *Science News* and was written by a professional science journalist. *Science News* is a weekly periodical as well as online newsmagazine published by the Society for Science and the Public, which was founded in 1921. It covers the latest developments in medicine, pharmacology, and the natural sciences. The articles vary in length, ranging from a single paragraph to several pages. The subscribers are primarily scientists who want a quick overview of what is occurring in other sciences. However, many nonscientists are also regular readers because the articles are well written and understandable to the lay reader. Subscribers also include professional and educational institutions.

Example Two

In a development that promises to ease structural analysis of proteins, British researchers have found a way to determine protein structures by using only basic and easy-to-obtain data complemented by theoretical calculations.

---

1. Barry, Patrick L. "The New Black: A Nanoscale Coating Reflects Almost No Light." *Science News* 171(9), 3/3/07, p.132.

The new approach, based on nuclear magnetic resonance (NMR) spectroscopy chemical shifts, is faster and simpler than conventional NMR methods.

Typically, NMR protein structures are based on interatomic distances, but these are difficult to measure. On the other hand, chemical shifts are the most readily obtained and accurate NMR parameters. They provide information about the molecular environment of atoms. They're used to determine structures of small molecules, and they're usually the first thing chemistry undergrads learn about NMR. . . .

Researchers have wanted to use chemical shifts to determine protein structures because that sidesteps the need to make time-consuming nuclear Overhauser effect (NOE) measurements. NOEs, which are pairwise distances between specific atoms, are currently the primary basis for most NMR protein structures.[2]

The article in example two appeared in *Chemical and Engineering News*, a member-supported weekly magazine of the American Chemical Society. This publication and online resource covers all the news of the chemical world, including recent advances in research, industry, education, funding, and regulations. The article was written by a staff correspondent who specializes in biochemistry, medicinal chemistry, analytical chemistry, organic chemistry, and combinatorial chemistry. Those who write for the magazine must be able to handle highly complex ideas and terms and still be able to write an interesting story that is easy to understand. The author of this particular article does have one distinct advantage: most of his readers are chemists. Nevertheless, few of them will have detailed knowledge about the field of work being described.

---

2. Borman, Stu. "Fast Route to Structures: Technique Defines Protein Structures from NMR Chemical Shifts." *Chemical and Engineering News* 85(23), 6/3/07, p. 10.

Example Three

> Some 10,000 years ago, somewhere in the Near East, an audacious wildcat crept into one of the crude villages of early human settlers, the first to domesticate wheat and barley. There she felt safe from her many predators in the region, such as hyenas and larger cats.
>
> The rodents that infested the settlers' homes and granaries were sufficient prey. Seeing that she was earning her keep, the settlers tolerated her, and their children greeted her kittens with delight.
>
> At least five females of the wildcat subspecies known as *Felis silvestris lybica* accomplished this delicate transition from forest to village. And from these five matriarchs all the world's 600 million house cats are descended. . . .
>
> Five subspecies of wildcat are distributed across the Old World. They are known as the European wildcat, the Near Eastern wildcat, the Southern African wildcat, the Central Asian wildcat, and the Chinese desert cat. Their patterns of DNA fall into five clusters. The DNA of all house cats and fancy cats falls within the Near Eastern wildcat cluster, making clear that this subspecies is their ancestor. . . .[3]

The paragraphs in example three are the beginning of an article by a scientific reporter and editor who is on the staff of the *New York Times* science section. The article goes on to discuss cat DNA and the animal's domestication.

You will notice the style of writing in this article is much more accessible to the lay reader, who does not need to have any particular training or knowledge to comprehend the topic. The *New York Times*, in which this article appeared, is a mainstream publication

---

3. Wade, Nicholas. "Study Traces Cat's Ancestry to Middle East." *New York Times*, www.nytimes.com/2007/06/29/science/29cat.html?ref=science, visited 6/29/07.

read by a much more diverse audience than those in the previous examples. The author of the article clearly understands his readership and has been able to craft his writing so that, although it includes technical terms and concepts, it is not so technical as to be not easily understood by the publication's average reader.

Example Four

> Explore the effects of color mixing with light with this eye catching demonstration.
>
> The fascinating phenomenon of color mixing is conveyed using LED technology. A great alternative to traditional ray box and filters, the ultra bright LEDs of the Color Mixing Apparatus prevent the need for full blackout.
>
> This apparatus is comprised of six large bright LEDs, two each of red, green, and blue. The brightness of these LEDs can be adjusted using the control box, and either the inner or outer ring of lights can be selected, for a full range of experiments. Set the apparatus in full rotation and use with the included screens to demonstrate both additive and subtractive color mixing. Using a blank white screen and the color mixer, you can highlight how color is perceived; use the black screen with aperture for projecting circular patches of light; or use a clear screen with an eclipse disc for blocking light.
>
> When you use the apparatus in conjunction with the various screens, you can highlight the way we see color and also how colored light is created. . . .[4]

Example four is a product description taken from an online catalog of scientific products. The catalog is intended to take the place

---

4. Sargent-Welch Online Catalog, www.sargentwelch.com/product.asp_Q_pn_E_WLS 1751%2D72%5FEA_A_CENCO+Color+Mixing+Apparatus_E_, visited 6/29/07.

of a salesperson by giving prospective buyers a brief, concise, and accurate description of a scientific apparatus. The catalog must give potential customers complete information on all its items so that they will be able to order precisely what they want. The emphasis in this type of writing is to provide necessary information using a minimum number of words. For this reason, complete sentences are not always used.

As you can see from the four preceding examples, the field of technical writing is broad and can cover preparing articles to go in everything from a highly specialized journal to a syndicated story in a large, influential newspaper.

Where to Find Jobs

Chapter 3 will cover the job hunt, helping you to learn what kinds of jobs are available and how to locate them. But as a starting point, one of the best ways to get a feel for the various types of work available to technical writers is to read job advertisements. They often list the duties and required experience and show you the wide variety of environments and specializations in which technical writers work.

You can find job advertisements in any Sunday newspaper or on the Internet. The Society for Technical Communication has an active database of job openings in eight different regions in the United States and Canada. Contact information is provided in the appendix.

Sample Job Advertisements

Note that the following job announcements do not have contact information because they have already been filled.

Position: Technical Writer
Job type: Permanent
Company: Technical publications firm
Location: Midwest
Duties: Preparing new and revised information for use in technical service manuals, user manuals, and operator manuals in the agricultural and heavy equipment fields. Technical writer will be responsible for coordinating material from engineers, dealers, and other sources. Other responsibilities include reading blueprints and detailed engineering documents, marking up artwork for illustrator, and interacting with engineers, product specialists, and other technical writers to learn about parts installation and operations.

Requirements: A high school diploma, in addition to vocational, career, or related technical studies in technical writing or other engineering discipline and one to three years technical writing experience. An understanding of hydraulic, electrical, and mechanical systems is required.

Tool skills: Proficient with a personal computer, copier/duplicator, and various software including desktop publishing, spreadsheet, word processing, illustration, and database programs.

Position: Technical Writer
Job type: Temporary/Contract
Company: A gateway security firm
Location: Southeast
Duties: Researching and writing technical information and procedures for manuals and online help; developing technical illustrations and graphics to support written material; editing technical documentation; and testing documented procedures.

Requirements: Bachelor's degree and four to six years of related writing or technical experience; excellent research and writing skills; background in high-tech industry, preferably with Internet and networking technologies.

Tool skills: Experience with RoboHelp, Word, and HTML highly desirable.

Position: Technical Writer
Job type: Permanent
Company: IT software firm
Location: Eastern Canada
Duties: Plan, organize, write, edit, and test software manuals, developer guides, and online materials; work closely with software development team to research documentation requirements and content; read code written by developers, as well as translate specifications written by developers into information that customers can use, and develop and maintain custom publishing tools.

Requirements: B.A./B.S. in computer science; electrical, civil, or mechanical engineering, or equivalent experience; experience writing user documentation and tutorials; ability to produce quality documentation with aggressive deadlines; and demonstrated ability to communicate technical information clearly.

Position: Technical Writer
Job type: Full-time
Company: Agricultural manufacturing firm
Location: Western Canada
Duties: The successful candidate will be responsible for writing all technical product documentation for clients, including generating manual content, technical writing, graphics, and layout. The position provides support to the Engineering Department.

Requirements: A diploma in technical writing, CAD/CAM technology, or mechanical engineering technology, as well as experience in designing and producing technical manuals for mechanical equipment.

Position: Medical Writer
Job type: Contract
Company: Pharmaceutical firm
Location: Southeast
Duties: Preparing, reviewing, and editing clinical regulatory documents and publications; preparing documents for regulatory submissions in collaboration with clinical research, medical, and

statistical personnel; and preparing, reviewing, and editing reports, study protocols, and manuscripts.

Requirements: B.A./B.S. in life sciences, five years' experience in preparation of clinical documentation; experience with regulatory commissions; overall knowledge of the clinical trial process.

Qualities Necessary for Success

The two most important questions you must ask yourself before embarking on a career in technical writing are, "What kind of person should I be to succeed in this field?" and "What kind of personality traits should I have?" Some of the answers are obvious and are similar to traits that make people successful in any business or profession. You should be persistent and forceful, but not overbearing, in seeking the information you need. It goes without saying that you should enjoy writing. You must be a self-starter with a keen analytical mind who is at ease with management and can speak its language.

You also must have the capacity to assume responsibility and be willing to learn continuously about your field. The refusal or inability to stay on top of your job is the quickest route to unemployment. Working in the field of technical writing requires constant self-improvement. This is a highly competitive field, and you will find that an employer will have little trouble hiring your replacement if you don't produce high-quality work and stay well informed.

To be sure that you have the qualities you'll need to succeed, it's a good idea to set up a program of constant self-improvement and stick to it. Here are some of the ways you can accomplish this.

- Enroll at a local college or university night school for an advanced degree.

- Enroll at a local college or university night school and take some relevant courses each semester.
- Keep up with the literature in your field.
- Enroll in any company-sponsored courses.
- Attend as many technical seminars and conferences and take as many short courses as you can.

Another personal quality that is essential for the technical writer might surprise you: it is an interest in both the arts and sciences. Technical writers often deal with graphic artists and technical illustrators, and having some appreciation of their skill and ability will make your interactions more successful. You should know the basic principles of good composition in an illustration or a photograph and why certain kinds of graphics are appropriate for one situation but not for another.

You must also develop a sense of objectivity and should be able to place things in their proper perspective, unaffected by personal bias. The new hire who starts out saying "This is not the way we did it at my other company" (or at school) is in for a rude awakening. Industrial publications must be processed in the shortest possible time, and the publications department has probably already established a procedure that fits the company perfectly. The new technical writer should be able to recognize this and adjust to it.

There are other things to consider as well. A private engineering firm, distressed at some of the personnel interactions, distributed this memo to its employees.

> The success of an engineering enterprise depends on the cooperation and interaction of administrators, engineers, and technical communicators. An engineering firm's administration must con-

sider the individual personalities and the interaction of all the people it has on board. We will endeavor to look for prospective employees with the following characteristics:

• **All members must regard themselves as being players on a team, with each one having a specific function.** A large part of participants' time may be spent outside their field getting information and data from engineers and working with other publications personnel, printers, and illustrators.

• **They must also be capable of dealing with details and minutiae.** Many times the technical writer is anxious to get the job done as quickly as possible, but quotations must still be authorized, statistics checked, and all kinds of calculations verified. Very often a highly technical scientific project will require gaining an intimate understanding of the subject before proceeding with the actual writing. The report that is subsequently written may require collecting and compiling large amounts of technically accurate, detailed data prior to its publication. If you are averse to working through the unglamorous aspects of writing, you probably will not make a good technical writer.

• **They must be tactful.** The job of editing requires a high degree of diplomacy. The less people write and the less skillful they are, the more sensitive they will be to criticism about their literary craftsmanship. For generations, engineers have been told they do not write well. Thus, they may resent being criticized by professional writers. Tactfulness does not imply cowardice. It simply means that the writer has to cultivate a rapport with engineers and scientists and know how to offer constructive corrections and suggestions about their writing.

Employers judge prospective employees by their training and education. But the best training in the world may not get you the job if you are lacking certain personality traits. Technical writers are people, not machines; they must work with other people.

The manager of publications and illustrations at a defense company emphasizes the importance of the interaction between technical writers and others in the company:

> Tact and diplomacy are so important to the writer-editor that too much cannot be said of them. When preparing an original manuscript, the writer must establish and maintain open lines of communication between himself and the source of the material. . . . In an editorial capacity, the writer-editor must rely on his power of friendly persuasion. . . . Initiative and an inquisitive nature are as important as a keen, well-developed sense of order. . . . The very nature of communication forces the writer-editor to work at once independently and jointly.

Most interviewers can accurately judge the personality traits of people who will be readily accepted by their fellow workers.

Advances in computers and software have raised the expectations of what is required and demanded of both novice and veteran technical writers. At a recent executives' meeting in a large company that employs hundreds of technical writers, a lengthy discussion ensued concerning what the company expects of its writers. The list of requirements and expectations was staggering. In addition to writing and editing skills, the company expects that its writers will become familiar with graphics management, especially the layout and design of documents. They must be able to turn out documents that the reading audience for whom they are intended will find acceptable. The company expects that its technical writers will be totally computer literate and use the latest hardware and software in performing their tasks.

Finally, to state the obvious, you must like to write! While this is certainly not a new idea, some people overlook it when choosing a career. The more skill you have with words, punctuation, and grammar, the more options you'll have to work in a variety of writing modes, and your chances for success also will be greater. It has long been known that writers who can prepare the most articulate oral and written presentations are better equipped for good jobs and for regular promotions than those who do not communicate well. Every report we have seen, every questionnaire filled out by technical communicators now holding important management positions, attests to this fact: the author knew how to write well, how to present proposals, and how to speak convincingly.

Problems Faced by Technical Writers

The phrase *media intake* implies that communication has at its disposal more media and channels of information than were conceived possible just a few short years ago. As with the scientist, more information reaches and is available to the writer than can be assimilated in a short period of time. This can frustrate a writer, who may feel inundated by this ever-increasing tidal wave of information. In this vein, the late President Kennedy is reported to have said, "I'm reading more and more and enjoying it less and less."

There isn't any simple or rational solution to this problem. Earlier in this chapter, you read that the most successful technical writer must necessarily become an eternal student. You will have to spend many hours reviewing mountains of information just to keep up to date. For example, consider the story of the Hollywood agent who was fired by an actor for failing to get him a choice role. The agent protested and proceeded to give the actor a long list of accomplishments on his behalf. The actor responded, "Yes, I know. But what have you done for me lately?" Unfortunately, this little vignette is true everywhere people work for others. So, to ensure your continued value and employability, you must stay current and on top of things in this fast-moving world, where employees can be quickly replaced.

Because your technical writing career will include dealing heavily in human communications, you must maintain effective personal interaction. If you find yourself wondering why you aren't getting responses to your requests, why you are not receiving the same information other members of your staff are getting, or why some of your meanings are being distorted by your readers, then it might be time to reevaluate the way you are communicating. To minimize these problems, you must keep all lines of communication open, and your communication must be clear and active.

Other communication problems may arise between you and the people you work with and write for. Don't be surprised if scientists and engineers think and behave differently than you do and if they apply different meanings to words. This also may apply to your readers. You will be expected to adapt yourself to them because most of them won't change their ways for you.

Marshall Field, the great entrepreneur, once said, "The customer is always right. So, give the lady what she wants." Because of this, you must learn how to address your words and writing and to use language that is appropriate to your audience. All of these issues emphasize that the field of technical writing is an ever-evolving profession with ever-changing demands.

2

TRAINING FOR
TECHNICAL WRITERS

EVERY PROFESSIONAL WORKING in a technical field—from the electronics engineer designing a user's manual for a new product to the biologist writing an environmental impact report to the accountant explaining an auditing procedure to a client—must be able to communicate ideas effectively.

There are two main ways to become a technical writer. The most traditional way has been on-the-job training; however, the ideal situation in which you can learn this field is to major in technical communications in college. This will help you to not only learn to master the mechanics and techniques of writing, but to be well-grounded in science and technology as well. Not every college and university offers such a curriculum, but with the large number of schools throughout the United States and Canada that do, finding a program shouldn't be too difficult.

Most technical writers are graduates of four-year programs and have earned bachelor's degrees. Some have master's degrees gained through specialized course work beyond their undergraduate study. However, a growing number of technical writers have graduated from two-year and community colleges.

It is, of course, possible to become a technical writer directly after high school graduation, as you saw in some of the job advertisements in Chapter 1. However, recent reports issued by the Society for Technical Communication show that the level of education for writers has risen considerably over the past two decades. Based on this information, you can see that most employers believe that someone fresh out of high school wouldn't have acquired the skills or experience necessary without further training to be successful at technical writing.

Background You'll Need

What constitutes good training? We have selected the views of two professionals whose years of experience in the field qualify them to address the educational needs of the prospective technical writer. Fred W. Holder, who has written a great deal about communication, has this to say.

> Ideally, a candidate should have a bachelor's degree in engineering (in the particular specialty with which you're dealing) and a master's degree in English, journalism, or another field requiring a sound background in written communication. . . . I've found that people with sixty to ninety credit hours of college work covering English, journalism, mathematics through calculus, physics, chemistry, and a wide range of other subjects make excellent technical writers.

Marguerite F. D'Amico, a director of technical communications for international corporations, expresses her views.

There are three essential requirements for those involved in translating and presenting technical ideas: a solid foundation in the basic sciences and some understanding of how they relate to technology; an understanding of how to organize and present concepts clearly, logically, and graphically; and a sensitivity to the standards and needs of those receiving and supplying the information.

What does it all add up to? It simply means that technical writers will need more and more formal education as time goes on. In discussing technical writing education, some general principles apply.

Differences Between Technical Writing and Technical Editing

Most companies differentiate between technical writing and technical editing. Editing requires a person who is adept at improving the composition end of writing by correcting grammar and punctuation, style, and construction of sentences and paragraphs. Technical writing, on the other hand, encompasses the whole process. It takes in editing, of course, but it extends to original writing as well as the rewriting of other people's manuscripts. The writer must have a firm grasp of the technical material to cope with this kind of assignment.

For the rather restricted job of technical editing, it is generally agreed that solid training in English composition will serve you well. A prospective technical editor also should, of course, have an affinity for technological subjects and familiarity with engineering and scientific terms. For the writer who must deal in-depth with technical subjects, a firm foundation in science and engineering is essential.

It almost goes without saying that to work as either a technical writer or editor, you must be computer literate. In addition to using word processing programs to write, you'll need the ability to use a variety of databases and software programs for research and information storage and retrieval.

Courses in Technical Writing

Depending on the university, you will find courses in technical writing offered in many different departments, including English and other humanities-based departments, communications, journalism, business, the sciences, and engineering.

In recent years, colleges and other schools have recognized that engineering students, for example, should be taught not only English composition, but should also be exposed to courses in technical writing. These courses are usually taught by members of the English department in an engineering college or by teachers of engineering who have an interest in writing. They deal with special forms of technical writing such as report writing and the preparation of scientific papers and magazine articles.

As a result of the formation of various technical writing societies and the great need for technical writers, industry and the technical press have taken more interest in what is being taught by colleges. Every year the Institute of Electrical and Electronics Engineers (IEEE), with more than 370,000 members, holds a special session titled "Engineering Writing and Speech." During this session, seminars and panel discussions on the training of engineers are held to foster clearer and more informative written communications and to improve the relationships between engineers and technical writers. The result of this two-way process has been the introduction of many fine technical writing courses and four-year programs into a number of colleges and universities.

In addition to technical writing courses, a considerable number of schools now offer majors in this specific discipline. The programs have various names and can be found in communication- or humanities-oriented departments under such course titles as science writing, science information, technical journalism, and technical communications.

Choosing the Right Program

There are two important things to consider when choosing an education program. First, you must determine which programs and courses are available; then you must decide whether they will provide the skills you'll need once you are employed.

We carried out a study of this very subject among a group of technical writers. These are the answers broken down into three categories:

What Are Your Present Duties?
Professional (preparation of):
  Computer manuals
  Hardware manuals
  Reports and proposals
  Audiovisuals
  Brochures
  Layout
Management:
  Writing
  Supervising
  Consulting

Production
Operations
Editorial management
Training programs
Publicity:
  Writing technical articles
  Placing technical articles
  Preparing brochures
  Preparing newsletters
Academic:
  Teaching technical writing
  Teaching media instruction
  Teaching English composition

What Other Courses Should Be Included in the Curriculum in Addition to Technical Writing?

Science or engineering courses
Media courses using CDs and DVDs
Oral presentations

What Courses Should Be Taken Outside the Technical Writing Field?

Management administration
Sociology
Industrial psychology
Computer science
Graphic arts
Photography
Printing

You may be able to extract a couple of pointers from this information. First, decide what kind of technical communication job you are aiming for—writing or editing. Then you need to know what area you think you are qualified for, such as dealing with reports, manuals, papers and articles, publicity, or advertising. You must also think in terms of specialization, whether in computers, science, medical, or any of the other areas discussed in Chapter 1. Finally, you should find a college that meets your requirements.

Peterson's Guide to Four-Year Colleges lists many schools in the United States and Canada that offer B.S. degrees in technical writing. Enough information about entrance requirements and approximate cost is included to allow you to decide which schools you wish to contact for further information. You can visit www.petersons.com to search for programs and schools. Once you've found schools that interest you, visit their websites and request catalogs to learn about course descriptions and other important information.

Sample Programs

To illustrate the variety of programs available, we have randomly selected a number of schools and briefly outlined their technical writing programs. Notice the diversity of departments that offer degrees in technical writing.

Undergraduate Programs

Brigham Young University
English Department
Provo, UT 84602
http://english.byu.edu/emphasis/technicalcommunications

Students can pursue a B.S. in English with a technical communication emphasis. In addition to English courses, the department offers classes in technical writing, editing for publication, document design and portfolio, studies in language and rhetoric, and an academic internship.

Additional courses are available in computers and academic publishing, oral business communication, desktop publishing, electronic publishing, elementary computer applications, and magazine writing, editing, and publishing.

Capilano College
Communications Department
North Vancouver, BC V7J 3H5
http://capcollege.bc.ca/programs/cmns

In addition to a B.A. with a concentration in technical writing, the department offers a fifteen-credit certificate program in professional communications, which teaches generalist communication skills for business, communications industries, or the applied arts.

Graduates have the skills needed to plan and write correspondence, business and technical reports, proposals, promotional materials, Web content, speeches, presentations, and visual media materials.

Carnegie-Mellon University
English Department
Pittsburgh, PA 15213
http://english.cmu.edu

The program includes two tracks, one in technical communication and one in scientific and medical communication. Both begin with a core of foundation courses in print and online communication as well as a shared set of prerequisites in math, statistics, and computer programming; then they branch out to include appropriate specialized courses.

Students work on real projects for actual clients to learn group interaction and management skills. Students who maintain a B average in writing courses may participate in internships for academic credit during their junior or senior year. These internships provide a minimum of 120 hours of professional experience as well as exposure to the broad range of career possibilities that technical writers can pursue after graduation.

Colorado State University
Department of Journalism and Technical Journalism
Fort Collins, CO 80523
www.colostate.edu/dept/TJ

The program prepares students for careers working in newspapers, magazines, broadcast and electronic reporting, public relations and technical/specialized journalism, and computer-mediated communication. Students may choose from the following concentrations: computer-mediated communication, public relations, news/editorial, specialized and technical communication, and television news and video communication.

Embry-Riddle Aeronautical University
Department of Humanities and Communication
Prescott, AZ 86301
www.erau.edu/omni/pr/academicorgs/prdohc

Courses are offered in technical writing, business communication, professional communications, and informational literacy, among others. Courses are designed to support language, literacy, and critical thinking skills needed both in courses offered by other departments and in advancing professional and personal growth.

Academic support is provided through the writing center. Students network with faculty in the College of Engineering and the College of Aviation to provide writing support across the curriculum. Opportunities also exist to network with professionals in business, industry, and government to keep abreast of their needs in language, literacy, and critical-thinking skills among potential employees.

Massachusetts Institute of Technology
Program in Writing and Humanistic Studies
Cambridge, MA 02139
http://web.mit.edu/humanistic/www

Program subjects are divided into four areas: exposition and rhetoric, creative writing, science writing, and technical communication. Introductory subjects in each area are designed for students with little writing experience; the advanced courses are for students who have mastered the basic elements of writing. The faculty includes novelists, essayists, poets, translators, biographers, historians, engineers, and scientists.

Students may also major in writing or develop a joint major with another discipline in the humanities or with the program in science, technology, and society.

Metropolitan State College
Department of Technical Communication and Media Production
Denver, CO 80217
www.mscd.edu/~techcom

The four areas of concentration in this department are corporate communication, multimedia production, technical media, and technical writing and editing. Students may also minor in technical communication or receive a certificate in technical writing and editing.

Michigan Technological University
Humanities Department (Scientific and Technical Communication)
Houghton, MI 49931
www.hu.mtu.edu

The program for a B.A. in scientific and technical communication requires forty-five hours in the core option, with courses in writing, editing, basics of photography, introduction to website design, publications and information management, engineering ethics, and usability and instructions writing.

University of Washington
Technical Communication Department
College of Engineering
Seattle, WA 98195
www.engr.washington.edu

The B.S. in technical communication program gives students a solid foundation in math and science coupled with strong communication skills. Students learn to design, write, edit, and evaluate technical and scientific materials and to gain an understanding of the rhetoric of technical discourse, public policy and technology, hypermedia and multimedia, publications management, and online support systems. There are more than twenty courses for students to choose from, including options for self-study and special projects, and many opportunities to work individually with faculty members.

Graduate Studies

The following is a sampling of colleges and universities that offer graduate programs in technical and scientific communication. Again, notice the range of departments offering graduate studies in this field.

Boise State University
College of Arts and Sciences
Boise, ID 83725
http://boisestate.edu/techcomm/ma.shtml

Students working toward the M.A. in technical communication study such disciplines as rhetoric and composition, linguistics, cognitive psychology, sociology, and gender studies as they apply to the theory of technical communication. They then progress through courses in writing, editing, oral communication, and ethics, followed by a course in visual rhetoric and information design and either a print or on-screen document production course. Students also complete a three-credit internship.

In addition, there are a number of elective courses, including Writing for the Computer Industry and courses in both print and on-screen document production covering topics of interest in desktop publishing, Web development, and online help authoring.

Boston University
Center for Science and Medical Journalism
College of Communication
Boston, MA 02215
www.bu.edu/com/jo/science.html

The M.S. degree, which is awarded by the college's journalism department, comprises forty-eight credit hours that are taken over three semesters. In addition to any required program courses, students may take electives throughout the College of Communication such as in screenwriting, literary journalism, or radio reporting. They may also take science courses in other departments or, under special arrangement, at other academic institutions in the Boston area.

During the summer between the second and third semesters, students participate in a professional internship that involves a journalism position at a newspaper, magazine, or radio or television station.

Illinois Institute of Technology
Department of Humanities
Chicago, IL 60616
http://grad.iit.edu/bulletin/programs/techcomm.html#department

The M.S. degree in technical communication and information design provides a thorough understanding of communication practices, familiarity with the information and communication technologies, and an awareness of and appreciation for the importance of collaboration in enhancing the flow of information throughout an organization.

Required courses include research and usability testing, online design, documentation and project management, entrepreneurship in technical communication, documentation design, technical editing, and an internship.

Elective courses include proposal and grant writing, indexing and information retrieval, language issues in international communication, intercultural communication, and computer-assisted instruction using multimedia.

Miami University
Department of English
Oxford, OH 45056
www.units.muohio.edu/english/Graduate/MA/matsc.html

The M.S. in technical and scientific communication prepares students to write, edit, or supervise the creation of instruction manuals, grant proposals, scientific research reports, or DVD presentations on technical subjects, to mention just a few possibilities.

The interdisciplinary program consists of eight required courses plus three electives. Also required is a one-semester internship in which students work as apprentice technical and scientific communicators in business and government. Students who are already working in the profession may perform the internship with their present employers; those with substantial professional experience may choose to write a thesis in lieu of the internship. Students in the program will prepare many of their assignments in the technical and scientific communication laboratory.

Rensselaer Polytechnic Institute
Department of Language, Literature, and Communication
Troy, NY 12180
www.llc.rpi.edu/programs/graduate_techcomm.shtml

Students enter the M.S. program in technical writing and communication with academic backgrounds ranging from education to engineering. Regardless of their academic backgrounds, students are required to take thirty credit hours beyond the bachelor's degree and can complete the course in one year of full-time study or several years of part-time study. Some of the courses included in this program are: Visual Communication, Film, and Fiction; Language:

The Cultural Milieu; Data Processing; Organizational Psychology; and Advertising Strategies and Promotion.

Applying to University Programs

When you decide on a school you'd like to attend, check to be sure that the program it offers meets your needs. In most cases, you can search the school's website to get extensive information about course offerings and admission requirements, or you can request a catalog from the admissions office.

If you are considering taking one or two courses without matriculating, determine whether you'll receive credits for any courses you complete. It's a good idea to accumulate credits, because they will count toward your major if you decide to pursue a degree. Find out whether any prerequisites are required; you may need to complete certain courses in English composition prior to taking the course.

In-Company Training

Although the shortest path to becoming a technical writer is by mapping out a clear-cut educational program, there is still another way, and that is through in-company training. Such programs will benefit you if you are an employee of the company and have had formal training but need to get actual writing experience.

In-company training programs for technical writers include a variety of practices. Some companies offer elaborate seminars that are taught by professional educators. Many of the nation's most progressive companies, large and small, offer such courses because they find that training programs are an effective way of keeping their people alert and up to date. They are also a means of attracting good personnel to the company.

Technical writing training programs fit into several categories. One of these is the formal course offered at regular intervals on company time and run by a company employee who is or has been a technical writer. Some companies take a less formal approach by bringing in outside consultants. These consultants are likely to be teachers of technical writing, report writing, and technical composition who are known for their practical experience in the industry.

Society for Technical Communication

The Society for Technical Communication (STC) is a membership organization dedicated to advancing the arts and sciences of technical communication in the United States, Canada, and around the world. Its eighteen thousand members work in every aspect of communicating technical information and include technical writers and editors, content developers, documentation specialists, technical illustrators, instructional designers, academics, information architects, usability and human factors professionals, visual designers, Web designers and developers, and translators.

STC provides support to teachers and students of technical communication through programs, scholarships, grants and loans, annual conferences, and seminars. It also maintains a database at its website where students can search for programs throughout the world based on a number of criteria.

Web and Telephone Seminars

Participants in a Web and telephone seminar listen to the presenter over the phone (much like a conference call) while viewing presentation materials over the Web. This format provides easier access to materials for reference during the presentation. Registrants are provided with a toll-free number, a secure URL, and passwords to access both the audio and online elements of the presentation, which are followed by live question-and-answer discussions.

Student Competitions

To promote the study of technical communication among students, STC sponsors competitions for high school and college students. The International Student Technical Communication Competition (ISTCC) recognizes excellence in technical communication at the high school level. Each year cash awards are presented to students in one of the last three grade levels before college whose papers demonstrate outstanding technical writing skills.

Entries are judged by a panel of professional editors, writers, scientists, and educators. Judges evaluate the quality of each student's writing, clarity of the purpose, significance of the topic, effectiveness of the organization, and soundness of the conclusions. They also appraise the use and documentation of reference materials, as well as the use of visual and graphic aids.

The International Science and Engineering Fair (ISEF) Competition recognizes excellence in communicating technical information through posters and technical reports submitted by high school students as entries in the International Science and Engineering Fair. Students compete for scholarships, tuition grants, internships, and scientific field trips. The grand prize is a trip to Stockholm to attend the Nobel Prize ceremonies.

The International Technical Writing Competition is sponsored by the Phoenix Chapter of STC. It is an opportunity for college students to be recognized for outstanding writing in technical communication. The competition is open to all STC student members around the world who are enrolled in college. A cash prize is awarded to the top paper, which may be published in STC newsletters around the world.

Honorary Fraternities

Sigma Tau Chi (STX) and Alpha Sigma (AS) are honorary fraternities of the Society for Technical Communication. They recognize students enrolled in a technical communication program who have a cumulative grade point average of 3.5 or above, are exemplary in participation in STC, and demonstrate a potential for significant contribution to the profession. Sigma Tau Chi recognizes students in baccalaureate and graduate progams; Alpha Sigma recognizes students in two-year and certificate programs.

Additional Training Options

There are other education options aside from the traditional undergraduate and graduate university programs.

Short-Term Courses

An outgrowth of education in the technical writing field has been a number of special institutes, seminars, and workshops. They provide short-term means of bringing technical writers up to date on current practices. For the most part, these institutes, especially those run by private institutions, appeal to already established writers. However, they are also valuable to new writers who want to find out what technical writing is all about, meet other writers, and make useful contacts.

It isn't possible to list all of the options in this book, but a search at www.Petersons.com will lead you to these schools.

Online Programs

Online services such as AOL offer short-term courses covering technical writing and business and academic communications. Some courses have live sessions held in online classrooms; others are conducted via e-mail. Instructors are all professional writers and instructors who work closely with students. Courses run from four to twelve weeks.

A twelve-week program in professional technical writing is offered by Online-Learning.com. Mentored courses allow students to work on their own with support and feedback from instructors. Students communicate with instructors and other students through e-mail, discussion boards, and audio and text chat sessions. A thorough search of the Internet will lead you to even more options.

Words of Advice

As a future technical writer, whether you are just starting your training or are planning to enter from another field, you should think in these terms:

- Be sure to take enough science courses compatible with the area of technical writing in which you are interested, whether it is chemistry, physics, electronics, mathematics, computer science, or engineering.
- If you are still in high school, take all available writing and composition courses. Although courses in creative writing are fine for some forms of professional writing, it is important that your

curriculum include courses in science and technology. If you are already familiar with the subject matter of science and engineering and join a company as a technical writer, you have an advantage over the graduate who is not trained in science.

• If you have already graduated from high school and cannot plan on the four years required to earn a bachelor's degree, see what courses are offered by two-year community colleges or adult education programs in your area, or investigate some of the additional training options discussed above.

• If you aren't able to find a definite technical writing program in your own college, consider creating your own program by majoring in a science and taking writing courses and elective subjects such as mathematics, economics, and statistics.

• If you have already graduated from college, consider pursuing a master's degree. As with your undergraduate studies, you may find a defined graduate program in technical writing, or you may design one yourself with a technical writing career in mind.

• You might also consider the various journalism programs available that have options in technical writing. They will give you good training for a career in the technical and scientific press.

• Gaps in your training can be filled in by extension courses, taken either during the day or the evening, and by correspondence and online programs.

If you choose the last option, be sure that the institution offering the course is well established, that it is properly licensed, and that it operates under proper state and federal regulations. A potential employer must have confidence in the sources from which you have received your education, so it is worthwhile to check the accreditation, reputation, and longevity of any correspondence school you are considering. Ask your career counselor or other school administrator for guidance.

Education Costs

The cost of obtaining a degree in technical communication, as with other professions, depends on the kind of school you attend and where it is located. Liberal arts colleges tend to have lower tuition than colleges of engineering and science. State universities and community colleges are less expensive than private schools, more so if you are a resident of that state.

Graduate education is run somewhat differently from undergraduate education. The principal difference lies in the fact that a great many students can afford to go to graduate school only with financial aid, such as tuition scholarships and fellowships offered by colleges and industries. A scholarship provides tuition only; a fellowship usually contains a modest living allowance as well as the stipend for tuition. In addition, there are assistantships for which the graduate student is assigned to a particular department to teach undergraduate classes, correct papers, or assist in laboratories. Sometimes, to fulfill these assignments, the student is not permitted to take a full academic load, which means that it will take longer than two or three semesters to complete a master's program and may take twice as long. Under these circumstances, it is impossible to know in advance exactly how much the program will cost.

Costs of education vary from year to year and are affected by the amount of financial aid available in the form of state scholarships, fellowships, and assistantships. In addition, part-time work in writing and editing may be available on campus, especially to technical writing and journalism students.

Scholarships, Fellowships, and Internships

You will find a variety of financial aid sources available at colleges and universities. The following is not a complete list, but it will give you some idea of where to apply for assistance.

Several professional associations offer scholarships through their education programs. For example, the Society for Technical Communication awards scholarships to students enrolled in technical communication programs at universities, colleges, junior colleges, and technical schools. See the appendix for the contact information of numerous organizations that might provide financial assistance.

It's also a good idea to check with community groups to see whether any offer scholarships. Rotary International and the Elks Club are just two organizations that offer scholarships. In addition, some unions offer scholarships and financial aid opportunities for children of members. Be sure to investigate all the options while making your plans.

3

GETTING STARTED

In Chapter 4 you will read about the actual work technical writers do, who hires them, and the types of places at which they work. But first, let's get an overview of the employment outlook in technical writing and some tips on landing the job of your choice.

Employment Outlook

The employment outlook for technical writers is good; in fact, it is the most promising of all writing professions. Several factors have contributed to the strength of this field.

One of these is that the well-trained technical writer is at the forefront of new and groundbreaking techniques. If you are a student, prepare yourself for this career by getting a solid background in the sciences, particularly in computer science. With this foundation, you should be able to fill the needs of industrial and government employers.

Another factor is that the well-trained writer can bridge the gap between technical subjects and nontechnical readers. One thing is certain—at some point, everyone must learn something about technology, even if only to use an appliance by reading an appliance user manual. The general public buys the products and services that technology makes possible, but it is the technical writer who informs and persuades the public through reports, manuals, news releases, articles, and advertising. This need for reader-friendly materials that can be easily understood and followed by the nontechnical public will keep technical writers in demand.

According to the U.S. Bureau of Labor Statistics, employment for all kinds of writers and editors is expected to increase between 9 and 17 percent through 2014, with technical writers leading the pack in employment growth. Employment of salaried writers and editors for newspapers, periodicals, book publishers, and nonprofit organizations is expected to increase as demand for these publications grows, particularly in the online environment. Magazines and other periodicals increasingly are developing market niches, appealing to readers with special interests. Businesses and organizations are developing newsletters and websites, and more companies are experimenting with publishing materials directly on the Internet. Online publications and services are growing in number and sophistication, spurring the demand for writers and editors, especially those with Web experience. Advertising and public relations agencies, which also are growing, should be another source of new jobs.

Opportunities should be best for technical writers and those with training in a specialized field. Demand for technical writers and writers with expertise in areas such as law, medicine, or economics is expected to increase because of the continuing expansion of scientific and technical information and the need to communicate it to others. Legal, scientific, and technological developments and discoveries generate demand for people to interpret technical information for a more general audience. Rapid growth and change in the high-technology and electronics industries result in a greater need for people to write users' guides, instruction manuals, and training materials. This work requires people who not only are technically skilled as writers but also are familiar with the subject area.

In addition to job openings created by employment growth, some openings will arise as experienced workers retire, transfer to other occupations, or leave the labor force. Replacement needs are relatively high in this occupation; many freelancers leave because they cannot earn enough money.

Researching the Field

Technical writing is a highly specialized profession requiring a combination of technical training and competence in communication. As part of your career preparation, you should begin to consider employment opportunities long before you graduate from college.

You can find a considerable amount of information about how to get started in technical writing from a number of sources, including ads in newspapers and journals, brochures prepared by professional societies, professional websites, and books. If you are seriously thinking about becoming a technical writer, you can take a number of steps that will help you obtain professional guidance and information.

• Explore the education portion of the website of the Society for Technical Communication. STC provides support to teachers and students of technical communication through programs, scholarships, grants and loans, annual conferences, and seminars as well as a database of academic programs worldwide. Contact information for the STC is given in the appendix.

• If you are still in high school, make an appointment with your guidance counselor to discuss the profession of technical writing. A lot depends on whether you are planning to continue your education by going to college or taking other specialized training courses. In either case, counselors should be able to guide you to resources about technical writing careers or tell you where it can be obtained.

Don't be shy about talking to professionals working in the field or professors of technical writing. Contact your local college and ask to set up an appointment with a professor who also serves as a student advisor. This type of information-gathering session will help make sure you're on the right track with your career choice.

• If you are in college, talk with the official in charge of the placement office. Job placement is a service provided by almost every institution these days. Throughout the year, college placement officers are in contact with the human resources managers of companies and other organizations that are looking for people to fill important technical writing jobs.

But don't depend entirely on the college placement office. There are many excellent teachers working in technical communications. If your school has a technical writing program, talk with the person who teaches it. Nine times out of ten, this instructor will have good contacts with business and industrial firms. Contacts of this kind are probably the most valuable way of getting started in the profession.

• Job contacts also can be established by directly contacting the supervisors and administrators of the publications departments of companies. To establish these contacts, read the large industrial ads for technical writers in the newspapers, as well as those published on the Web, especially those in highly developed industrial areas. If you can't find a specific name to send your inquiry to, send it to the director of publications. In time, your letter will filter through to the right person, and you will be able to set up an informational interview, which could possibly lead to a job contact or a full-time job.

• Surf the Web for ideas. Websites and databases are updated on a regular basis. The following are agency and organization websites that will help make your job search a bit easier.

The Computer Merchant Ltd.
www.tcml.com

Documentation Strategies, Inc.
www.docstrats.com

Essential Data Corp.
www.essentialdata.com

PVA Global
www.pvaglobal.com

STC Career Center
http://jobs.stc.org/home

Researching the Jobs

If you would like to enter the industrial world, or any other occupation for that matter, you should do some groundwork. First assess what you have to offer, and then do some research into the company in which you are interested to see whether you can meet its requirements.

You can do much of your own research. Remember that certain kinds of companies, such as chemical, electronic, and aeronautical industries; contracting companies; research institutes; and government agencies are more in need of technical writers than others.

Most libraries have a copy of *Standard and Poor's Index*. This reference book lists a great deal of information about major companies, such as where they are located, what they manufacture, divisions in the company, and branches in various cities and countries. You can also visit its website at www.standardandpoors.com for information.

There are other helpful books and publications that you can consult for valuable career information. Plan to spend some time in your local public library, university library, or a community college library getting the information you need.

As mentioned earlier, the Society of Technical Writers maintains a database of job openings. Other sites do, too. See the appendix for a list of professional societies.

Don't forget about Internet job sites. Both Monster.com and Careerbuilder.com are examples of sites that allow you to post a résumé, search for jobs, and even get help in preparing your résumé and conducting your job search.

Sample Job Titles

Here are some job and title samples taken from ads in various professional journals.

- Editor for consumer electronics
- Senior editor for trade magazine
- Editor for medical journals; monographs on clinical medicine

- Editor, nursing journal
- Editor/writer to report on technology in robotics field
- Editor/writer for medical journal
- Business writer for management consulting firm
- Editor to coordinate production of proposals for computer services
- Experienced writer of government proposals
- Newsletter editor for part-time work in university for space research group

The Career Center of the STC website is a tremendous resource for anyone seeking a position in this field. Society members can post résumés, view job listings, and create a personal job alert and a career account to track their job search.

Letters of Application

Once you have the name of a potential employer, you are ready to write a letter of application with which you will include a résumé of your accomplishments. There are various ways to write this letter, which is also called a cover letter, but regardless of the format you use, certain points should be followed.

The application letter should be short, but it should include pertinent information about your background and the type of position you are seeking. If you are sending the letter in response to a specific ad, mention the date, publication or website, and job title. If a mutual friend or professional contact has suggested that you contact the company, you should mention it. Strive for a tone of enthusiasm, knowledge of the requirements of the company to which you are applying, and adequate training, all of which will catch the eye of the recipient.

Your application letter will be accompanied by a résumé, but it is best not to mention the attached résumé until the end of the letter. If you point it out too soon, the reader of your cover letter will turn to the résumé before finishing what it is you have to say about yourself.

Résumés

Preparing a résumé falls outside the scope of this book, but there are many resources you can consult on résumé writing and formatting. The Recommended Reading section at the end of the book includes some titles that can help you choose the best format and style.

Whichever type of résumé you decide to prepare, remember that, like your cover letter, it must be perfect. You can't proofread either document too many times, especially since you are applying for a writing position. A sloppy presentation or poor writing will not convince employers that you're the technical writer they are seeking.

Be sure to submit your letter and résumé in the format requested. For example, if an employer requests electronic résumés, don't mail a hard copy instead. Following that initial instruction is important, so be prepared to submit your credentials as requested.

Salaries

According to the Society for Technical Communication, the median annual salary for entry-level technical writers was $42,500 in 2004. The median annual salary for midlevel nonsupervisory technical writers was $51,500, and for those in senior nonsupervisory positions, $66,000.

The U.S. Bureau of Labor Statistics reports that during the same period, median annual earnings for salaried technical writers were $53,490. The majority earned between $41,440 and $68,980, while the lowest 10 percent earned less than $32,490, and the highest 10 percent earned more than $86,780.

As you are looking at salaries, remember that certain basic principles do apply:

• Graduating with a bachelor's or master's degree in engineering or science can help you to command a higher beginning salary than a degree in English or some other nontechnical subject.

• A degree from certain prestigious colleges also usually adds to your marketability and may bring a higher salary than a degree from a lesser-known school.

• The higher your course grades, the more summer experience you've had, and the more you can display characteristics of ability and initiative, the higher your salary is likely to be.

• With a degree in an area such as electrical engineering and electronics, you may be in greater demand than students with training in other areas.

• As a beginning technical writer, you will most likely be evaluated very closely on the basis of your educational record, writing ability, and potential for being promoted.

4

Duties of the Technical Writer

With a degree in technical writing, you will be qualified to pursue any one of the career paths listed in Chapter 1, but some specializations seem to offer greater opportunities than others. In this chapter we examine the different specializations and the opportunities they present.

Technical Presses

Technical journalism surrounds us; in fact, the number of publications, periodicals, magazines, trade journals, and newspapers is so great that we take their existence for granted and hardly notice their presence. There are so many scientific and trade publications that it is impossible to cite a number with which everyone will agree. In addition, new publications are constantly appearing.

Scientific Journals

The text and subject matter of these publications range in complexity from the highly scientific *Journal of Organic Chemistry* to the very simplistic magazine *Popular Mechanics*. The *Journal of Organic Chemistry* is found only on the bookshelves of chemistry and technical libraries and in the offices of chemists. Naturally, most of its readers are organic chemists, and it is not generally available to the public at large. Similar journals would be the *American Journal of Physiology*, the *Journal of the American Medical Association*, the *New England Journal of Medicine*, *Chemical Engineering*, *Brain Research*, and many others.

The articles published in scientific journals are generally written by the scientists who are involved with the work. In most cases, the articles present the findings of extensive research projects. The authors' names appear directly under the titles, followed by the institutions with which they are affiliated. In academic institutions, papers presented for publication often are written by the graduate students who actually did the work, while the professors in charge provide guidance and lend their names to the final publication. Sometimes, professors who did their own research hire or supervise graduate students to do the actual writing, although the students in this case would remain anonymous. In industrial concerns, the preparation of papers is usually done by technical writers to enable the authors to engage in "more productive work."

Papers presented to scientific journals for publication undergo a process called *peer review*. After the paper has been submitted to a journal, the managing editor sends copies to recognized authorities in the field who carefully examine the paper for originality of work, correctness of experimental procedures, and validity of the claims. Very few manuscripts are accepted after an initial review. In the majority of cases, the paper is returned to the authors for revision, based on the constructive comments of the reviewers. If the reviewers have major objections to the paper, they recommend rejection and state the reasons for their decision, telling the authors what they must do to satisfy the objections. The majority of authors will comply with the reviewers' comments and do additional work to make the paper acceptable for publication. If a paper has been rejected by one journal, it is not acceptable for the authors to present it to a different journal without disclosing the first rejection. It is not unusual for a paper to be presented and rejected several times before it is finally published. This process reduces plagiarism and fraud and ensures scientific integrity.

Scientific journals are vitally important to the community they serve. They allow the dissemination of valuable information and research results that can aid other scientists in their own work. In addition, researchers whose work is funded by grants are obligated to write up and submit the results of their work, and the number of accepted papers serves as a strong recommendation when the scientist applies for future funding. The same is generally true for those employed by academic institutions, where promotions and tenure can be influenced by the number of an applicant's publications. "Publish or perish" is a popular expression in both settings.

Trade Magazines

There are many scientific and technical magazines that are sold to the general public. These include *Scientific American, Science, PC World, Psychology Today, Popular Science,* and the aforementioned *Popular Mechanics.* The first two magazines often contain articles every bit as sophisticated and mathematical in content as those published by scientific and medical associations. Magazines like *Popu-*

lar Science and *Popular Mechanics* are intended for people who may know little about science or technology but who are interested in these subjects. The writers for these magazines must be able to interpret and present scientific material in such a way as to make it understandable and attractive to their lay readers. The success and longevity of these magazines speak for themselves.

Company Magazines

Your first job as a technical writer may be with a company magazine, such as Raytheon's *Technology Today*, which highlights the company's technological projects. Sometimes the table of contents contains a wide variety of articles on technology. At other times, an issue is devoted to discussing a particular field in depth. In either case, you would probably be writing some articles of your own or editing other people's articles.

The primary reason engineers and scientists write articles is to communicate knowledge. They may be engaged in research, may have developed a new technique, or may have been called on to publicize something for their companies. There is also the prestige factor—the author's professional reputation is enhanced when his or her articles are accepted and published.

In working on a company magazine, you will be helping others prepare their articles. Most of these magazines consist of three departments: editorial, advertising, and production. As a writer, you will be assigned to the editorial department, but if you should demonstrate advertising or production ability, you may be able to transfer to these departments.

One of the best features of working for company magazines is that they are likely to operate with small staffs on a fairly informal basis. This often results in interesting working conditions, and you may find yourself doing a variety of things, such as writing original articles, editing articles written by others, editorializing, and carrying out special assignments.

Sometimes a company magazine can be published by only one or two people working with a printing firm and outside advertising staff, or it may be produced in-house using computers and laser printers. It can have a much larger staff, including editors, proofreaders, copyreaders, illustrators, office support staff, and an editorial board.

Working on a company magazine will bring you in contact with many people, which will require patience and tact on your part. In the first place, you must persuade the engineers and scientists to write for you, and they can be very busy people who often are not particularly interested in whether they get published.

Most editorial boards start preparing an issue of a magazine by having a "think session." From this starting point, many of the things said about company magazines can be equally applied to commercial technical magazines.

A think session occurs when the magazine's staff gets together to decide what will go into a particular issue. And you may be surprised to learn that magazines work six, seven, or eight months in advance. It takes weeks and weeks to produce an issue, from the idea for the first article until the magazine is wrapped up and sent to the mailroom.

One of the most fruitful sources for papers and articles is conferences attended by company employees. Papers delivered at these gatherings often turn up as magazine articles. But such selection is planned with several factors in mind. The editor may decide to consult the public relations department to determine what is going on in the company that will appeal to readers. In addition, management must be consulted, because in the long run, responsibility for the magazine rests with the company's administrators.

Once you have received a manuscript from an author, the real job of writing and editing begins. This is when the experience you have gained in your writing classes will come into play. Although the people from whom you get the material may (or may not) know how to write, it is very likely that they haven't paid attention to their potential readers. So determining the audience becomes your job, and you must fit the style and tone of the piece to the audience you are trying to interest. For example, you may have to write a completely new opening for an engineer's paper to attract readers' attention. Here is where your job is perhaps most satisfying—and sometimes most frustrating—as you try to weld unorganized material into acceptable form. Changes of any sort, of course, necessitate conferences with the author, who must be as satisfied with the final product as you are.

The manuscript must be reviewed to be sure it fits the prescribed editorial format. It is then turned over to the appropriate staff members for illustration and layout.

Professional Magazines

Professional magazines are published by professional societies. Some examples of these are the *Journal of Chemical Education*, published by the American Chemical Society; *Civil Engineering*, by the American Society of Civil Engineers; and the *American Journal of Nursing*, by the American Nurses Association.

A great many journals are read by audiences outside of the company. For this reason, a technical journalist must be able to gauge the interest and needs of these external readers and to produce material that is "reader friendly." The ability to analyze these readers becomes of paramount importance. If you think that you have this ability, together with imagination and proper motivation, technical journalism may be your career goal.

In general, the technical press—magazines, journals, and publishing houses—employs fewer writers than other areas. However, interest in this field is increasing as publishers realize that second-best writing on technical subjects is not enough, and that in a highly competitive field, they must employ technically trained writers.

One professional in the field has noted that an increasing number of journalistic jobs are open to engineers and scientists. Some of these opportunities include science reporting for newspapers; professional and trade journal writing and editing; technical and industrial publicity work; science writing for radio and television; and freelance technical writing.

This increase reflects a growing interest in engineering and scientific news at both the lay and technical levels. Advertisers also have realized the potential in the technical advertising field, which makes the technical writer almost indispensable. The same thing is true of technical publicity, as advertising agencies are trying to locate technically trained writers or engineers with a flair for writing.

Promotional Writing

Advertising brochures, pamphlets, and catalogs are published and distributed by companies to sell their products and to attract new customers. The job of a technical advertising copywriter is closely related to that of a promotional and publicity writer. The technical writer who works in this area is usually employed by an independent advertising agency whose clients are companies that need outside help in advertising their products.

An example of this type of writing is the literature that pharmaceutical salespeople give to physicians along with free samples of their companies' products. Similarly, salespeople for agricultural companies visit farmers with advertising material to induce them to use their seeds, fertilizers, pesticides, herbicides, animal feeds, and farm implements. Although this promotional material does contain a lot of factual, reliable data and information, it must, nevertheless, be classified as self-serving.

Many technical writers prepare sales or promotional literature for a variety of merchandise such as automobiles, home appliances, and consumer electronics goods. Brochures are printed by the manufacturer for potential customers, and these brochures contain lots of technical data about the products that customers are considering buying. The brochure also will contain other information describing the products' virtues and attractiveness. This is best illustrated by what happens when you visit an automobile showroom to buy a new car—not only does the salesperson describe the merits of the car you are interested in, but he or she also hands you a very attractive brochure that describes its engineering, performance, safety, and appearance features. The salesperson then points out certain items in the brochure, hoping to make the car purchase irresistible to you.

Technical sales literature comes in many forms. In addition to the auto brochure described above, it could be a pamphlet describing the construction of a turbine for a government project. Or it could be information for a new product soon to be released to the industrial market. The publicity department of a company may handle all of these activities—preparing news releases for trade journals, newspapers, and magazines as well as brochures to be sent to potential customers. These written items usually combine sales appeal and technical information.

The procedure for preparing a sales brochure is about the same as for other pieces of technical writing. First the project itself must be authorized, in this case, by management. Then a number of things take place, sometimes concurrently.

You will first collect all the information about the product or equipment that you possibly can. To become totally familiar with the background of the project, you may have some earlier publications to serve as guides. You will visit the departments responsible for the design, construction, and manufacturing of the product to get its views on the consumer, the kind of company it is, and anything else that will help the booklet put across its message.

To work on sales literature, you must be aware of how much money can be spent on the brochure and how many copies are going to be distributed. These two factors will sometimes determine whether the brochure is to be printed by the publications department or given to an outside printer.

You will then design the brochure, working in close cooperation with a designer. This is where this kind of publication differs from some others. In sales literature, the layout of the brochure is extremely important, involving questions of shape, size, color, and illustrations.

The copy in an advertising brochure is frequently subordinate to the illustrations, and the writer must decide how much copy to write to support the illustrations. At this point the actual writing of copy begins, followed by checking and revising and all the other stages that go into any industrial writing.

Technical Advertising

Manufacturers of machines, instruments, and other industrial products spend millions on another kind of promotion—technical advertising. Sargent-Welch, a supplier of science education equipment and apparatuses, placed this ad in an issue of *R & D* magazine.

> A Pump for Every Vacuum Range: You've got the vacuum requirements—we've got the pumps. Pick your own range and there's a Sargent-Welch pump right there ready to go to work—from the famous Duo-Seal oil-seated rotary vane pump line to the ultra-high, ultra-clean vacuum Turbomotor line of turbo-molecular pumps with capabilities to 1,600 liters per second. Or maybe one of our New Director direct drive pumps will fit your application better.

What we have given you is only the copy, or description, written by a technical writer either in the company's advertising department or in an agency hired by the company. The ad also features illustrations, various kinds of type, and other attention-getting devices.

It should be apparent that to write copy for technical advertising you must know something about the technical part of the product. You also should know enough about graphics, illustrations, and charts to give directions to the printer. And you should have some familiarity with composition, how various items are positioned on the page.

So, as a technical writer in advertising, you may work in the advertising department of a company or you may get a job with an outside agency specializing in technical advertising. In either case, your job duties and projects will be similar. One private advertising agency lists the following specialties.

- Market research
- Program planning
- Publication advertising
- Direct mail advertising

- Publicity
- Technical literature
- Merchandising aids
- Power Point presentations

As a writer of technical advertising, you may be involved in institutional advertising, for example, by writing general copy that creates a favorable image of the company in the public mind. New products must be advertised or the marketing of old products changed to such an extent that they seem new. The advertiser also may call attention to the service and maintenance offered by the company.

Robert D. Towne, an advertising executive, has outlined some points that help to explain the duties of the technical advertiser, as summarized here.

- Advertising writing is different from other kinds of writing because it is persuasive. In other words, even though information is at the heart of advertising, its main purpose is to persuade people to buy a product or a service or to have a problem solved. To many writers, this offers an interesting switch from the usual technical writing.
- The technical copywriter must think not only in terms of writing, but also in terms of two other factors: the sales idea and illustration. These will bring the writer in close contact with the sales force of a company and provide the stimulating experience of working with fine illustrators.

Technical advertisers also have their think sessions, as ideas are tossed around for review and the objectives of the advertising campaign are discussed. Dozens of ideas will be looked at and discarded, but somewhere will be the one that will please most everyone, especially the client.

News Releases

Another kind of technical promotion is the news release, which may be in the form of a news story or an article for a magazine or website. The real reason for preparing a news release is to supply information (and advertising) that editors will want to include in their publications. It must be carefully written to present the information clearly and concisely, with language chosen to interest and impress the editors to whom it is submitted.

The technical writer often gets involved in news releases, operating from either a regular publications office or an advertising department. The considerable skill involved in preparing news releases is acknowledged by one editor, who points out that the presentation to the editor is as important as the news contained in the release. The most successful news releases are those that are run in the greatest number of beneficial spots.

If you work in this area, you must ensure the consistent acceptance of your news releases. You can do this by knowing the interests of the particular editors and of the magazines' readers; by preparing valid, newsworthy releases; and by submitting the releases in the proper, easy-to-use format that facilitates their use.

For individual readers, the news release often comes in another form called *new product information*. This variation must be short and to the point, demonstrating confidence in the product, describing it briefly, and requiring a minimum amount of space. Here is an example of new product information.

> This Hand-Held Anemometer will easily measure air speed wherever your hand can reach. The accurate hand-held one-piece unit weighs only three ounces and requires no external probe. Running on sapphire bearings, its freely turning turbine will rotate at a speed directly proportional to wind speed. The rotation is passively sensed by an infrared light beam, which adds no friction. An integrated circuit even converts the signal to your choice of units (feet per minute, mph, meters per second, or knots) and feeds it to a three-digit LED display. This cleverly designed instrument, which operates with three AAA batteries, measures 4½ by 4½ by 1⅛ inches.

It has been estimated that daily newspapers receive from 25 to 250 news releases a day and that approximately one of every 25 is used. As you can see, dealing with news releases requires special skills, and many of them were learned on the job.

Public Relations

As a member of a company's public relations department, you may be asked to determine what customers think of the company's products. Working with others in your department, you can expect to be given the assignment of planning a sales promotion campaign not only to maintain the loyalty of your customers but also to win over the affections and dollars of your competitors' clients. Here are a few examples of some representative projects.

- Developing brochures, press releases, and other materials that explain technical products and processes
- Preparing feature articles for trade and technical magazines that describe new technologies

- Writing speeches and presentations that will be delivered by organization executives at various meetings
- Preparing the company's annual report
- Developing audiovisual presentations
- Preparing position and technical papers for presentation to governmental agencies

Today's corporate managers and executives seldom have time to get involved in the actual work of speech writing and preparation details. They will decide on the theme and the main topics to be stressed, and they may offer guidelines as to how they wish to present and embellish their speech. But the rest is up to the publicity department to "give the boss what he wants." If the speech is deemed important enough, outside resources and assistance may be enlisted for the preparation.

Instruction Manuals

Publications departments engaged in producing manuals and instruction books show the most expansion and turnover of personnel for technical writers. You will find that when you apply for a job, the greatest response will come from employers needing technical writers who specialize in either manuals or research reports.

The need to transform masses of data into structured, intelligible information has created the ever-growing information industry. Without any identifiable plants, buildings, offices, or factories, the information industry exists in myriad companies, governmental agencies, laboratories, colleges, and universities in the form of individuals and departments whose sole function is to produce objective, understandable information for laypeople, regardless of the subject at hand. Consequently, technical writing is not limited to topics connected with science, technology, and engineering. The ability of technical writers to convert raw data into usable information has received widespread recognition as a special skill and a talent. Companies that must sell the products they manufacture realize the importance of having technical writers on staff, and service organizations likewise must inform the public about their activities to sell what they have to offer.

A table of contents of a typical industrial manual that accompanies every manufactured item usually includes a general description; a theory of operation; instruction on installation, adjustment, and operation; and finally several drawings of the item. An instruction manual must be prepared to tell the customer how to install and operate the product safely and often includes troubleshooting suggestions.

The people who prepare these manuals are among the most skilled in the technical writing profession. To work in this area, you must be thoroughly familiar with the equipment and must write in a clear, concise, simple, and unequivocal manner for those installers and operators who may have a limited education and vocabulary or even limited knowledge of English. It is ultimately your responsibility to oversee the manual from inception to final pages for printing. Approximately one-third of all those who are employed as technical writers work exclusively on instruction and maintenance manuals.

Even before an instruction book can be started, a number of steps must be considered and the duties of each staff member must be well defined.

1. When a new instruction book has been authorized, the manager reviews what is required, issues a project work order, and assigns various people to work on it.

2. The writer prepares a preliminary outline of the instruction book based on predetermined specifications. This will include not only what must be written, but also a proposed list of illustrations.

3. The manager calls a conference, which includes the writer, illustrator, copyeditor, production editor, and, if possible, the project engineer.

4. All of these people consider the following: scope and contents of the outline, date on which the equipment the instruction book is supporting must be delivered, where the instruction book fits into the overall schedule for all publications, existing workload in the department, amount of work required to complete the instruction book, time required to have it printed and reproduced, and the deadline date for each section of the book.

5. The manager informs the person or department that originally ordered the instruction book when it can be delivered.

6. The production editor draws up a schedule for the work to show how the various staff members will contribute to it.

Who are the staff members we have been mentioning? The production editor is in charge overall and sees that the particular instruction book is worked on, completed, and delivered on schedule. The technical editor, or copyeditor, edits the written part of the instruction book and, in general, reviews it for style, accuracy of expression, grammar, and punctuation. The product engineer is in direct charge of the device or system for which the instruction book is intended.

Following are the procedures that the writer may follow when handed an assignment to put an instruction book together.

1. Collect and study available production drawings (schematics, wiring, and assembly diagrams). Obtain related written informa-

tion already in existence (development reports, test procedures, and instruction books on similar equipment). If possible, obtain the equipment for further study.

2. Meet with the project engineer and other responsible personnel to obtain additional data.

3. Based on information from steps 1 and 2, review the preliminary outline and list of illustrations. Revise this preliminary outline to make a working outline.

4. Deliver the list of required illustrations to the illustration section and discuss how they will be produced.

5. Begin writing the instruction book. During the writing procedure, prepare sketches, revise existing production drawings, and describe requirements for illustrations. Identify illustrations by figure number and title and forward them to the appropriate illustration section.

6. As writing continues, check the illustrator's rough drawings.

7. Make arrangements with the photography section for necessary photographs.

8. Review the completed draft. Edit the copy for technical accuracy, format, content, and correct references to illustrations and paragraphs.

9. Submit corrected draft to the editorial section for preliminary review.

10. Following conferences with the copyeditor, prepare final draft and forward it to the editorial section.

11. After receiving the reviewers' copies of the final draft, check and incorporate reviewers' comments into the master copy.

12. Review the manuscript completely, rechecking all illustration and paragraph references, format, and paragraphing for technical accuracy.

13. Send the completed manuscript to the editorial section.

14. When galley proofs have been received from the printer, review carefully, correct, and forward the corrected galleys to the editorial section. The importance of careful proofreading cannot be overemphasized.

In any publications department that prepares instruction books, the writer is involved in the following four phases.

1. **Research.** The writer analyzes the requirements of the project, collects the preliminary data, examines and interprets the data, and prepares the outline.
2. **Development.** In the development stage, the outline prepared in the research stage is used by the writer as a guide in writing the text and in determining the illustration requirements of the first draft.
3. **Prototype.** The research and development stages produce a prototype or model of the instruction book.
4. **Production.** In the production stage, all effort is concentrated on mechanically producing the book.

These, then, are the specific duties of the manuals writer; but in terms of procedures, they are fairly representative of any kind of job the technical writer may tackle.

Proposals

Writing proposals is very important to most manufacturing companies. In general, a contract usually precedes the start of any manufacturing operation. The contract may be between the company and a government agency, between the manufacturer and a supplier of parts and materials, or between the manufacturer and the company that is buying the finished product. A contract proposal is prepared in which the product and the standards to which it is supposed to adhere are submitted to the purchaser. The two parties to the contract then work out the final purchase terms. Contract proposals probably rank next in number to reports and manuals.

Government agencies, frequently branches of the military, as well as private industries and foundations regularly solicit proposals from suitable companies to conduct research on a particular problem or to design a mechanism or facility. These requests for proposals (RFPs) may involve anything from investigating the socioeconomic impact of a new manufacturing facility through developing new traffic control patterns. They may even involve the design and manufacture of new military equipment.

Companies responding to RFPs must design proposals, often several volumes long, which convince the government agency or industry that their company's suggested research project or design best fits their requirements and is worthy of funding. Often these proposals must be submitted within a short time after receipt of their request, so expertise in proposal writing is essential.

Proposals may seek funding in the millions of dollars. A company's success and its continued existence depend upon having its proposals accepted and funded. Without funded projects, there is no new business and no reason for the organization to continue to exist. Academic research units are in much the same position: without funding obtained through proposals, they cannot continue their work.

In all companies involved with proposal preparation, the technical writer serves a crucial function, and the ability to write concrete, persuasive proposals within tight deadlines is a highly marketable skill. Later, of course, these same writers may be involved in the preparation of the report and impact statements growing out of the research projects.

Regardless of the type of proposal involved, it is a vital element in all companies, large or small, in government agencies, and in universities. So, when you read that General Electric or Lawrence Livermore Laboratory or Lockheed has received grant money, you may be sure that a proposal writer was involved in obtaining the grant.

Research and Development

Research and development is the starting point of manufacturing; therefore, there will always be a place for technical writers in public and private research institutes. Research reports of all kinds must be written to provide vital information for product development and manufacturing.

Government-Sponsored Activities

Opportunities for technical writers are also available with programs that are sponsored by the governments of the United States and Canada. Good starting points are the U.S. Department of Defense and the Canadian Department of National Defence.

As an example, the U.S. Department of Defense maintains a Defense Technical Information Center (DTIC), which provides centralized operation of department services for the acquisition, storage, retrieval, and dissemination of scientific and technical information to support the department's research, development, engineering, and studies programs. Many universities and private research foundations also have government-sponsored programs. Additionally, the DTIC reports on all writings that it deems significant, even on work that was not government funded. This is a staggering task. In this country alone, there are thousands of industrial concerns ranging in size from Lockheed Martin to small shops that manufacture just one or two specialty items.

Employees of DTIC work in one of seven major categories, with the classification *technical information specialist* of particular interest to technical writers. The job is described as follows.

> Technical information specialists are primarily concerned with the direction, administration, development, coordination, and performance of work involved in processing and transmitting scientific, technical, or other specialized information. Requires a broad knowledge of one or more professional, scientific, or technical disciplines or fields of interest to understand the significance and relationship of the concepts and ideas contained in the information area and a practical knowledge of documentation or library techniques.

DTIC headquarters is located in Fort Belvoir, Virginia, and there are five additional locations throughout the country. Visit www.dtic.mil for complete information on this interesting career option.

In both Canada and the United States, many of the larger companies that manufacture highly complex machines, such as combat aircraft, computers, and nuclear power plants for submarines, also maintain huge research laboratories. Written reports on all of their activities, including ideas for new or modified products, must be submitted to the government. The organizations that submit these reports do so not only because they are required to, but also because they hope that this information will lead to new contracts and revenues.

Trade Journals and House Organs

Almost every technical, commercial, and trade organization, and business association, no matter how small, publishes a monthly magazine that contains material of interest to its members. The articles included may discuss such subjects as the effects of crime, tax laws, or new marketing techniques on business.

Every company that has publicly traded stock issues an annual report to its stockholders. Some of these reports are magnificent beyond imagination and are often a staggering twenty pages long. A lot of work, money, and effort are expended in preparing these annual reports, which are intended not only to inform but to impress the reader.

Many large companies also publish and distribute *house organs* (technical magazines the companies produce) to their stockholders and libraries. An example is *The Lamp*, published by the Exxon-Mobil Corporation. This magazine presents articles in a narrative form about its far-flung operations, new technology it is adopting, its research projects, and its pro bono activities. These magazines are printed to present a favorable image of the company.

Special Projects

The wide variety of industrial concerns has created a need for special project writers. The vast field of research depends on the interchange of ideas, and because of this, many companies encourage their engineers and scientists to write papers for presentation at conferences and seminars. The preparation of a paper is a very time-consuming process.

Some companies, particularly those with large research staffs, have a technical publications department whose function is to assist employees in preparing and presenting papers. The writers may use report drafts to write the entire paper, subject to editing by the presenter. Graphs, photographs, and digital images are often an integral part of the presentation. In addition, the writer may coach the presenter in delivering the talk if he or she is shy or a novice public speaker. Many executives now employ technical writers as special assistants. By combining a flair for writing with a sound scientific background, these assistants help top management officials by writing progress reports for them or reviewing their speeches.

With the continuous introduction of new technology, the communications field is an ever-changing and expanding field. Technical writers will be preparing lectures and instructions to be delivered from DVDs, developing programs for data storage and retrieval systems, and performing a multitude of other communications jobs too numerous to mention. To succeed, the writer must be able to learn new communications and computer techniques as they occur.

Technical Reports

Technical reports are found in any library, especially those in universities and government installations that conduct research. The number of these reports on file throughout the world is staggering and requires advanced storage and retrieval systems to reduce the space that all of this written material requires and to make it more accessible to users.

Technical reports represent a very large part of an organization's publication output. They also represent a great amount of the time devoted by many technical writers and editors.

A final report is usually preceded by a series of progress reports, which are short documents indicating what has been accomplished at stated intervals and submitted to the contracting agency. Sometimes a technical writer helps with this work; at other times it is done entirely by the researchers. If the project is complicated and takes a long time to complete, a periodic report is written that consolidates a number of individual progress reports. The periodic report also may be edited by a technical writer. A technical editor will work on the project once the material submitted by the scientists is put together into a report. For example, the National Air and Space Administration (NASA) spells out certain specifications for the format of its reports. This format must be checked by the editor, along with grammar, punctuation, and other stylistic features.

Report writing is one of the main categories of technical writing. As technology matures and as companies continue to grow, the volume of records and communications also grows. Reports are the usual method for many of the larger companies to coordinate their various activities, especially if research is a primary occupation. The publications department will be responsible for the reporting, and a technical editor will be assigned to supervise the undertaking.

Some engineering and scientific organizations exist primarily for testing, research, and experimentation. Their main product is not the manufacturing of goods, but the production of reports and papers describing research procedures and results. In this endeavor, the technical writer is as necessary as the researcher.

There are many kinds of reports, depending on who will use the information being reported. External reports go outside the company to clients, government bureaus, and libraries. They become the basis for further research. Internal reports are written solely for use within the company. They may be service reports, progress reports, and maintenance reports, to name only a few.

The reporting skill of the technical writer is important to most technical fields because reporting is basic to the success of the enterprise. The techniques of reporting are the foundation of instruction books, technical papers, and various forms of promotion and publicity.

A basic approach to technical writing is suggested by Matt Young in *The Technical Writer's Handbook*. In his preface he states: "It would be very easy to show how technical or report writing differed from other writing. My purpose, however, is to stress the similarities. Writing is for communication." Along these lines, he presents a few simple rules.

1. Write the way you talk; then polish.
2. Be explicit.
3. Write for the uninformed reader.

He continues by stating, "Many technical writers, unfortunately, seem to forget that their intention is to communicate, and they write as if for themselves. Their papers are insufficiently explanatory, and they are written with little or no regard for style or clarity. . . ." Even relatively good technical writing is frequently characterized by long, complicated sentences and difficult prose.

Young even points out that important papers may be ignored because no one can understand them, so the work about which they are written remains to be discovered independently by someone else!

Audiovisual Scriptwriting

You might not realize that technical writers can work in scriptwriting, but they are important contributors to training, instructional, and documentary films. And while many technical writers remain anonymous, those working in scriptwriting generally receive credit along with everyone else who worked on the project.

In general, these projects are produced by private film and television studios or even by large companies that have their own production facilities. The films and tapes are broadcast by private or public television stations. Some films, such as the Civil War documentary by Ken Burns, are so well done that they attain widespread fame.

Training Films

Audiovisual productions cover a wide range of topics. They are used for training personnel in industry, hospitals, and the armed forces. Private companies produce films that are distributed to their customers to teach their personnel how to install and operate newly purchased equipment. Schools use disks, tapes, and films for instructional purposes. Audiovisual presentations are popular at all educational levels from elementary through graduate school and for adult education.

The most popular method of training had long been the video, but that has now been largely replaced by the DVD because of its effectiveness in holding the viewer's attention. As a technical writer working on such a project, you need to remember that the DVD must complement the printed material so that it becomes a visual aid to encourage the viewers to think about what they have just seen. Also, consider how the visual presentation will provide the basis for class discussions about its subject matter, which is the purpose of audiovisual projects.

In preparing a script, think about how it will look to the viewer and what effect your material will have on the audience. Once the script is written, consider what cinematography techniques you could employ to enhance the value and effectiveness of your work. This is an opportunity to give your creative imagination a workout. To create a great script, consider the following suggestions.

1. Determine the nature of your audience.
2. Do extensive research on your subject before you write a single line.
3. Simplify your message.
4. Tell a creative, visual story.
5. Write narration with eloquence, and dialogue with character.
6. Work with the director and the production crew throughout the entire filmmaking process.

A smart scriptwriter will take advantage of the expertise of all who are associated with the project. By soliciting their advice, cooperation, and suggestions, you will make your job easier and ensure the success of your film. A successful DVD will make the members of your audience receptive to your message and leave them feeling that they have learned something valuable.

Technical Films and DVDs

The technical or scientific film can be an effective way of selling a company's services or products. Film and DVDs play an increasingly important role in the training of technical and nontechnical employees and present another area in which the trained technical communicator can find stimulating employment. Scriptwriters do most of the technical writing in the production of films and discs. This position can be interesting because it involves a multifaceted medium—communication that is linked with visual aids. Technical films are used for a variety of reasons:

• A film or DVD cuts across many audiences. It may be interesting to a large group of people and yet, at the same time, have a more specialized appeal to a particular smaller group.

• It can accomplish things that the product by itself may not be able to do and that a still photograph can do in only a limited way. Through drawings and cartoons, the film or video can enlarge views, reduce them, allow one to see inside a device, linger over it, and repeat it—all in motion.

• Films and DVDs have impact. Research has revealed that the combination of sight and sound impresses ideas and facts most emphatically upon the audience.

Once the central idea for the film has been determined, the manuscript is written that will be put together with action shots to make the final film. As the scriptwriter, you must decide what type of audience is being targeted—whether it is a group of specialists, managers, or people who are unfamiliar with the subject. This is a most critical stage for the technical scriptwriter.

Motion picture production is a complicated and costly procedure. If you decide to pursue a career in scriptwriting, it would be a good idea to get some training in this kind of writing in high school or college. And, although it isn't absolutely necessary, you will certainly benefit by knowing something about photography. Courses in cinematography would be advisable as well.

You'll have to visit shooting sites to become familiar with the location to be described in the script. And just as with any other writer, you must have an in-depth understanding of the product.

The story line is usually developed first. This is a kind of synopsis, or highly concentrated version of speech, action, and narration. Next, the actual motion picture shooting begins, scene by scene. Then the film will be reviewed, and as the scriptwriter, you may be asked to write a narration, which is an accompaniment to what the action means, usually spoken by a professional actor or reader hired for the purpose. Words must be written that are easily spoken and understood and that synchronize with the photographed action.

Technical Translation

When most of us think of technical writing, we probably think of writing in English for an American audience about American technology, or perhaps writing in French for Canadian readers. But technical writing is universal, and a growing number of technical writers must work with translations—reading them, evaluating them, and sometimes retranslating them from poorly written English into usable prose.

If you can write in Spanish, German, French, Japanese, Chinese, Hindi, or any other major language, you may find a job waiting for you in technical communications.

You can see the importance of technical translations as a career in the science or business sections of the *New York Times* or the *Wall Street Journal*. It is also evident in the technical magazines found in engineering libraries or in online publications, where you can find articles that have been translated from foreign languages into English.

Most major businesses and industries are global in nature, and the majority of large American and Canadian companies could not exist in their present form if they weren't able to communicate with companies and people in other countries. The electronics, chemical, and transportation industries and computer hardware and software manufacturers, among others, need manuals, reports, research papers, and technical advertisements that can be translated into foreign languages.

Industry professionals agree that global companies must publish in a variety of languages to reach a world market. Customers want to read instructions and manuals in their own languages and are more likely to purchase a product that offers this option. This is something to keep in mind as you study to become a technical writer. If you have any facility in a foreign language, continue to develop it. You never know when it may be a skill that appeals to a prospective employer and will give you an advantage over other applicants.

Document Coordination

Many technical writers and editors move beyond technical writing into document coordination. This role is frequently a management position and may include responsibility for the entire document production process. This involves following each document from the initial meeting with the client, in which the document's specifications are determined and the various activities of the researchers clarified, to the final publication and presentation to the client. The document coordinator also is involved in any modifications made in response to suggestions from the clients.

This function demands strong interpersonal and managerial skills, because document coordination requires the ability to elicit material from the technical staff (who are often reluctant to write their research results), to interact with clients who may be uncertain of their actual needs in a particular document, and to work within personnel and budget constraints imposed by the company's administration.

The document coordinator often is required to visit job sites, help with data gathering and analysis, monitor the production of graphics, perform public relations functions on behalf of the company, control production costs, and perform a multitude of other activities. You may think these duties are beyond the scope of technical writing, but they quickly become great sources of challenge and satisfaction to the able individual.

Technical Editors

As in any editorial field, the primary responsibility of a technical editor is to constantly make decisions. Working in this field, you will have to decide whether the draft you are reviewing meets the quality criteria of the organization. You will make the final decision of whether to accept, reject, or revise the material, all with an eye to meeting a deadline. In effect, the quality of the final draft rests with you.

Among the many decisions a technical editor makes every day, a good number concern the form of a document rather than its substance. The editor must decide whether the words in the draft are the best ones to convey the author's meaning.

A technical editor at the Naval Explosive Ordnance Disposal Facility in Maryland has offered some thoughts about the profession. We think his words are a fitting summary for this section:

> We can say that the qualified technical editor is a sort of specialized jack-of-all-trades. He or she melds literature and science,

understands people, implements management policy, is objective, steers steadfastly toward a goal, and remembers minutiae. He or she can adroitly answer the writer's questions such as: Why are you taking the zap out of my draft? Why are you asking me what the test objectives are when I've already explained them in my report? What is your reason for requesting a rewrite with different conclusions? Why are you deleting the entire paragraph on potted electronic circuits?

Sample Job Advertisements

The following want ads show that interesting opportunities await those who have the requisite skills.

Video Scriptwriter

Firm that consults in corporate training and development is looking for a scriptwriter to create scripts for short video vignettes for a brand new project. Project would require full narrative scriptwriting for two to three key characters (project leader, their manager, and mentor) taking them through an entire project. Previous experience in creating client specific training or scriptwriting for similar projects is required.

Advertising Copywriter

Interested in fine and performing arts, foreign films, documentaries, and business training programs? Video distributor seeks versatile and self-disciplined copywriter with college degree and three to four years' experience to write copy and assist with video scripts and preparation. Applicant must have excellent verbal and written English skills and be detail-oriented.

The following job description is from an institute that serves a number of companies in the construction business.

> Secure and write construction-related articles through visits to design offices, building sites, and individuals involved. Report construction news including that obtained at sponsored conventions.
>
> Rewrite and amplify press release material received from outside sources. Edit construction-related papers and articles obtained from outside sources. Applicants should have experience or training in technical writing as well as in engineering and science.

To show the widespread opportunities in technical and professional writing, here is a sample job description from a pharmaceutical company.

> A leader in manufacturing and marketing pharmaceutical products on a worldwide basis, we seek a scientifically oriented writing professional who can initiate, develop, and coordinate our various communication requirements as follows: prepare scientific reports from raw medical data, investigators' brochures, package inserts, medical abstracts, and product information summaries. Review manuscripts for publication and marketing pieces for technical accuracy. Successful candidate should have a B.S. in chemistry, biology, or pharmacy, plus three years' writing experience.

Large vs. Small Companies

Large companies produce specialists. One person writes theory, another assembles parts lists, another coordinates with typists or illustrators. Most people are not involved with tasks outside their small area of activity.

In a smaller company (which is where many jobs may be located) a publications person, particularly a writer, must be a generalist. In a smaller publications department, one with perhaps from five to fifty people, a writer is usually responsible for a project from scheduling through printing. This includes outlining, writing, laying out rough schematics and drawings, coordinating with clerical help, directing the photography of equipment, making parts lists, planning the final layout of the book, and preparing the printer's assembly sheets.

A human resources manager in an electronics company states that the increased need for technical writers can be attributed to a growth in the use of computers by relatively unsophisticated employers. Computers are used in virtually every business, no matter how small. While large companies can afford to employ computer specialists, in small companies the employees themselves must become the specialists with the aid of properly written instructions.

This presents another possible employment situation to explore. If you are particularly interested in computer science, try the smaller companies, and make sure that you include computers in your technical writing curriculum.

Opportunities for Advancement

To move up the career ladder, the technical writer can become a supervisor or a department manager. Managers may supervise not only technical writers, but also the people engaged in illustration, graphics, photography, and distribution. In short, supervisors mobilize their departments to produce the specified printed matter, be it a report, manual, or technical article.

The technical writer works at the center of advances in communication. When you join an organization, you may find yourself learning new methods of using graphics, transferring ideas and facts to paper using current technology, and translating from one language to another. You will become a member of an organizational team, using your technical communications skills to assist engineers in presenting their ideas and designs. By interacting with the marketing staff, you'll find out what research is being done and help plan for new products.

Once you have become fully integrated into the organization and have mastered the skills mentioned above, you may find that one of the best opportunities for advancement involves becoming a supervisor or a department manager. Managers may supervise not only technical writers, but also the people engaged in illustration, graphics, photography, and distribution. In short, supervisers mobilize their departments to produce the specified printed matter, be it a report, manual, or technical article.

Importance of Teamwork

During their careers, technical writers come in contact with the management, research, and production divisions of their companies. This contact emphasizes the fact that the technical writer is part of a team.

You may wonder just what is meant by teamwork. In brief, it means contributing your skills as a writer or editor to a project at the same time that other people you are working with contribute theirs. Here are a few examples.

• You will undoubtedly have to work with nonwriters, people who may do very little technical writing throughout their careers. They may be engineers, managers, personnel people, artists, or audiovisual experts. Remember that they are experts in their fields, even if they aren't writers. Sometimes you may have to call on these colleagues to provide the basis of a report or a research project or to suggest an illustration to go along with an important piece of work. They may give you sketchily produced work: the sentence structure may be poor or confusing; the style may not be your idea of good writing; the grammar may violate what you have learned in school. And this is where you act as part of a team, by acknowledging that each of you excels in your own area. You'll soon learn that the illustrator is a far better illustrator than you will ever be; the researcher is a far better chemist than you will ever be. Each contributes his or her special knowledge and experience to produce a successful project.

• You will frequently work with people who have given little thought to the kinds of readers they need to attract. In this case, it would be up to you to ask the author of a scientific paper you are editing such questions as: How much do your readers already know about the subject? How "technical" must your terminology be? Do you have to spell out everything? These are the questions of a team worker, and they must be asked with much tact and a great deal of consideration for people's feelings.

Suppose you have been given the job of coordinating a proposal that is submitted to NASA. Your company thinks that it can produce a superior electrical system for a missile, and NASA is definitely interested in hearing about it. It is up to you to get all the technical data on the electrical system from the engineers who have designed and tested it. Their data probably will be in the form of reports, test sheets, and innumerable calculations. Your job will be to sort out this huge amount of communication and present the most important information to impress upon the NASA people that your company is well qualified to handle the job.

But this isn't the end of your assignment. You will have to attend meetings of the sales force so they can help you put your proposal across, giving it sales appeal. Then somewhere in the process, probably after you have written the first draft, you will have to meet with your company's top administrators, who will want to scrutinize your proposal backward and forward, inside and out. They must pass final judgment on what you have written, for the reputation and strength of the company depend on your effort, at least in the eyes of NASA.

Or, suppose that you have been assigned to write a manual. This can be a big job, requiring four or five people—a technical writer, an engineer, a designer, and an illustrator. Writing a manual is usually a long-term project. Although the material will originate with the engineers who worked on the equipment the manual describes, the technical writer must consult many other people as well.

You may be the person in the publications department who is responsible for the production of articles and papers. The basic material will come from the engineers and research people, but you will work closely with the public relations staff in trying to place the articles in national magazines. To get a single article in shape, you may meet with a veritable barrage of management executives, patent lawyers, and supervisors of one kind or another.

You can see, then, that the technical writer is not isolated in a tiny cubicle, working alone. Many hours must be spent on preparing and writing, and the writer will become adept at interviewing and attending meetings and become thoroughly familiar with the divisions of the company.

Final Words

You now know the many types of jobs that are available for technical writers and editors, and you can see that there is a good deal of variety in the possibilities that await you. In summary, let's review the distinctions between writers and editors and the general makeup of a publications department.

A technical writer prepares technical reports and articles for specific audiences, usually based on existing reports and on information obtained directly from the personnel involved. Typical documents may be highlights of research progress reported by many groups, slanted for management information; overall status reports; and technical papers or chapters of books, where expedient.

A technical editor is responsible for expediting or managing the writing and production of reports and papers required by management in the company's established forms and styles. The editor's responsibilities include editing rough drafts prepared by the technical personnel and coordinating illustration, proofreading, printing, and initial distribution. The editor may also prepare or coordinate style manuals and technical writing courses.

A typical publications department consists of editors and writers, photographers, illustrators and other graphics people, reproducers, printers, and production staff, all of whom contribute their expertise to prepare a publication for print. For example, take the idea of a writing-illustrating team—the art is not added as an afterthought but represents a complete integration of team effort throughout the project. The technical writer has conferred with each supervisor and has consulted the graphics department about pictures of the research involved and any charts or graphs that must be drawn.

Deadlines must be set with all of the people involved with the project, from the researchers to the graphic artists to the printers. If the schedule has been planned to allow enough time, there will be less chance of a bottleneck in distributing the final report. The pressure of deadlines can be formidable at times, and the ability to function well under such pressure is a prime requirement for technical writers and editors. When the proposal or report you are preparing could mean many thousands of dollars in business to your employer, you can be sure the deadline won't be taken lightly by management.

5

EMPLOYERS OF
TECHNICAL WRITERS

IN THE PREVIOUS chapter, we discussed the different types of duties technical writers might perform. Now let's look at some specific employers and their technical writing staffs.

A survey conducted by the Society for Technical Communication asked publications managers about the depth and breadth of technical publications in the United States. These are just a few of the conclusions.

• Most technical publication work is done in industrial multi-division corporations.

• Most publication work comes from organizations with more than two thousand employees, and the publications departments report primarily to engineering, administration, and marketing.

• The most common job titles are *technical writer*, *technical editor*, and *technical illustrator*.

- An organization that requires personnel with degrees will hire those with a B.A. or B.S. in technical communication and others with a B.A. or B.S. in English or journalism. The majority of managers believe that employees with degrees in technical communication are better prepared.

The diversity of skills required by employers is evident from the many types of technical writing and editing that we examined in Chapter 4.

Industrial Companies

Almost all government research contracts contain a clause that requires industrial companies to provide periodic reports of progress, indicating the need for technical writers and editors as liaison between research and administration. An authority on technical writing offers this observation.

> Today, government contracts account for as much as 90 percent of the total business of many of the larger companies. Because of these contracts, the volume of progress reports, correspondence, and interplant communications has expanded enormously. The result has been that since 1945, industry has attempted more and more to employ professional writers with scientific backgrounds to take the load of product explanation off the already overburdened engineers.

IBM is an excellent example of industry's heavy reliance on technical writing staffs. IBM is a very large company, manufacturing a wide variety of products in plants all over the world. Technical writers are employed in each of its plant locations to write reports that are distributed internally among departments. For example, reports are circulated between laboratory and top management and from domestic to international branches to prepare sales literature when the company introduces new products and to propose new ways of handling great masses of technical information.

IBM has offered many opportunities for success in the field of technical communications. For example, one young man who completed a tour of duty with the U.S. Army in Europe started and organized the publications department at IBM's Stockholm facility. With his fluency in several languages, he became a manager in the Far East Corporation of IBM.

Not surprisingly, the electronics industry employs many technical writers. An example is the Northrop Corporation, which needs technical communicators in many areas. One department that needs technical writers is avionics, which deals with the parts of an aircraft concerned with how the plane gets from one place to another, how the flight crew can communicate with various planes, and how the plane is controlled while it is in flight. Because it is so technologically complex, a great mass of reports and papers is generated by technical writers in this branch of electronics.

IBM and Northrop are only two of the many industrial companies throughout North America that employ large numbers of technical writers. One of the primary areas in which these companies use technical writers is internal communication. In such large companies, it is essential that employees on all levels and at all locations be kept informed about company news. This information is circulated by a variety of communication techniques such as in-house newsletters, faxed memoranda, e-mail reports, and internal group meetings.

As one of the largest single sources of technical papers for engineering and scientific journals, General Electric Company provides its scientists and engineers with a wide range of supporting services.

The company encourages employees to publish technical work and attend professional conferences, while remaining relatively free from the pressure to prepare routine reports. This means that technical writers relieve the engineers of the responsibility to write reports and assist in the preparation of their papers for presentation.

A look at the General Electric website also reveals the work of technical writers. Clicking on the "products and services" link will take you to descriptions of the company's many offerings, from the components of lighting control to the workings of a jet engine.

Technical writers also have found a secure niche in the chemical industry. A technical writer for Allied Chemical Corporation describes a publications job as editing technical and safety analysis reports, describing design criteria, and helping to write and edit journal articles, papers, and brochures.

A job description from a chemical company illustrates the duties of technical writers in these corporations. This company's technical writers are expected to do the following.

- Research journals, magazines, and the publications of other companies to locate technical literature that would be useful to the service and sales groups.
- Direct the preparation of rough drafts by the technical employees responsible for developing new products for the industrial market.
- Edit copy and supervise the layout and printing of technical literature.
- Prepare articles for technical magazines and speeches for technical conferences.
- Coordinate the literature output of the research departments.

Don't let all of this convince you that only large companies employ technical writers. With the increase of small companies as subcontractors, their volume of paperwork has increased greatly. Small companies are not necessarily selling their products to technical companies; many sell directly to the public. Because consumer products are increasingly complicated to operate, even smaller companies are compelled to furnish well-written instructions. It is a good idea to consider a variety of companies of all sizes when you are looking for a job. Remember, the directions for do-it-yourself kits for household equipment had to be written by someone.

At the same time you are thinking in terms of smaller companies, consider other places for employment. Some technical writers prefer to work for agencies producing services rather than goods. Technical writers have worked for such agencies as the Travelers Insurance Company in the capacity of senior technical writer in the engineering division. Another agency known to hire technical writers is the National Oceanic and Atmospheric Administration.

Research Groups

Research organizations are another excellent source of employment opportunities for technical writing positions. Some are part of the companies themselves, some are supported by universities, and others are privately endowed.

Regardless of their management, all research groups have one thing in common—they work to find new ways of doing things, whether that means developing new products, designing new communication systems, or treating diseases. Frequently their efforts do not show results for many years, but they generate an incredible flow of reports, science and engineering papers, and presentations before technical audiences.

Consider the ongoing research conducted by pharmaceutical companies, which work to develop medications and products that are vital for the public's health. For example, Pfizer Inc. employs more than one hundred thousand workers and twelve thousand medical researchers and currently manufactures over fifty prescription medications. If you were a technical writer for Pfizer, you would collaborate with chemists and biologists trying to identify new methods of treating illnesses, with geneticists who study issues of heredity, with neuroscientists who research the brain's involvement in illness and its response to drugs, and with engineers who produce the drug based on the research results.

Since it is vitally important that medications are safe and effective, you can only imagine the number of reports that the company must prepare throughout the research and development process of a new drug. These include internal communications within the company, progress reports, reports to government regulatory agencies, and papers presenting research findings. We've all filled at least one prescription and hopefully have carefully read the patient product information that accompanied the medicine. The need for technical writers and editors is evident given the variety of information that must be communicated.

Some research organizations are not affiliated with large industrial concerns. An example of this special type of research institute is Battelle Science and Technology International. Battelle contracts with both industry and government to develop scientific and technological innovations and manages research laboratories for its customers. With the national labs it manages or co-manages, Battelle oversees nineteen thousand staff members and conducts $3.7 billion in annual research and development. The company also works with more than eight hundred federal, state, and local government agencies to provide science and technology in the areas of national security, homeland defense, health and life sciences, energy, transportation, and environment. Given all of these activities, you can see that the scope of activity for a technical writer associated with Battelle is almost endless.

Many universities also have large research organizations that are heavily dependent on government contracts. One is the University of Dayton Research Institute; another is Lawrence Livermore National Laboratory, affiliated with the University of California.

Government Agencies

Government units employing technical writers usually fall into two categories: federal and state or provincial groups that use technical writers for their own work, and agencies that work closely with companies and industries.

The governments of both the United States and Canada maintain websites through which you can search for and apply for federal jobs. A quick search of the U.S. site, www.usajobscom, shows that at this time positions for technical writers and editors are available with the Department of Agriculture, the National Archives and Records Administration, the Federal Reserve System, the National Institutes of Health, and the Air Force Personnel Center, to name just a few. The Canadian site, www.jobs-emplois.gc.ca, shows availabilities with Defence Construction, Parks Canada, and the National Research Council.

In general, technical writing jobs for the federal government are classified as those that provide internal communications and those that deal with external contacts. Writers working on internal communications can be described as follows.

- **Public information specialist.** This category includes writers who not only collect information about the many activities of the commission, but who also write and disseminate information about the many programs available in federal government. As an information specialist, you could be involved in writing for a variety of public communications media, including newspapers, television, magazines, and the Internet.
- **Writer-editor.** This job should appeal to you if you have substantial knowledge in the areas of engineering or science. The federal government employs writers and editors to produce articles, press releases, periodicals, pamphlets and brochures, speeches, and scripts for radio, television, and film.

As a writer or editor for the federal government, you would research the subject to be described, select the information to be included, and write or edit the final manuscript. Many in this group specialize in technical fields such as engineering, science, or the social sciences.

Technical writers and editors working in the second category deal with strong industrial contacts. Some government agencies work so closely with private companies that it is hard to distinguish between the two. One example of this relationship is the Mound Plant at Miamisburg, Ohio, operated for the U.S. Department of Energy by the Monsanto Research Corporation.

Mound Plant is in the forefront of energy research, providing leadership in such areas as polonium technology, thermal diffusion, and reactor fuel studies. This complex and extensive research requires the services of many skilled technical writers. One writing group is responsible for the preparation of the manuals that must accompany every project before its results can be implemented.

Another group, the Technical Information Office, is responsible for the preparation of technical papers for publication in journals, for answering inquiries of a technical nature that are received by Mound Plant, and for editing and publishing periodic progress reports.

Government research groups are not all run by large companies. Some government agencies are found in the military itself, developing weapons, missiles, and equipment for space exploration. The Adelphi Laboratory Center (formerly the Harry Diamond Laboratories), part of the U.S. Army, is one of these agencies, as is the Naval Air Weapons Center at China Lake, California. These military agencies provide numerous career opportunities for civilian and enlisted technical communication specialists.

Journals and Magazines

As we have discussed previously, the technical writer working in the journal field is usually required to edit someone else's work and prepare articles for publication. In doing this, the writer works closely with the author, restructuring ideas and checking grammar, punctuation, and spelling. Eventually, the technical editor may be asked to write original articles in some specialized fields. A brief discussion of the different categories in the technical magazine market should help illustrate the variety of career opportunities available.

Journals

First are the journals, sponsored by professional societies. You are probably familiar with a number of these, and you may even belong to a chapter of an engineering society, such as the American Society of Mechanical Engineers.

Practically every professional association publishes its own journal. *Aerospace America* is self-descriptive, as is the *American Journal of Agricultural Economics*. Two of the better-known ones are the *Journal of Chemical Education*, published by the American Chemical Society, and *Engineering Times*, the journal of the National Society of Professional Engineers.

These journals have several common features: they usually publish papers based on original research, they operate with comparatively small staffs, and they are mainly read by people in the same field as the sponsoring society. Regardless of its individual makeup or audience, the technical journal must be edited by skilled technical writers.

One of our former students, for example, is an assistant editor of *Theriogenology*, an international journal of animal reproduction. She is responsible for editing (including visual aids) all articles submitted. Many manuscripts, especially some submitted by foreign authors, require extensive revision. She also indexes the volumes of the journal, compiles the front matter, and corresponds with authors and reviewers.

Commercial Magazines

Commercial magazines are found in technical libraries in every country. McGraw-Hill publishes several technical, scientific, and business magazines, including *Aviation Week and Space Technology*, *Engineering News-Record*, and *Architectural Record*. Penton Media Inc., another well-known publisher of technical magazines, produces *Electronic Design* and *Ward's Auto World*, among others.

Most editors of commercial technical magazines are interested in interviewing qualified technical writers for staff positions. These editors realize that their competitive journalism field requires fresh talent, which means hiring new people with good technical training and the ability to write.

But you should realize that there are differences between working on journals and working on commercial magazines. The latter are money-making concerns, employing large editorial staffs. For this reason, the chances of obtaining a job with a McGraw-Hill or Penton magazine are greater than with such specialized publications as *Journal of Nuclear Materials* or *Neuroscience*.

Company Magazines

As previously mentioned, one particular form of technical magazine, the *house organ*, is put out by a company's publications department. House organs usually fall into two classes: those for outside readers and those for internal readers. The *RCA Engineer*, published by the Research and Engineering Division of RCA, is a highly technical publication. On the other hand, Oak Ridge National Laboratory publishes *Review* largely for internal readership, and it is distributed to employees and others associated with the laboratory. The staff writes and edits a variety of articles: some deal with interesting people employed by Oak Ridge National Laboratory; others with work in progress in the research area. A magazine like *Review* could offer an opportunity for a writer with a combination of training in technology and journalism.

Trade Journals

Another class of magazine is the trade journal. While it can be a little difficult to define, a trade journal bears the same relation to a technical magazine that a trade bears to a profession. It features down-to-earth articles on how things are done, methods of production, and tips to readers in various trades. There are trade magazines for a variety of occupations, such as *Restaurant Report, Women's Wear Daily, National Jeweler,* and *Mortuary Management.*

Books

Although we've been talking about magazines, we shouldn't forget book publishers as potential employers. John Wiley and Sons is one of several large publishers of engineering and science textbooks that require editing by highly qualified people who act as liaison between the company and its authors. The *McGraw-Hill Encyclopedia of Science and Technology* is a twenty-volume work containing over seven thousand articles contributed by five thousand internationally known researchers. A graduate of Rensselaer Polytechnic Institute's master's program in technical writing worked as a staff editor on the most recent revision, handling most of the field of physics, plus aeronautical and nuclear engineering and space technology.

More and more publishing houses that produce technical and scientific books are looking for specialists, technical editors who can help authors and who are familiar with the content, vocabulary, and audiences of technology.

Support Companies

There is a growing industry of small businesses that might be called *support companies* and that produce technical brochures, manuals, and other publications and materials under contract with larger manufacturing firms. They generally fall into two groups: those that serve as consultants and help promote company products and those that act as contractors by doing the actual writing.

An example of a consulting business is industrialpublicity.com, a business-to-business Internet publicity service. With a staff of experienced technical news writers and editors, the company serves its clients by reaching the publications, industrial newspapers, Internet news sites, and electronic media that correspondingly reach a customer's market base.

An online publicity service, industrialpublicity.com was founded by Allan G. Hall, who has worked in industrial publicity for over twenty years. He has a degree in manufacturing engineering from Miami University and completed the General Electric Manufacturing Management Training Program. He is a member of both the Society of Manufacturing Engineers and the Society of Automotive Engineers. He also has written hundreds of technical feature articles in the industrial and metalworking industries. He is joined on the editorial staff by a full-time freelance writer who specializes in the automotive industry; a manufacturing engineer who has written and presented technical papers and is a past editor of *Tooling and Production Magazine*; the current editor of *Powertrain International*; a professional in production, account services, and public relations who specializes in industrial publicity; and an experienced copywriter who works on advertising, brochures, mail kits, newsletters, videos, and websites.

Based on the collective experience of the staff of industrialpub licity.com, you can get a sense of the various opportunities for technical communicators with small companies.

Although the line between consulting companies and contracting companies in technical writing can be blurry at times, some distinctions can be made. A contractor is essentially a specialized organization that handles publication projects for larger companies that either don't employ a publication staff or are too busy to complete the work in-house.

Suppose that Radio-Electronics Company has received a large order from the government for a fire control system on a line of navy ships. Radio-Electronics is prepared and able to manufacture the system, which will require operating and maintenance manuals. Rather than overtax its publications department, the company contracts with Roberts Technical Writing Service to prepare the necessary manuals. This outside company now adds Radio-Electronics to its list of clients for this job only. Perhaps it will be the only job on which the two companies will ever work together, or it might be the beginning of a profitable professional relationship.

A successful technical publication contracting firm must be able to provide specialized services in the preparation of catalogs, brochures, or training manuals, and it must be able to work in any media, including print, electronic, and video. The company can hire additional staff on a temporary basis for large projects, which helps to keep a lower overhead.

A contracting writing service will plan the entire publication effort for a particular project, doing all the necessary writing and editing. It will offer a complete illustration and graphics service and will either do the printing or have it done. It will deliver the final product to the client or distribute it as contracted. In the long run, the contractor supplies a complete communications package to its client, with little responsibility on the client's part beyond the necessary input and final approval.

Higher Education

Many colleges and universities are engaged in industrial research and development, particularly those with strong science and engineering faculties. Just think of Stanford University's Research Institute, MIT, and CalTech.

There are hundreds of institutions throughout North America whose teaching staffs are active in either government- or industry-sponsored research. As the number of academic discoveries and inventions increases, so does the need to convey information to industry and government, as well as to the general public. This policy of sharing results is known as "technology transfer."

An independent study of several such college research groups shows a trend toward hiring technical writers to prepare reports. Over half of the respondent groups employ one or more writers. Most of the technical writers work in public relations, a small number work in research, and some are employed by the university press. Many of the writers are graduate students studying communications; others have come from industries that have publications departments. The variety of qualifications required include five or more years of professional writing experience, a B.S. or B.A. degree, an interest in science and technology, and a flair for technical writing.

The results of this study show that there are many places in academic life for technical and scientific communicators. For example, the Child Development Institute at the University of North Carolina at Chapel Hill employs a writer and editor who collaborates with other technical communicators and develops programs for assistance in using media devices.

Teaching Technical Writing

More and more colleges are offering communications courses for students whose major fields of study are engineering, sciences, and liberal arts. At the University of Florida, for example, all future engineers are required to take basic technical writing. This alone has increased the enrollment in the course by some four hundred students a year.

We mention this to indicate that colleges teaching technical writing need more teachers. Some of these teachers have already prepared themselves by obtaining special degrees at such schools as Rensselaer, Carnegie-Mellon, and Colorado State. Others are branching out into what is a completely new field for them.

Schools of journalism recognize that their graduates may get jobs in science writing for newspapers and journals. They also may end up in publicity or advertising with a heavy science slant. All of these students of technical journalism must be instructed by qualified teachers, which creates more opportunities for technical communication instructors.

You will find that most positions require an M.A. or Ph.D. degree and that administrators favor applicants with some experience in teaching technical writing. So how can you qualify for these positions, especially if you are coming from a traditional English department?

Some universities offer English courses, particularly at the graduate level, in the practice and teaching of technical writing. A typical graduate-level course of this kind would offer instruction in business and technical communication, providing you with basic texts, study outlines, and assorted assignments and exercises.

If departmental courses are not available, you have other options. Several universities offer week-long institutes and seminars. These present opportunities to network with many people, trade ideas, and get a real feel for the discipline. The institutions and seminars regularly cover useful classroom topics, such as types of technical writing courses, designing objectives for technical writing courses, report writing topics and assignments, evaluation and grading of student papers, and computer-assisted instruction.

Frequently these programs will include information about resource material available to technical writing teachers, areas of needed research, and consulting possibilities. Most of the programs include workshops in which the participants practice various technical writing skills to give them a better understanding of some of the problems their students may face. Any technical writing teacher will gain valuable experience and acquire much useful information by attending such a program, and the teacher seeking a technical writing teaching position will enhance his or her credentials by participation.

The annual conference of the Society for Technical Communication (STC) is also an excellent source of information. What better way to learn than to talk with professional writers and well-known teachers? You also may learn about the prevailing job market and meet with potential employers. In addition, associations such as the Modern Language Association and the Popular Culture Association have begun to include panel sessions on various aspects of teaching and research in technical writing in their national and regional meetings. This is concrete testimony of an increased awareness of the importance of technical writing teaching at a time when there are many cutbacks in other teaching areas.

Teacher Resources

The new teacher can draw on a variety of resources. A basic exposition syllabus, coupled with a reliable technical writing text and any supporting materials gathered from the sources already mentioned, is a starting point. *Technical Communication Quarterly*, a journal published by the Association of Teachers of Technical Writing, provides many useful suggestions contributed by experienced teachers. In the same category is the *Journal of Business and Technical Communication*, which includes articles by both teachers and industrial writers. You can easily carry over into your classes many of the ideas suggested by practicing writers.

The STC provides much useful information through its magazine *Technical Communication* as well as a series of specialized collections including *Teaching Technical Writing* and *How to Teach Technical Editing*. The National Council of Teachers of English has put out several pamphlets on teaching technical writing, and its journal, *College English*, publishes some fine articles on technical writing that the new or experienced teacher will find useful. A bibliography of references for many areas of technical writing, as well as a list of periodicals and journals, is included in the Recommended Reading section at the end of the book.

Consulting and Freelance Writing

Much has been written about the possibilities of consulting in technical writing—going into a company to help it solve its writing problems, perhaps through a series of in-house training courses or through individual work with the company's writers and editors. Other articles discuss possibilities as a freelance technical writer. *Technical Communication*, for example, has explored consulting in depth.

If working as a consultant in technical communication interests you, first consider the amount of competition in the field. You'll need a reputation or some recognized affiliation, with a university for example, to get work. It is very difficult to develop a lucrative consulting business when several large communication consulting firms already exist and many highly experienced technical writing instructors offer their services as consultants. Consulting has long been seen as an added benefit of college technical-writing teaching, but recently we have seen numerous advertisements for consultants to work with national companies. Usually these positions require some teaching background, most require a Ph.D., and all require extensive travel. In such positions, your duties would include offering intensive short courses for various industries and organizations throughout the country and, possibly, in foreign countries. This is demanding work, is usually high paying, and may represent a career choice for those unable to gain secure university teaching positions.

Freelance technical writing may offer more possibilities for the newer professional. Often small organizations that cannot afford permanent full-time technical writing personnel will hire others on a temporary basis or will have work available for writers to do at home.

For several years, one of our students supplemented her income by documenting computer programs at home, using a terminal supplied by the company. Another student gained valuable experience writing and editing study guides for the Certified Public Accountant exam and the LSAT. Part of her job was to design reading comprehension tests (for the LSAT), which included selecting relevant passages and making up reading questions that were followed by the correct answers and explanations of the answers.

This can be a good way to begin if you are still a student or are new to the field and wish to develop some credentials. For the experienced professional who prefers on-call work or to work in his or her home on a variety of projects for a variety of clients, freelance technical writing offers worthwhile possibilities.

Summer Employment

Opportunities for students to find summer employment in technical writing generally vary according to the national economy. Nevertheless, well-trained students who are willing to look for work should be able to find summer positions. A technical communication student who worked during the summer for IBM described his work as follows:

> Our first big project was to edit and revise a manual describing the testing process used to warm up a computer for full-on operation. . . . As it was essential in this writing project to become thoroughly familiar with the equipment, we visited the site where the equipment had been designed and built and was being tested. We talked with the engineers on the project in order to completely understand the equipment. Finally, we took the existing manual, deleted much of the material from it, and added quite a lot of new material.

Ask yourself a few questions to determine whether you should pursue summer employment. Has your educational background prepared you to handle the products of science and technology? Are you a good enough writer to handle the communication phases? Do you live in or near an area that needs technical writers, or are you willing to relocate temporarily?

Some people argue that summer employment in technical writing is a waste of time; that in such a specialized job, a major part of the summer may go by before you can really become productive. Despite this opinion, if you can find a summer job in the field, by all means take it. It will offer you the chance to get your foot in the door, giving you a decided advantage over other applicants with no experience who must start from scratch after graduation.

A summer job will also give you a chance to see if you are really suited for a technical writing career and whether the working conditions are what you expected them to be. Most employers will give you on-the-job evaluations of the work you have been doing and will let you know whether there will be a permanent job available after you graduate.

No organization, however, is willing to give you a free ride for the summer. You must demonstrate ability to get the work done, enthusiasm, and a desire to learn. Among the principal academic requirements today are a sound science background, competence in writing, and computer skills.

Working Overseas

In addition to the United States and Canada, there are technical writers working for companies in South America, England, Europe, Israel, India, Japan, and other countries all over the world. If you speak or write a language other than English, you may be qualified to work in one of these countries.

The best place to start to locate overseas jobs is on the Internet. A search will reveal databases of job listings, employment agencies, and many free job-placement services.

6

RELATED FIELDS AND GROWING TRENDS

TECHNICAL WRITING IS only one part of a larger picture of professional writing and that encompasses the skills applied to such professions as medicine, pharmaceuticals, public health, and business.

The two kinds of professional communication that bear the greatest resemblance to technical writing are medical writing and business writing. Each has its own professional society: the American Medical Writers Association (AMWA) and the International Association of Business Communicators (IABC), both of which serve members in the United States and Canada (addresses are given in the appendix). Some writers belong to both of these organizations, as well as to the Society for Technical Communication. Because of their common characteristics, what we have already said about technical writing can certainly be applied to medical and business writing.

Medical Writing

Medical writing is a wide-ranging field that covers the many different areas of medicine, including the science and allied health professions. Medical communicators may work on a variety of documents and projects specific to the field. Like their counterparts in technical writing, they also have the option of working in different areas of communication.

Duties of Medical Editors and Writers

According to Dr. Eric W. Martin, past president of AMWA and author of the association's code of ethics, the duties of medical editors and writers may include the following:

- **Clinical brochures.** These publications contain the all the data gathered by a company from years of research on new drugs.
- **Case report forms.** With these forms, medical writers help clinical investigators report on the medical histories of patients.
- **Clinical research reports.** Medical writers prepare these summaries of research and clinical data that are important in determining whether drugs will be available for patient use.
- **Clinical papers.** In the preparation of these papers, the medical writers give editorial and writing help to busy scientific investigators.
- **Physician brochures.** These brochures specify dosages, side effects, and other pertinent information that doctors must have to safely and effectively treat patients.

- **Official brochures.** These are commonly known as package circulars or package inserts, again for the benefit of the physicians.
- **Abstracts.** Medical writers screen hundreds of important journal articles and condense them for scientists and researchers.
- **Guides.** The manufacturers of medical products must follow strict federal and state government regulations. Medical writers frequently prepare manuals to interpret these controls for company employees.
- **Media preparation.** Medical writers coordinate the preparation of motion picture scripts and digital presentations.

If you have a strong background in chemistry or biology, investigate the possibility of working in the pharmaceutical rather than the chemical industry. If the ultimate consumer of the company's products is the public, then as a communicator for such a firm, you would be classified as a medical writer.

Medical Journalism

If you visit a medical library, you will be overwhelmed by the number of journals available there; a trip to the stacks will find you surrounded by thousands of volumes covering every possible aspect of medicine. Perhaps you'd like to contribute to this incredible wealth of information. What we have already said about technical journalism in previous chapters pretty well applies to medical journalism. If you join the staff of the *Journal of the American Medical Association* or a more general magazine such as *Today's Health*, you will be writing articles, editing other people's work, and acting as a liaison with artists and production personnel.

Freelancing

Many freelancers work in medical writing. The majority work from home offices on manuscripts and reports originally written by doctors and researchers who are too busy or lack the writing skills to produce a final manuscript. Frequently these freelancers are highly qualified scientists who wish to do only part-time work. If you are trained in biology, chemistry, or in one of the more specialized sciences, you may wish to consider this very important kind of medical writing. It may be just the right kind of employment for you.

Medical Advertising

You may find a niche in medical advertising. Just as there are many technical advertising firms and public relations firms, there are also many advertising companies that specialize, at least in part, in drawing the attention of the public and of physicians to the availability of new drugs.

Medical Writers at Work

To illustrate some of the opportunities in medical writing, here are brief accounts of two professionals working in this field.

A young woman who earned a B.A. in psychology and English and an M.A. in psychology was hired by a large army medical center as a technical publications editor. The center was issuing an increasing number of scientific papers and was about to publish its own journal. This position led to a more challenging one in an army research institute. In addition, this medical writer has been made an associate editor of a journal of sports medicine and an editorial consultant to the Eisenhower Medical Center.

Another writer who has a B.A. in journalism worked briefly as editor of a trade publication and later became an editor for a publishing firm that produces technical books and pamphlets. He then joined a state health department as an editor of its monthly magazine. His current duties include writing and editing pamphlets, booklets, and brochures for all units within the department; preparing the annual report; and preparing news releases concerning department activities and providing information for the press. When asked to classify his position, he describes himself as a public health writer.

Many physicians have become medical writers, just as many engineers have become technical writers. For example, one writer received a degree in pharmacology from one college, a B.S. degree from another, and a medical degree from a third. He has been both a practicing pharmacist and a physician and has also served as medical director and director of research for a large chemical manufacturing company. He is now employed by a New York advertising firm as medical director in charge of clinical research. It is the job of his department to delve into the research and manufacture of the drugs and chemicals of his client firms so that they may be advertised intelligently and accurately in the medical journals.

American Medical Writers Association

The aim of the American Medical Writers Association is to bring together all North Americans who are employed in the communication of medicine and allied sciences in order to maintain and advance high professional standards. Its purpose is educational, scientific, and literary. At an annual meeting addressed by distinguished authors, editors, and teachers, members have the opportunity to keep informed on the progress being made to maintain and advance high professional standards and thus to aid in general medical advancement.

The association publishes the *AMWA Journal*, which is delivered quarterly to members and subscribers. It is an authoritative, comprehensive source of information about the knowledge, skills, and opportunities in the field of medical communication worldwide.

AMWA offers an extensive continuing education program that allows professionals in the medical and allied scientific communication fields to explore new areas of expertise in order to enhance their skills. More than one hundred educational sessions are offered during a three-day annual conference, including curriculum workshops that can also be applied toward AMWA's certificate programs. Earning an AMWA certificate is considered part of a career path in the field and is required by some employers.

Workshops are also offered at AMWA chapter-sponsored conferences presented at various times during the year, and approximately twenty workshops are available for on-site presentation at companies' facilities. There are also a number of self-study workshops available that include a combination of a workbook and CD-ROM. Two examples are *Basic Grammar and Usage* and *Punctuation for Clarity and Style*, which can be ordered through the AMWA website.

AMWA Certificate Programs

AMWA offers three certificate programs: core, advanced, and science fundamentals. Participants in core workshops can learn how to improve editing, writing, communication, and bibliographic skills; how to develop and manage a freelance business; learn the skills necessary for writing for the pharmaceutical industry, public relations/advertising/marketing, or Web/multimedia; discover the latest methods for educating writers and editors; and brush up on statistics. Advanced workshops provide experienced medical communicators with in-depth consideration of issues in writing, editing, management, bibliographic research, education, and other topics of interest. Workshops in science fundamentals offer participants an opportunity to deepen their understanding of basic concepts in science and medicine. This curriculum is designed for medical communicators who do not have a university background in science and for those educated in science who wish to learn more about areas outside their specialties.

Core Certificate

Participants can earn a core certificate in one or more of five specialty areas: editing/writing, educators, freelance, pharmaceutical, and public relations/advertising/marketing. To receive a certificate, participants must successfully complete four general workshops and four additional workshops from the specialty area of their choice. Participants may also earn a multidisciplinary core certificate by successfully completing four general workshops and six specialty workshops chosen from three or more of the specialty areas.

Multiple Certificates

After earning their first core certificate, participants can earn additional certificates in different specialty areas. For each new certificate, participants must pay an additional enrollment fee and then complete four more workshops from the new specialty area. The work for each new certificate must be completed within four years.

Science Fundamentals Certificate

Participants must successfully complete four general science workshops and four additional workshops from specialty areas such as body systems, diseases, or diagnostics and therapeutics.

AMWA Advanced Certificate

The advanced workshops are designed for those who have earned AMWA core certificates or have a minimum of five years of experience in the topic covered by the specific workshop. Earning an advanced certificate requires the completion of eight advanced workshops. Some advanced workshops require core workshop prerequisites that cannot be waived. Therefore, in choosing core workshops, participants should consider which advanced workshops they may eventually want to take.

Business Writing

If you choose a career in business writing, you may be dealing with readers ranging from business managers to the general public and with such topics as human resources to consumer relations.

In planning a career in business writing, you should study business and the communication of business. Since business writing is highly specialized, it is important to carefully select the kind of writing or editing you will train for. It's one thing to write repair manuals, but something else altogether to write training materials for the sales personnel. You should assemble a portfolio of samples of your work, and you should learn to write good letters of application to accompany your professional portfolio.

Types of Business Writers

Business writers fall into a number of classifications, including the following, which are adapted from the IABC.

- **Informal auditor.** Performs operational reviews and reports on recommendations for management
- **Financial analyst.** Does analytical reporting
- **Accountant.** Writes company policies and procedures
- **Researcher (advertising).** Gathers, organizes, and writes final reports; makes formal presentations of findings to clients
- **Product advertiser.** Plans and coordinates product development; composes literature and sales aids
- **Community planning specialist.** Writes, edits, and reports on community concerns
- **Planning director.** Oversees and prepares copy for promotional literature
- **Publications specialist.** Prepares original copy, graphic arts, and layouts
- **Corporate relations officer.** Writes news releases and edits materials
- **Proposal specialist.** Plans, writes, and produces contract proposals

This is only a partial list of the possibilities for business writers. In all the descriptions, you will find that, once again, there is an overlapping of job duties among business, medical, and technical communicators.

International Association of Business Communicators

IABC is the professional organization for business writers. Its more than fourteen thousand members are from seventy countries, and they work in every aspect of business communication.

The aims of IABC are similar to those expressed by STC and AMWA: to promote professional standards and provide a forum for its members. IABC carries out its purpose through an annual national convention and regional meetings and seminars offered throughout the year by individual chapters.

IABC publishes *Communication World*, its magazine for members that offers articles written by leaders in the field of business communication. *CW Bulletin* is an e-newsletter supplement to the journal that is sent to all members every month.

The association also sponsors Student Connection, a variety of resources and opportunities for students who plan to enter the communication profession. It allows students to gain insights from leaders in the profession, make valuable contacts, and supplement their academic education with practical training.

IABC Training

The IABC offers training opportunities ranging from in-depth conferences and seminars to convenient distance-learning sessions delivered directly to your office. The options in distance learning include teleseminars, Web seminars, and online seminars. Teleseminars are sixty-minute telephone sessions led by IABC conference speakers and include downloadable handouts. Web seminars are ninety-minute telephone sessions with visuals presented on the Web. Online seminars consist of ten hours of training taken during a two-week period. Members who complete four seminars earn a professional certificate in strategic communication management.

Accreditation

Accreditation is an IABC professional development program that allows communicators to demonstrate their ability to think and plan strategically and to successfully manage the skills essential to effective organizational communication, which could include internal communications, media relations, crisis communications, and external relations.

To earn the designation of accredited business communicator (ABC), you must be a professional communicator with a minimum of five years of experience in business communication (organizational communication, public relations, or communications management) and a bachelor's degree or a total of nine years of combined postsecondary education and/or experience.

There are three steps to the accreditation process, each of which must be successfully completed before proceeding to the next. The steps are an application, qualification (the portfolio), and written and oral examinations. Each portion of the process contributes to your score—the portfolio grade counts for 25 percent of the total, the written exam counts for 58 percent of the total, and the oral exam counts for 17 percent of the total.

• **Application.** Your application should be a comprehensive summary of your professional experience and qualifications; it will be used to determine your eligibility to proceed with the accreditation process. Several IABC chapters offer accreditation workshops and local mentoring programs to help candidates present the most compelling applications.

- **Qualification: The portfolio.** Your portfolio must include two work samples, with work plans to demonstrate the range of communication projects or programs you've been responsible for and your ability to plan and work strategically. Candidates must receive a passing score of 4.0 or better (using a 0–7 scale) on the portfolio to qualify to take the examination.
- **Examination.** The examination tests your knowledge of communication and management skills. The exam is four and a half hours long and includes a written and oral test.

Visit www.iabc.com for complete information about the accreditation process and the dates and locations of upcoming exams.

Trends in Professional Education

More and more colleges, universities, and technical schools are offering courses and programs in technical communication, making it easier than ever for you to find the curriculum you want in a school near you.

Another trend in professional education is employers' increasing interest in graduates with master's degrees. An advanced program of this sort will give you the time to acquire more skills and is frequently a step toward a supervisory or management job. Human resources interviewers are always looking to the future—do the candidates for a job have the characteristics and skills that will favor promotion into managerial positions?

Global Information

Companies also are looking for applicants who can handle worldwide documentation systems. Technical writing students must be trained in the operation of these communication systems and on procedures in sorting out data and dealing with foreign countries that need the data.

If you examine the course listings of most colleges, you will find classes that address the subject of global information. Communication systems are now standard in many colleges, and courses in technical German, French, and other foreign languages are available, too.

Machine Translation

If you have knowledge of one or more foreign languages and are skilled in technical writing, you should be well equipped to work with translating equipment to convert foreign languages into English and vice versa.

Machine translation (MT) is a subfield of computational linguistics that investigates the use of computer software to translate text or speech from one natural language to another. At the most basic level, MT performs simple substitution of words in one language for words in another. Using advanced techniques, more complex translations may be attempted, allowing for better handling of differences in phrase recognition and translation of idioms.

Current machine translation software often allows for customization by domain or subject area, which improves output by limiting the scope of allowable substitutions. This technique is most effective in domains where formal or formulaic language is used. For example, machine translation of government and legal documents more readily produces usable output than conversation or less standardized text.

To give you some idea of how translators and technical writers may work in machine translation, we contacted William L. Benzon, a renowned expert in technical communication. Dr. Benzon is associate director of the World Development Endowment Foundation and a former assistant professor of communication at Rensselaer Polytechnic Institute. He said:

> As high technology spreads across the globe, the need for rapid, reliable, and relatively cheap translation of technical documentation grows proportionately. Translation, however, is slow, boring, but highly skilled work, which adds up to its being very expensive work as well. On the other hand, computers are fast and they don't get bored. If they can be programmed with skills sufficient to the task, then fast and cheap translation may be possible.

Whether translation can be done by machines depends on the fact that most of the decisions to be made in translation are, in principle, as routine as the multiplication tables. Those decisions can be made quickly and accurately by a computer with the requisite software. However, many of those decisions depend on prior decisions of a different class, decisions that cannot be specified by some routine procedure. These decisions concern the meaning of the text and seem to require encyclopedic knowledge of the text's content. Current software provides literal, not idiomatic (everyday) language translations, so its use is restricted. Translated text must be converted into good idiomatic language, and there is an ongoing effort to solve this problem.

To illustrate the difficulty of idiomatic versus literal translation, consider the phrase, "the coast is clear." In Spanish, the equivalent phrase is *no haber ningunos moros en la costa*, whose literal translation is "there are no Moors on the shore!"

At present there are more practical machine aids to human translators, called MAT (machine-aided translation). Several MAT systems are in use by government agencies and private corporations, and this subfield of technical communications should grow rapidly. Machine translation is an exciting employment possibility for translators—those people gifted in more than one language and with the ability to write well.

You may be more familiar with CAT, computer-aided translation. To aid in the usage of CAT, companies are approaching translation in stages. First a glossary, or vocabulary, of the most common technical terms used by that company for foreign translation is drawn up for the translators as well as for other writers. This glossary is entered into the database, followed by, for example, a page of a manual. This is pre-edited and then applied to the glossary. Words in the original piece of work are now transformed by the glossary, or *glossarized*, and the piece of writing is returned to the translator for its completion and final editing. Of course, this is an oversimplification of the process, but it may provide you with some idea of what is meant by CAT and machine translation. This development is by no means foolproof, but it does show the direction translation efforts are taking.

Systems of oral dictation to the computer also are being developed for translation purposes. Eventually, words spoken in one language may be computer processed and translated into another.

Computer Documentation

Computers are certainly no longer novel, but their increased use in every area has presented a challenge for the technical writer to produce clear and usable computer-related documents. Lack of adequate documentation, that is, the written form of all the available information about a particular computer, computer program, or set of programs, is a major problem in modern industry. Documentation in its many forms, such as operating instructions, troubleshooting and repairs, user guides, and so forth, is essential for management information on systems development and for proper coordination of subsequent phases of systems development and use. This documentation is often not thorough, nor is it done at the same time that the system is developed. Sometimes it is never done at all. The technical writer must be able to step into the complex documentation process and quickly and accurately prepare such forms as the job run manual, the job control language manual, the balancing and control manual, the key processing manual, and the job scheduling manual.

Obviously, special training is necessary for the technical writer to function effectively in preparing systems documentation. Some schools offer training programs that train technical writers for the computer industry. Most such programs offer computer science courses and training in writing operating instructions and programming reference manuals. This is just the beginning of the experience a technical writer must accumulate to function effectively in the area of systems documentation.

Many technical writers today are deeply involved in computer programming and able to analyze databases, while they are also familiar with software psychology, human factors, and ergometrics (the study of the ability of humans to adjust to their environment). The preparation of manuals for people unfamiliar with data processing and programming is a continuation of what has long been a major role of the technical writer, bridging the information gap between the technical and the nontechnical person.

Some professionals feel that technical writers are well suited for program design because they are best qualified to design the information package for the beginning user. For instance, IBM hires technical writers to produce user manuals for their personal computers. The writer must learn what kinds of documents best fit the needs of the home computer buyer and what form would be best for these documents. This may require analyzing existing documents, interviewing users and designers, and generally converting technical and highly specialized language to language that the nonspecialist can understand.

Looking Ahead

The need for technical writers should remain steady because technical writing is not a routine job. As you have seen, new developments in communication are continually occurring, and it is widely accepted by industry that communication is the pipeline to global business.

You now know about the training and qualifications you'll need to pursue a career in technical communications and the many areas in which you might find work. If this is the profession that interests you, be confident that the opportunities are there for a serious, well-trained technical writer.

Professional Associations

FOLLOWING IS A list of associations that serve the field of technical communication.

Society for Technical Communication

The official society of the technical writing profession is the Society for Technical Communication (STC). Members have opportunities to exchange ideas, express their views, and utilize programs that benefit them in the advancement of their careers. Some regional chapters have been very active in their industrial communities in bringing business and education together, presenting important speakers, and developing writing workshops.

Whether you are a student or a practicing technical writer, you should plan to attend the annual conferences of the Society for Technical Communication, which is held each spring in various locations around the country. Conferences generally attract thousands of members and feature speakers from around the world. Presentations are made on every aspect of the profession, and you will have the opportunity to learn firsthand from experienced technical communicators.

For complete information on membership and other society information, contact:

Society for Technical Communication
901 N. Stuart St., Ste. 904
Arlington, VA 22203
www.stc.org

Other Professional Associations

There are a number of professional societies devoted to more specialized forms of technical communication, as well as others that cover more general aspects of education.

Accrediting Council on Education in Journalism and Mass
    Communications
Stauffer-Flint Hall
1435 Jayhawk Blvd.
Lawrence, KS 66045-7575
www2.ku.edu/~acejmc

American Advertising Federation
1101 Vermont Ave. NW, Ste. 500
Washington, DC 20005-6306
www.aaf.org

American Agricultural Editors Association
P.O. Box 156
New Prague, MN 56071
www.ageditors.com

American Association for the Advancement of Science
1200 New York Ave. NW
Washington, DC 20005
www.aaas.org

American Association of Advertising Agencies
405 Lexington Ave., 18th Fl.
New York, NY 10174-1801
www.aaaa.org

American Chemical Society
1155 16th St. NW
Washington, DC 20036
www.chemistry.org

American Medical Writers' Association
40 W. Gude Dr., Ste. 101
Rockville, MD 20850-1192
www.amwa.org

American Society of Indexers
10200 W. 44th Ave., Ste. 304
Wheat Ridge, CO 80033
www.asindexing.org

American Society for Information Science and Technology
1320 Fenwick La., Ste. 510
Silver Spring, MD 20910
www.asis.org

American Society of Journalists and Authors Inc.
1501 Broadway, Ste. 302
New York, NY 10036
www.asjamail.org

American Society for Training and Development
1640 King St., Box 1443
Alexandria, VA 22313-2043
www.astd.org

American Translators Association
225 Reinekers La., Ste. 590
Alexandria, VA 22314
www.atanet.org

Association of American Publishers
50 F St. NW, 4th Fl.
Washington, DC 20001
www.publishers.org

Association for Business Communication
P.O. Box 6143
Nacogdoches, TX 75962-0001
www.businesscommunication.org

Association for Computing Machinery's Special Interest Group on
    the Design of Communication
2 Penn Plaza, Ste. 701
New York, NY 10121-0721
acmhelp@acm.org
www.sigdoc.org

Association for Educational Communications and Technology
1800 N. Stonelake Dr., Ste. 2
Bloomington, IN 47404
www.aect.org

Association of Teachers of Technical Writing
http://cms.english.ttu.edu/attw

Association for Women in Communications
3337 Duke St.
Alexandria, VA 22314
www.womcom.org

Authors Guild Inc.
31 E. 32nd St., 7th Fl.
New York, NY 10016
www.authorsguild.org

Canadian Association of Journalists
Algonquin College
1385 Woodroffe Ave., B224
Ottawa, ON K2G 1V8
www.caj.ca

Canadian Association of Teachers of Technical Writing
http://cattw-acprts.mcgill.ca

Canadian Authors Association
www.canauthors.org

Canadian Science Writers' Association
P.O. Box 75, Station A
Toronto, ON M5W 1A2
www.sciencewriters.ca

Council for the Advancement of Science Writing
P.O. Box 910
Hedgesville, WV 25427
www.casw.org

Council for Programs in Technical and Scientific Communication
www.cptsc.org

Council of Science Editors
CSE Headquarters
c/o Drohan Management Group
12100 Sunset Hills Rd., Ste. 130
Reston, VA 20190
www.councilscienceeditors.org

Dow Jones Newspaper Fund
4300 Route One North
South Brunswick, NJ 08852
http://djnewspaperfund.dowjones.com/fund

Editorial Freelancers Association
71 W. 23rd St., 4th Fl.
New York, NY 10010
www.the-efa.org

Health and Sciences Communications Association
39 Wedgewood Dr., Ste. 1A
Jewett City, CT 06351
www.hesca.org

Human Factors and Ergonomics Society
P.O. Box 1369
Santa Monica, CA 90406-1369
www.hfes.org

IEEE Professional Communication Society
http://ieeexplore.ieee.org/iel5/47/29409/01331587.pdf

Institute of Electrical and Electronics Engineers
445 Hoes La.
Piscataway, NJ 08854-4141
www.ieee.org

International Digital Enterprise Alliance
IDEAlliance
1421 Prince St., Ste. 230
Alexandria, VA 22314-2805
www.idealliance.org

International Federation of Agricultural Journalists
www.ifaj.org

International Society of Logistics
8100 Professional Pl., Ste. 111
Hyattsville, MD 20785
www.sole.org

Literary Translators Association of Canada
LB 631 Concordia University
1455, Blvd. de Maisonneuve ouest
Montreal, QC H3G 1M8
www.attlc-ltac.org

Magazine Publishers of America
810 7th Ave., 24th Fl.
New York, NY 10019
www.magazine.org

National Association of Black Journalists
8701-A Adelphi Rd.
Adelphi, MD 20783-1716
www.nabj.org

National Association of Government Communicators
201 Park Washington Ct.
Falls Church, VA 22046-4527
www.nagc.com

National Association of Hispanic Journalists
1000 National Press Bldg.
529 14th St. NW
Washington, DC 20045-2001
www.nahj.org

National Association of Home and Workshop Writers
www.nahww.org

National Association of Science Writers
P.O. Box 890
Hedgesville, WV 25427
www.nasw.org

National Council of Teachers of English
1111 W. Kenyon Rd.
Urbana, IL 61801-1096
www.ncte.org

National Federation of Press Women
P.O. Box 5556
Arlington, VA 22205
www.nfpw.org

National Writers Union
113 University Pl., 6th Fl.
New York, NY 10003
www.nwu.org

The Newspaper Guild
501 3rd St. NW
Washington, DC 20001-2797
www.newsguild.org

Professional Writers Association of Canada
215 Spadina Ave., Ste. 123
Toronto, ON M5T 2C7
www.pwac.ca

Public Relations Society of America
33 Maiden La., 11th Fl.
New York, NY 10038-5150
www.prsa.org

Science Fiction and Fantasy Writers of America
P.O. Box 877
Chestertown, MD 21620
www.sfwa.org

Society of Professional Journalists
Eugene S. Pulliam National Journalism Center
3909 N. Meridian St.
Indianapolis, IN 46208
www.spj.org

Usability Professional's Association
140 N. Bloomingdale Rd.
Bloomingdale, IL 60108-1017
www.upassoc.org

Writers Guild of Canada
366 Adelaide St. W, Ste. 401
Toronto, ON M5V 1R9
www.wgc.ca

Recommended Reading

The following are some suggestions for additional reading on the profession of technical communication.

Society for Technical Communication Publications

Intercom, the Society for Technical Communication (STC) magazine, provides various examples and applications of technical communication that will promote readers' professional development. It includes articles on new tools and technologies, columns edited by technical communications experts, society news, and a calendar of industry-related events. It is published ten times a year and is free with membership.

Technical Communication, the STC journal, publishes articles about the practical application of technical communication theory and serves as a common arena for discussion among practitioners. It includes quantitative and qualitative research, as well as book reviews. The journal is published quarterly and is free with society membership.

Proceedings comprises more than two hundred papers given at the annual STC conference's educational presentations, known as "technical sessions." Your conference registration includes one copy of that year's *Proceedings*.

The "Business of Technical Communication" is a monthly online column that covers the business aspects of the profession. Articles discuss such areas as employment, salaries, job search techniques, and marketable skills.

The STC also publishes several informational brochures that are geared toward explaining and promoting membership. They can be purchased from regional chapters.

Journals and Periodicals

This is a short list of periodicals that are most likely to feature articles of interest to the technical communicator. You may find additional publications at your public or school library. A list of current articles also should be available. Consult a librarian for sources.

American Medical Writers' Association Journal
AMWA
www.amwa.org

Business Communication Quarterly
Sage Publications
www.bcq.sagepub.com

College English
National Council of Teachers of English
www.ncte.org/pubs/journals/ce

Editor and Publisher
VNU Business Publications
www.editorandpublisher.com

IEEE Transactions on Professional Communication
Institute of Electrical and Electronics Engineers
www.ieeexplore.ieee.org/xpl

Journal of Business Communication
Sage Publications
www.job.sagepub.com

Journal of Technical Writing and Communication
Baywood Publishing Co.
www.baywood.com/journals/PreviewJournals.asp?Id=0047-2816

Library Journal
Reed Business Information
www.libraryjournal.com

Publisher's Weekly
Reed Business Information
www.publishersweekly.com

Technology Review
Massachusetts Institute of Technology
www.technologyreview.com

Writer's Digest
F and W Publications
www.writersdigest.com

Books

Alred, Gerald J. et al. *Handbook of Technical Writing*, 8th ed. New York: St. Martin's Press, 2006.

Ament, Kurt. *Single Sourcing: Building Modular Documentation*. Berkshire, United Kingdom: Noyes Publications, 2002.

American Medical Association Manual of Style: A Guide for Authors and Editors. Philadelphia: Lippincott Williams & Wilkins, 1998.

Anderson, Paul V. *Technical Communication: A Reader-Centered Approach*, 6th ed. Belmont, Calif.: Heinle, 2006.

Beer, David F., ed. *Writing and Speaking in the Technology Professions: A Practical Guide*, 2nd ed. New York: Wiley-IEEE, 2003.

Bennett, Scott. *The Elements of Résumé Style: Essential Rules and Eye-Opening Advice for Writing Résumés and Cover Letters that Work*. New York: AMACOM/American Management Association, 2005.

Blum, Deborah et al. *A Field Guide for Science Writers: The Official Guide of the National Association of Science Writers*, 2nd ed. New York: Oxford University Press, 2005.

Bly, Robert W. *Careers for Writers and Others Who Have a Way with Words*, 2nd ed. New York: McGraw-Hill, 2003.

Brasseur, Lee E. *Visualizing Technical Information: A Cultural Critique*. Amityville, N.Y.: Bayville Publishing, 2003.

Bridgeford, Tracy. *Innovative Approaches Teaching Technical Communication*. Salt Lake City: University of Utah Press, 2004.

Burnett, E. *Technical Communication*, 6th ed. Belmont, Calif.: Heinle, 2004.

Camenson, Blythe. *Great Jobs for Communications Majors*, 2nd ed. New York: McGraw-Hill, 2001.

Carlson, Mim. *Winning Grants, Step by Step*, 2nd ed. San Francisco: Jossey-Bass, 2002.

The Chicago Manual of Style. Chicago: University of Chicago Press, 2003.

Coghill, Anne M., and Lorrin R. Garson, eds. *The ACS Style Guide: Effective Communication of Scientific Information*, 3rd ed. Washington, DC: American Chemical Society, 2006.

DeGalan, Julie, and Stephen Lambert. *Great Jobs for English Majors*, 3rd ed. New York: McGraw-Hill, 2006.

Dubinsky, James M. *Teaching Technical Communication: Critical Issues for the Classroom*. New York: Bedford/St. Martin's, 2004.

Goodman, Neville W., and Martin B. Edwards. *Medical Writing: A Prescription for Clarity*, 3rd ed. New York: Cambridge University Press, 2006.

Hancock, Elise. *Ideas into Words: Mastering the Craft of Science Writing*. Baltimore: Johns Hopkins University Press, 2003.

Hargis, Gretchen, et al. *Developing Quality Technical Information: A Handbook for Writers and Editors*, 2nd ed. Lebanon, Ind.: IBM Press, 2004.

Harty, Kevin J. *Strategies for Business and Technical Writing*, 5th ed. Boston: Longman, 2004.

Harvard Business Essentials. *Business Communication*. Cambridge, Mass.: Harvard Business School Press, 2003.

Herrington, TyAnna K. *A Legal Primer for the Digital Age*. Boston: Longman, 2003.

Hirsch, Herbert. *Effective Communication Strategies*, 2nd ed. New York: Wiley-IEEE Press, 2002.

Johnson-Eilola, Johndan, and Stuart A. Selber, eds. *Central Works in Technical Communication.* New York: Oxford University Press, 2004.

Kynell-Hunt, Teresa, and Gerald J. Savage, eds. *Power and Legitimacy in Technical Communication: Strategies for Professional Status.* Amityville, N.Y.: Bayville Publishing Co., 2004.

Lipson, Charles. *Cite Right: A Quick Guide to Citation Styles— MLA, APA, Chicago, the Sciences, Professions, and More.* Chicago: University of Chicago Press, 2006.

Matthews, Clifford. *A Guide to Presenting Technical Information: Effective Graphic Communication.* New York: Wiley, 2005.

Microsoft Manual of Style for Technical Publications, 3rd ed. Microsoft Press, 2003.

Mirel, Barbara, and Rachel Spilka , eds. *Reshaping Technical Communication: New Directions and Challenges for the 21st Century.* Mahwah, N.J.: Lawrence Erlbaum Associates, 2002.

Montgomery, Scott L. *The Chicago Guide to Communicating Science.* Chicago: University of Chicago Press, 2002.

Munger, Roger. *Document-Based Cases for Technical Communication.* New York: Bedford/St. Martin's, 2004.

New, Cheryl C., and James A. Quick. *How to Write a Grant Proposal.* New York: Wiley, 2003.

Oliver, Vicky. *301 Answers to Tough Interview Questions.* Naperville, Ill.: Sourcebooks, 2005.

Pfeiffer, William S. *Technical Communication: A Practical Approach*, 6th ed. Upper Saddle River, N.J.: Prentice Hall, 2005.

Pringle, Alan S., and Sarah S. O'Keefe. *Technical Writing 101: A Real-World Guide to Planning and Writing Technical Documentation*, 2nd ed. Research Triangle Park, N.C.: Scriptorium Press, 2003.

Reep, Diana C. *Technical Writing: Principles, Strategies, and Readings*, 5th ed. Boston: Longman, 2002.

Reinking, James A., et al. *Strategies for Successful Writing with 2001 APA Guidelines*, 6th ed. Upper Saddle River, N.J.: Prentice Hall, 2002.

Rosenberg, Arthur D., and David V. Hizer. *The Résumé Handbook: How to Write Outstanding Résumés and Cover Letters for Every Situation*, 4th ed. Cincinnati: Adams Media Corp., 2003.

Rosenberg, Barry. *Spring into Technical Writing for Engineers and Scientists*. Upper Saddle River, N.J.: Addison-Wesley Professional, 2005.

Rubens, Philip. *Science and Technical Writing: A Manual of Style*, 2nd ed. New York: Routledge, 2000.

Rude, Carolyn D. *Technical Editing*, 4th ed. Boston: Longman, 2005.

Simons, Warren, and Rose Curtis. *The Résumé.com Guide to Writing Unbeatable Résumés*. New York: McGraw-Hill, 2004.

Sun Technical Publications. *Read Me First! A Style Guide for the Computer Industry*, 2nd ed. Upper Saddle River, N.J.: Prentice Hall, 2003.

Taylor, Alan, and James R. Parish. *Career Opportunities in Writing*. New York: Checkmark Books, 2006.

Van Wicklen, Janet. *The Tech Writer's Survival Guide: A Comprehensive Handbook for Aspiring Technical Writers*, 2nd ed. New York: Checkmark Books, 2001.

Weiss, Edmond H. *The Elements of International English Style: A Guide to Writing Correspondence, Reports, Technical Documents, and Internet Pages for a Global Audience.* Armonk, N.Y.: M. E. Sharpe, 2005.

Wysocki, Anne. *Writing New Media.* Salt Lake City: University of Utah Press, 2004.

Young, Matt. *The Technical Writer's Handbook: Writing with Style and Clarity,* 2nd ed. Herndon, Vir.: University Science Books, 2002.

Zobel, Justin. *Writing for Computer Science,* 2nd ed. New York: Springer, 2004.